The Murder of Fatty Fuller

John Sturgeon

Black Rose Writing | Texas

ISBN: 978-1-68433-321-9
PUBLISHED BY BLACK ROSE WRITING
www.blackrosewriting.com

Printed in the United States of America
Suggested Retail Price (SRP) $18.95

The Murder of Fatty Fuller is printed in Calluna

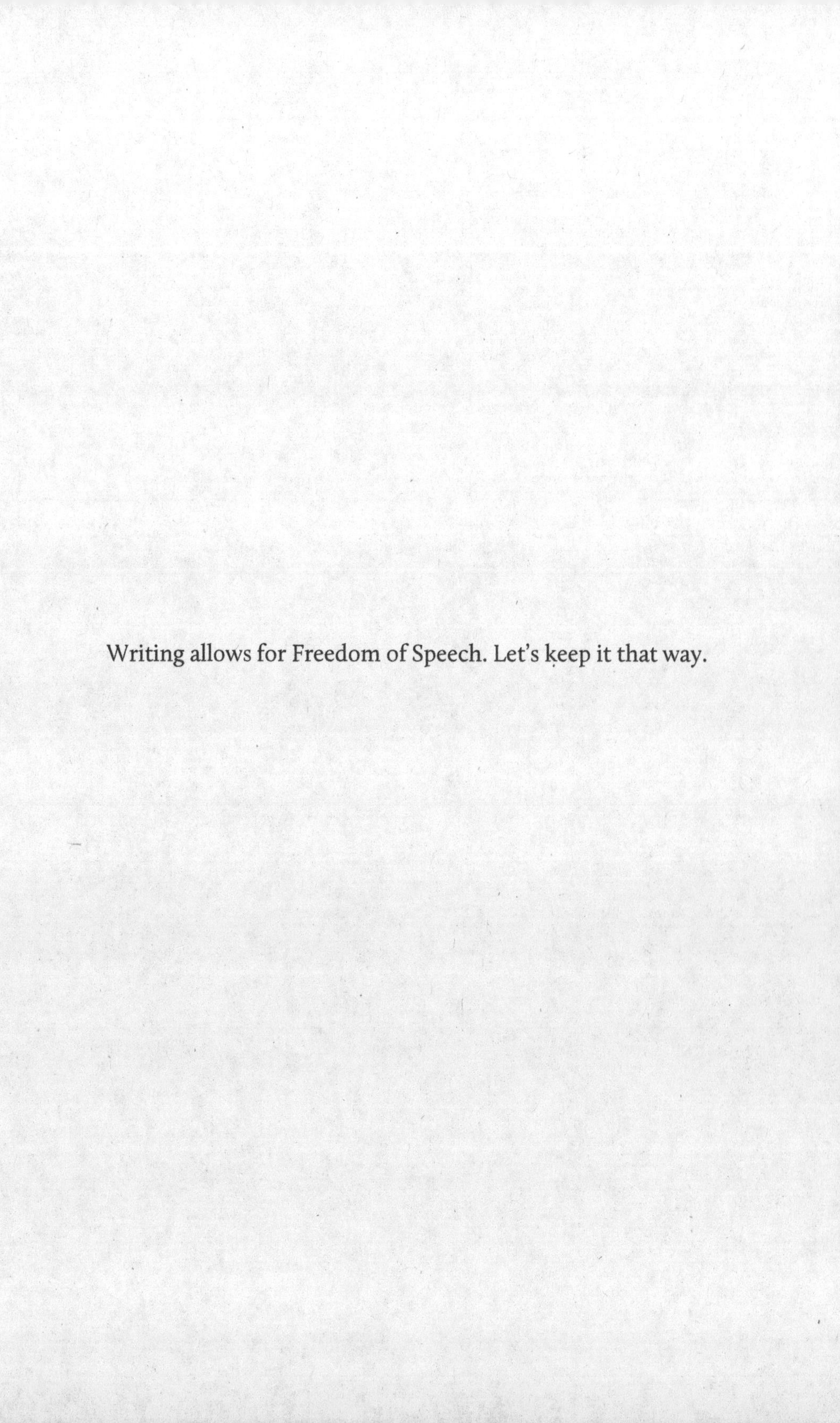

Writing allows for Freedom of Speech. Let's keep it that way.

The Murder of Fatty Fuller

Milton

On a sunny October afternoon, from the western side of the Mississippi, just east of Dubuque, you can get a very good look at the town of Milton on the Illinois side of the river. Milton was once a lead mining town; there were always a number of boats ready to take the precious metal from the town and carry it to other places in the states, but those days are long gone. From the Iowa side, you can see that the banks of Milton are covered with trees of all types, all now showing the yellow, golden and red leaves of fall. Occasionally a bald eagle would fly into view, but usually, the most exotic bird was a blue heron. This tranquil picture doesn't give an accurate view of the town. Forget the rusted barges that would lumber into view as they trudged along the great river. That might have added to the ascetic pleasure of the viewer. What stood out was the hulking figure of the old riverboat casino still docked on the shore. Illinois had long ago done away with the law that required gambling boats to be offshore when operating, but the Trips Aces was still in business down there in Milton. These days she never left the dock. She had also not lost many of the visitors who came to see her daily.

What you couldn't see was Brewster Way, the wide avenue that ran behind the boat and all along the western edge of the town. Brewster was where you found legal poker rooms, slot parlors, vape lounges, and bars and, of course, strip joints. These establishments lined Brewster on both sides of the street. Brewster Way ran for nearly a half a mile. Behind the buildings that were on the eastern side of Brewster ran the Amtrak rail lines that served the town and others east and west. Beyond the tracks was where the residents of Milton lived, almost twenty-seven thousand of them. A lot of the citizens of Milton worked in the businesses along Brewster. Many worked at the casino or across the river at the dog track when it ran. Most people from Milton, especially those that worked along Brewster or at the

Aces, knew not to get in any trouble down there. It simply wasn't worth it.

It's not that there wasn't trouble at the casino, the bars or especially the strip clubs. There was all the time. If you were a Milton resident and got caught starting trouble along Brewster or at the Aces there would be hell to pay as the saying went. People who weren't from Milton and got arrested for any kind of criminal activity usually never came back to Milton. Many times they told their friends and families not to go there either. The primary reason for this was Chief Teddy Brown and the Milton Police Department.

Teddy Brown, until the stroke this past March, had been the Chief of Police for almost forty years. Crime in the residential areas of the town was non-existent. No one wanted to deal with Teddy or any of his lieutenants. None of the residents seemed to mind it either. Most loved Teddy and the way he managed the town. Crimes that were committed along Brewster or at the casino were dealt with quickly and often times harshly. This was no secret. Don't come to Milton if you plan on being drunk and disorderly, get in an argument with a dealer or hassle with one of the dancers at Satan's Palace. Again, it wasn't worth it, but that didn't stop it from happening.

Crimes of any type were very low for the entire town of Milton. Serious crimes were almost non-existent. The Milton PD was well staffed and equipped. The town was well protected. Serious crimes just didn't happen very often. In the last forty years there had been two murders in Milton. In 1981 a redneck, corn farmer had come into town and hassled a black man who was talking to a white woman. The black man, Arthur Kimbro, told the farmer to go back to his fields. The farmer, Herb Varner, shot Kimbro dead in the middle of Brewster. Herb Varner made it back to his car where he tried as hard as he could to get over the Mississippi and back into Iowa. Unfortunately, he blew a tire before he could get onto Route 20 and over the bridge. Teddy Brown, Jack Davis, and Ben Smith were the three Milton cops who caught up with Herb as his car spun off the side road and rammed into a tree. Herb scampered out of the car but was knocked down by Ben Smith, the former Iowa linebacker. Herb was able to get up on his knees and began to say he was sorry, didn't know what got into him, and just didn't like seeing that nigger talking to a white girl. Teddy, who'd just seen his no murder record blemished, took out his service piece and fired two bullets into the back of the head of Herb Varner.

"Jesus Christ, boss," Jack Davis said.

"Oh shit," Ben Smith said.

"Shut up," screamed Teddy. "You two get this son of a bitch buried back there away from the road. Dig a deep trench. I don't want anything digging this bastard up. When you're done, we'll call it in that we found his car, but no driver. No fucking idea where he went. This is the only way to deal with these white trash farmers who come to town."

So the murder of Arthur Kimbro went unsolved. Every state trooper in Illinois and Iowa were looking for the murdering farmer, but no one ever caught him. No one found his rotting corpse either. Jack Davis and Ben Smith, the newest gravediggers in town, were promoted to Detective Lieutenant the next week. Both remained with Teddy.

The only other murder to occur in Milton had occurred fifteen years ago. That had been the murder of Fatty Fuller. Fatty had been born with Down Syndrome and had been almost fourteen at the time of his death. He had gone fishing in the early evening on one of the last days of summer at Whisper Creek. Fatty fished a lot and knew that the smallmouth liked to feed near the creek. He left his house around six-fifteen. When he didn't return by eight-thirty, his sister, Cynthia, called the police.

Cynthia told the police the three top spots where Fatty liked to fish. It was at Whisper Creek where they found his body, face down in about two feet of water. The coroner determined that Fatty died by drowning. It didn't help that Fatty's head had been bashed in by a large rock. The only motive that the police could come up with was theft. All of Fatty's fishing tackle, some of it expensive, had been stolen.

Unlike the murder of Arthur Kimbro, Fatty's murder was solved and quickly. The police received a "tip" that some of Fatty's fishing gear was in the shed in the back of the house owned by Skitch Grayson. Without a warrant, but with good cause, the Milton Police descended on Skitch's place, were able to open the shed and found a good amount of Fatty's equipment. Skitch, a known drunk and sometimes handyman, was arrested. He had no alibi but claimed total innocence. His trial, six months later, was short. The jury, based solely on the evidence found in Skitch's shed, found him guilty of the murder and the theft. The judge, Henry Fillson, gave Skitch life in prison. The case was officially closed. After serving almost fourteen years, Skitch was diagnosed with lung cancer and released on parole. His health is failing and he is living out his days at the Marymore Nursing Home in nearby Platteville, Wisconsin.

First Notice

When he first heard the cell phone ring, he thought someone was playing the radio. Maybe setting your ring tone to an old Beach Boys' song was not such a good idea. When the phone kept playing the same verses over, TH Brown knew it was his phone. He rolled his body towards the table on the side of the bed. The clock there read 5:05. The total darkness in the room told TH it was AM. He grabbed the phone and checked the Caller ID. It read Rachel Brown, his sister. This, he reasoned, couldn't be good.

He touched the talk button and thought before speaking. "Hello, Rachel. Everything okay?"

As soon as his words were out of his mouth, he heard his sister sobbing. "I didn't mean to call so early, TH. I wanted to wait until seven, but you have to come home."

TH didn't know if she meant seven in Illinois or California. He wondered if his father, who'd had a stroke this past March, had gotten worse or maybe even died. "Is it dad?"

"No, TH. It's not dad," Rachel said through sobs. "It's Melissa."

Melissa was a thirty-nine-year-old school teacher with two normal kids and a drippy husband who sold real estate. "What's wrong with Melissa?"

"She did something bad, TH, real bad."

Now he sat up in his bed. "So is she in jail? Call one of dad's old cronies and get her out of there."

"It's not that," she said. She paused, and he could hear her blowing her nose. "TH, Melissa hanged herself last night. She committed suicide."

Those few words were stronger than a punch to the gut. TH felt all of the air leave his body. Melissa had been his pretty sister, his successful sister and the one with the least complicated life of all. "Why?" was the only word he could manage.

"Nobody knows. Nobody knows anything especially her dumb shit husband, but you've got to hurry home. I spoke to Richie, but he can't come until tomorrow, late. I need you to come right away."

His older brother, Richie, was a detective in Kansas City. "I can come, but why do you need me right away?"

"I have to tell dad, and I can't do that alone. I need you to come with me, TH."

He understood now, and he nodded to himself. "Let me get showered and find a plane out of LA. I'll let you know when I have more details."

"But you'll come today?" she blurted.

"Rachel, I'll be there sometime today."

•   •   •

For as far back as he could remember, TH Brown had always been a thief. Some of the time he stole things because he wanted them, but most of the time he stole things to see if he could get away with it. It was hardly ever a question of need or want. TH's father would buy him just about whatever he needed, but the thrill of stealing something and getting away with it was another topic.

In his early days, TH would steal small things, candy, toys, pens, and money. There wasn't much of a challenge to it and very little thrill. When he was eleven, he decided to challenge himself with an epic theft, one that would convince him that he was truly a professional. He tried for the longest time to think of something that would be both difficult to steal and rewarding. The best thought he could come up with was inspired by the Alpert family. They lived on Grace Street, and TH went to school with Martin Alpert. The Alpert's father, Randle, had run off ten years ago, leaving his wife Lauren and their three kids alone in the small house. Lauren worked as a secretary during the day, and at night she would clean offices in the town for extra money. With three children, there was always the need for extra money. TH was pretty sure that their holidays weren't as grand as they were at his own house. He could just tell by the way Martin dressed. The kid was an ad for Hand Me Downs.

What TH decided to do was to steal the biggest turkey he could find at the A&P and to give it to the Alperts. Part of the heist was a bit of a sham because everyone in the A&P knew who TH was. He was Teddy Brown's son, the Chief of Police's son. They all knew him and said hello to him whenever he came into the store. Things weren't any different when he entered the store the Wednesday, a week before Thanksgiving. Everyone he saw when he came into the store greeted him warmly. No one questioned the large ski jacket that he wore. It was twenty-eight degrees outside. TH calmly walked down the aisles and picked up a box of stuffing and two cans of green beans. He then walked over to where the turkeys were displayed in a freezer bin. He scooped up a twelve-pound bird with one hand while cradling the stuffing and beans in the other. Finding himself in the bread and cereal aisle, he saw that it was empty. He quickly slipped the turkey under his coat and inside the sweat pants he wore. Other than the fact that the bird was freezing it wasn't that uncomfortable. He didn't look any fatter as the coat had plenty of room underneath it. TH then walked calmly up to the register where Mrs. Gates was working. There was a woman with a small child in line in front of him, but TH waited patiently, putting his goods on the conveyor. When his turn came, he smiled widely at Mrs. Gates.

"How are you today, Mrs. Gates?" he said.

She returned his smile. "I am fine, Theodore." Quite often, older people wouldn't call him TH. "What have you got today?"

"Just a couple of things we forgot to pick up."

Mrs. Gates rang up the stuffing, and the beans and TH paid her for them. She gave him his change and the receipt. "Still real cold out there?" she asked.

"Yes, mam. Feels like it's getting colder."

"Well, say hi to your father and brother and sisters."

"Thank you very much, Mrs. Gates."

By the time TH got to the parking lot, he was laughing so hard tears were rolling out of his eyes. He looked around and found an extra plastic shopping bag. He quickly placed the turkey inside of it and headed for the Alpert's house. When he got there, he walked up the steps and rang their bell. Luck was on his side as Martin was the one who answered.

"Hello, Marty," TH said.

The two boys were not friends, so Martin Alpert looked at him warily.

"I've got something for your family, a donation from the Rotary." TH held out the plastic bags, and Martin took it from him. "It's a turkey, beans and stuffing for Thanksgiving."

Martin Alpert still said nothing, but a broad smile crossed his face. "Mom didn't know if we could afford a decent turkey this year."

"Well, your mom doesn't have to worry about that now. Happy Thanksgiving, Marty."

Martin Alpert smiled again. "Happy Thanksgiving, TH."

When he was walking home, TH realized he'd done wrong by stealing the turkey, but did it really hurt the big chain A&P store? He remembered how his heart had thumped in his chest as he waited in the checkout line and how he acted so normal with Mrs. Gates. He really felt good when he saw Martin smile when he handed over the groceries. He wondered if there was a way that he could always help people by giving them things, a little like a modern Robin Hood. He smiled as he thought about that.

•   •   •

"Welcome to Chicago," the flight attendant said. "It is currently cloudy outside and a crisp thirty-eight degrees."

"Oh shit!" TH said, maybe a bit too loudly for the woman with the small child across the aisle from him.

He had been able to get a seven-thirty flight from LA which got him into Chicago at just past one-thirty. He only had his two carry-on pieces, and the rent- a car went faster than he expected, so he was on the road to Milton by two-fifteen. The flight attendant had not been lying. It was cold and dreary looking outside. He turned on the heat in the rental, found the classic rock radio station and settled in for the two-hour ride.

Without talking to Rachel, TH had made the decision to stay at one of the motels along Route 20. He could have stayed at her house, but the thought of a few days with his slightly unstable sister and her brood of kids was too much. Obviously, Melissa's house, where he had stayed when visiting in the past, was out of the question. Even more so was the family home, not yet sold by his ailing father. There were too many bad memories from that house to consider staying there. The Red Roof would do.

He took a corner room on the second floor. A con man had told him once these were the best rooms. Trouble didn't like coming at you up the stairs and from only one direction. TH never knew when this action would apply, but he'd since followed the man's instructions. When he was settled in, he called Rachel.

"Are you here?" she said, answering after only one ring.

"I'm at the Red Roof out on 20."

"You could have stayed here," she said. "We have plenty of room."

"I didn't want to inconvenience anyone. Probably best that I just stay out here."

"Can you come over to talk? I want to go see dad in the morning, and I'd like to fill you in on a few things and talk about how we are going to tell him."

"I'll be there in about fifteen," he said. TH wondered what "few things" she needed to fill him in about. He also wondered how his father would take the double whammy of the news of Melissa's suicide and of seeing him for the first time in two years. Probably not all that great.

·　　·　　·

The house that Rachel Brown lived in with her three children was on the outer edge of Milton. The house was exactly like TH remembered. In the fading light of the day, he could see where the grass was dying, and the lawn was covered with bare spots. All of the bushes in front of the house were void of leaves and TH could see areas where the foundation of the home was visible. The exterior of the house needed painting, and the roof was missing several shingles.

At thirty-six, Rachel was three years older than TH. She had been married three times with a child by each husband. She was twice divorced. Her third husband had left in the middle of the night with only their pickup. That had been several years ago. Rachel worked full time at the Walmart over in Dubuque. This was never enough to cover all the bills. TH knew that their father sent her money each month. TH sent her extra money every now and then.

TH pulled the rental into the driveway behind the old Ford sedan that Rachel drove. He took a deep breath and stepped out into the crisp October air. He closed the car door just as Rachel stepped out of her house. She walked towards him and smiled. TH noticed that she might have put on a little weight, but she looked pretty good.

"This what you're used to driving out in LA?" she asked, pointing at the rented Chevy.

"I don't live in LA. I live in Costa Mesa and, yes, I do drive an old Chevy Suburban."

"Still stealing stuff for a living?"

He shrugged. "I am a repo man. To my clients, I am a repossession expert. I only steal what does not rightfully belong to people."

She laughed and gave TH a big hug. "Let's go inside and talk. The kids are all out right now, so it's a good time."

The inside of the house didn't look much better. The place needed decorating, the furniture was old, and the house had a constant musty odor to it. The inside air made TH's nose tickle.

"You want a beer," Rachel asked. In the light of the kitchen, TH could see her better and make out the lines on her face and shadows under her eyes. Now she looked older than thirty-six.

"A beer would be good. It's already been a long day."

She grabbed a beer from the fridge and placed it in front of TH. "I didn't mean to wake you so early. The time change thing gets me. I just wanted somebody else here with me. I freaked."

TH nodded. "It's okay. I wouldn't have been able to get here today if you hadn't woke me up."

She sat across from him, and he could see her lip begin to quiver a bit. A single tear rolled from her left eye, leaving a trail in her makeup. "It's such a shitty thing. I mean, of all of us, who's the least likely to kill themself? I thought Melissa had this kind of easy-going, mostly trouble free life. I mean, Bob's an idiot, but he's always been a good provider and a good dad. It doesn't make sense." Bob Booker was Melissa's husband.

TH opened the beer and took a long sip. It was a watered down light beer, but it was cold. "Nobody has any ideas?"

"Bob says she went to school yesterday like any other day. When he got home, they decided to order pizza for dinner. Bob said they had a half-hearted fight about what kind of pizza to get and then she went upstairs to change. When the pizza came, and Melissa hadn't come down yet he went up to get her and found her. She used a cloth belt to hang herself from the ceiling fan in their room. She was dead when he got up there."

The second swig of the beer didn't go down as easily, burning at the top of his throat. "Bob doesn't know if anything else was bothering her?"

"Not that he knows of. I know that they rarely fought. A little spat here and there, but nothing major."

None of this made any sense to TH. "When was the last time you saw her?"

Rachel looked to the ceiling, considering the question. "Maybe a month,

month and a half."

TH nodded again. "Wake and funeral?"

"Wake's tomorrow. Funeral the next day."

"And dad knows nothing?"

"Not a thing. I called the staff down there and told them not to say anything until I could get there. That's why I called you."

"Richie?"

"He's coming from Kansas City tomorrow. He'll be here in time for the wake."

"Dad behaving himself these days?"

She laughed. "Again, that's why I called you. He gets worse every day, meaner. He likes one nurse out there. Her name is Sheila, a big black lady. Most of the others he treats like shit. Sheila is the only one that can keep him in line."

"How often do you go see him?"

"Every two weeks. I'd go more often if he wasn't so nasty. It's not always a pleasant experience."

"How do you think he's going to treat me?"

"What do you think? It's been a couple of years; I have the feeling that he is going to be a real asshole to you. I go see him, and he's not always nice to me."

"So it's our job to tell him Melissa killed herself?"

"That and to make sure the staff has him ready for the wake. The Three Amigos said they would pick him up and take him to Keifer's."

Now TH laughed a bit. The Three Amigos were the three ex-cops who worked for their dad for over thirty years. "This sounds like it has the making for an all-around good time here in Milton."

"That's why I called. I didn't want you to miss any of it."

•   •   •

TH's sister Melissa had lived in a newer home on Short Street with her husband Bob and their two boys. In contrast to Rachel's house, the front lawn was well groomed, and all of the bushes and shrubs were trimmed to perfection. The street light in front of the house showed there were no noticeable bare spots anywhere on the lawn. It was dark when he pulled into their driveway, and it was noticeably colder when he stepped out of the car.

There were no outside lights on, but there was one small light shining from within the house.

He thought he should have called first, but it was too late for that. He walked up to the front door and rang the bell. After a wait of several moments, he rang the bell again. Maybe there was nobody home. After the second ring, the door was slowly opened. The man that opened the door did not resemble the man TH knew as Melissa's husband.

Bob Booker had always been a meticulously groomed man. None of his clothes ever seemed out of place, and his hair was always perfect. Today the man that stood in the door wore a battered pair of jeans, an old sweatshirt and a two-day growth of stubble. It was hard to tell if his hair was clean, but it hadn't seen a brush or comb today. The face did manage a smile.

"Hello, TH," Bob said.

With those few syllables, TH could tell that Bob had been drinking. The alcohol stench that came from the man was strong. "Hello, Bob. Mind if I come in for a bit?"

Bob looked confused for a moment, but he did push the door open further and let TH into the house. Like he remembered, the house was a picture of order. Everything looked neat and clean. The light TH had seen was from the kitchen. He followed Bob in that direction.

The only light burning was a small one over the stove. On the kitchen table, TH could see a glass and a bottle of Jim Beam. Bob quickly sat down in the chair with the glass in front of it. He pointed at the bottle of whiskey.

"If you want some the glasses are in the first cabinet above the sink. Ice is in the freezer," Bob said.

"I'm good," TH said, taking a seat next to Bob. "The two boys around?"

Bob shook his head. "By my parents. Too much to be in this house. My mom picked them up this morning. Dad went to Kiefer's and took care of the arrangements."

TH felt his temper rising. Bob couldn't even get over to the funeral home for his own wife. His dad had to do that for him, too.

"It was too much for me, TH," Bob said, answering TH's thoughts. "I couldn't do it. I woke up today and thought that was the worst dream I'd ever had. I went downstairs to look for Melissa. She always made the coffee and got the paper." He shook his head as if to rid a bad thought. "Today, there was no coffee and no paper. No Melissa either. It wasn't a bad dream, TH."

TH got up from the chair, found a glass and filled it with ice. He sat down and poured a good inch of whiskey into his glass. He added a little bit to the glass that Bob had. He took a sip of the whiskey and felt the warmth of it hit his body. It felt strangely good. "So what happened, Bob?"

Bob looked like the question shocked him. "That's it in a nutshell. What happened? What a simple question, but there is no answer. Melissa was a great mom, a great wife, and a great teacher. She balanced all of her jobs expertly, never complained, and never missed a day. She didn't get sick; she didn't get down. There was no depression. No anger. She was as steady as you could want. She was really quite remarkable."

TH took another sip. "Why don't you tell me what happened last night?"

Bob picked up his glass and twirled it in his hands, the ice rattling against the glass. "Nothing happened. Nothing. Both boys had football practice, and I picked them up like always. Melissa was going to stay a little later at school and grade some papers. We all got home around six-thirty.

"We had talked in the morning about ordering a pizza for dinner. I had forgotten to do so, apologized and said we could get one delivered in probably twenty minutes. She said fine, but then she said we should just get cheese. Cheese pizza and a salad. She said the sausage and pepperoni on pizza was not good for you. For one time we just needed to get a plain cheese pizza." Bob stopped and took a gulp of his drink; some sloshed down his chin. He poured more into his glass.

"Well, this announcement about eating healthy didn't go over too well. Both boys love pepperoni, and I love sausage with everything else. We all started kind of yelling at her but in a friendly way. Nobody wanted cheese only, Melissa looked at us for a minute and said, 'Just get what you want' and then she went upstairs. I thought she was going upstairs to change. Anyway, like I said, the pizza came in about twenty-five minutes. I yelled for Melissa to come down. When she didn't come down or answer, I went up there. That's when I found her."

TH shifted nervously on his chair. "That's it?" he asked.

"That's the whole story. We had a half-baked argument about pizza, and she went upstairs and did that. I'm just glad neither boy saw her. I wish I hadn't."

TH thought about finding a loved one like that. "This doesn't make any sense. Nothing else seemed to be bothering her?"

"Not that I could tell. I talked with her in the morning. Everything seemed fine at school, and she might have been a little miffed when I forgot to order, but come on, TH. A disagreement about pizza and then that?"

"I hear you, Bob. It doesn't make any sense. Stupid question, but anything I can do?"

"It's not stupid at all." He tilted his glass towards TH. "Can you or anyone else tell me how I can explain to my two boys why their mom went upstairs and hanged herself with a belt from a ceiling fan? So far, no one has given me one good answer, and you know why? Because there isn't one."

•　　•　　•

TH ended up in a bar on Brewster called Lifer's. A lot of the people who worked for the city, county, police department and fire department came there to drink. It was always locals. TH stopped there because he thought he might run into somebody that he knew. The bar was old and was never very fancy, but they had upgraded all of the televisions recently. TH grabbed a spot near the corner of the bar and ordered a Bud Light.

The beer came, and he thanked the bartender, a guy of about forty, who he didn't know. The TV in front of him had on an NBA game, but that didn't interest TH. He looked around the bar, saw maybe ten to twelve patrons and knew this stop wouldn't be long.

He was about half-way through the beer when the door opened, and two burly men and one small, skinny guy entered the place. TH recognized them at once. The Three Amigos. Jack Davis, Ben Smith, and Logan Aft had all been detectives under his father. They had all been with him for over thirty years, and all were retired. They were all tough. Davis and Smith were big; Logan Aft was small and wiry. Logan Aft had a reputation for being the meanest. They went to the opposite end of the bar and ordered drinks. They hadn't noticed TH, and he hoped it stayed that way.

He quickly finished his beer and was thinking about how he could get out the front door without being seen. It seemed like an impossibility, but then the thought became moot.

"Is that the great TH Brown sitting down there?" The voice was loud and scratchy, the voice of a heavy smoker, Logan Aft.

TH looked down to that end of the bar just as Logan was coming around it and towards him.

"I'll be damned. It is TH Brown. Milton's long lost son," Aft said. He had

Davis and Smith following.

"Mr. Aft," TH said politely. "Mr. Davis, Mr. Smith."

"I was wondering if you'd make it back in town," Logan Aft said. "I just didn't know if your sister dying was important enough for you to return to Milton."

"Leave him alone," Ben Smith said. Jack Davis was just smiling.

"No, I'm serious," Aft continued. "His father had a stroke about seven months ago, and he couldn't find the time to come back and see him. I'm just trying to figure out young Mr. Brown's priorities. I know it's important for you to be here for your sister, but wasn't it important to be here for your dad when he was struggling?"

TH stared at Aft but kept his cool. Even in the dim light, he could make out his acne-scarred face. He could see the mean smile, the thin mustache. This was Logan Aft's game. Get you riled up to where you said or did something to get you in trouble.

"Don't know the answer, TH?" Aft said.

"I just stopped to have a beer, Mr. Aft. I have done that, and now I'm going to head back to my hotel. It's been a long day, and there's another long one tomorrow."

"You know, the last time I was talking to your dad, he was telling me how disappointed he was in you. Told me it's been going on since the middle of high school. Then you left home for California and can never find time to come see your old man. That and the repo business you have. Not the best reputation you have out there TH."

"It's not the kind of job that gives you a good reputation."

"Thieves generally don't have a good reputation. A repo man. A tough business. I never figured you'd get into a tough business, especially after I heard the hunting story. You were there, weren't you, Ben."

"Logan, you're just being an asshole," Ben Smith said. He turned and returned to their corner of the bar.

Both Aft and Jack Davis laughed. "Story I heard was that you were a real pussy out there in the woods. Crying because daddy wanted you to shoot a deer. Problem killing Bambi, TH?"

TH stood quickly, and Aft backed up a couple of steps. "I've got to get going. It was nice seeing you guys, and I'm sure I'll see you tomorrow. I'll tell my dad when I see him in the morning that we had a nice visit."

Aft took one step forward. "Yeah, you tell him that, TH. You tell him we had a real nice visit."

"Good night, guys."

"Hope you didn't have too many drinks, TH. I hear the local cops can be assholes out on Route 20 with drinkers."

He walked past the two men and out the door. He was just outside when Ben Smith called his name. He turned, and the former Iowa linebacker was walking towards him.

"Don't listen to Aft. He's just a jerk sometimes."

TH laughed. "I'm not even sure my dad ever liked him."

"Maybe not," Ben said. "I saw an old friend of yours this morning at Aces. Remember Cindy Fuller?"

Remember Cindy Fuller, TH thought? Cindy had been his all-time crush in high school, but she was a year younger and had never shown any interest in him. She was also the sister of Fatty Fuller who had been murdered right before TH's senior year. "I remember Cindy," he said.

"We were talking by the blackjack tables. You know she deals out there now. She was just wondering if you would come back based on what happened to Melissa. I just thought I'd mention it to you."

TH smiled. "Thanks, Mr. Smith."

"She's still a cutie, TH, and she finally dumped that idiot Stripling."

Troy Stripling had been the loser of a boyfriend, and then husband of Cindy Fuller.

"I'll keep that in mind."

"No disrespect. I know you're here to bury your sister."

"None taken."

"And, TH. Don't take what your father says too literally. He's a little off since the stroke. The whole thing just frustrates him, and he gets angry. Sometimes he says some crazy things."

"I understand."

"And definitely don't listen to Logan."

"Don't worry, Mr. Smith. I never do."

•   •   •

Good Ole Dad

Maybe it was the time change, or it could have been the encounter with The Three Amigos, but TH didn't sleep well. He would doze off for about a half hour but would awake and take a look at the bedside clock. Time wasn't moving very quickly. In the dark and staring at the ceiling wasn't doing much for TH's mood. That had been spoiled by Logan Aft. The guy was just an old, frustrated asshole. Of the three he was the most unstable. He was divorced and had no kids. As far as TH knew, he lived by himself. All of that could make you a little cold.

Speaking of cold, TH found himself thinking about the hunting trip that Aft had mentioned. He was twelve years old at the time. It was in early November, and it was TH, his father and Ben Smith. They drove Ben's old Dodge truck into a heavily wooded area in Wisconsin that ran along the banks of the Mississippi. When they got out of the truck, there was thick frost covering everything. When TH blew air out of his mouth, it seemed to crystallize right in front of his face.

They walked along the river and up into the woods when they had to. Ben had told them on the ride up that there were two spots that he knew of that were guaranteed to get you a deer. Now, as they walked, there was no talking. They moved quietly, in search of their prey, stopping every so often for Ben and his father to share a slug from the flask Ben carried. TH was freezing. His face was stinging.

TH had shot a lot of guns in his life. Every child in the Brown family had. He was very familiar with the rifle he carried that day. What happened next had nothing to do with inexperience.

They came over a small ridge and spotted the young buck drinking from the cold river. TH's father made a motion with his fingers to be quiet and signaled TH to come forward and take the shot. The deer was oblivious that they were near.

TH stepped forward and raised the rifle to fire. The deer stopped drinking for a moment and seemed to look right at him. TH swallowed hard. His hand trembled. The deer looked away, and TH sighted him. His hand shook worse. He couldn't do it and faked a hard sneeze just as he fired. The shot went high above the buck's head and sent him scurrying into some deep woods.

"What in the hell was that, TH?" his father boomed.

"I'm sorry," he said. "I just sneezed."

Ben Smith roared with laughter.

"Jesus Christ. A three-year-old girl could have made that shot. Don't let that shit happen again."

His father started up the trail again. TH put the safety back on the rifle.

"Don't let it bother you," Ben said. "You'll get the next one."

When Ben set off after his father, TH smiled and slowly followed.

It took another hour, an hour after TH had lost the feeling in his toes, but they did come upon another buck. This one was much older than the first, an eight pointer. He was slowly walking through the woods and coming right at them. TH thought his dad would ask him to take the shot again, but this time Teddy raised his own rifle, released the safety, aimed and fired. TH saw the buck get a startled look on his face and then drop into the brush.

The three of them hurried ahead to the spot where the deer had fallen. As they got there, the deer raised his head to look at the men who had killed him. His eyes fluttered a bit, and then his head fell to the ground.

"Now that's a fucking deer," Teddy bellowed. "What do you think, TH?"

There were no words from TH. As his father looked at him, tears began to stream down his face. He told himself he would never kill anything again.

Later that night TH was in the kitchen, eating some leftover stew that his sisters had made. He still had some tingling in his fingers and toes from the cold of the hunting excursion. He flipped a page in the magazine he was looking at when he felt the smack of getting hit in the back of the head. He turned quickly, figuring it was one of his sisters. It was his father.

"What the hell kind of shit was that out in the woods today?" Teddy said. TH could smell whiskey on his breath.

TH shrugged. "I don't know."

"You don't know! You faked a missed shot and then there you are bawling like a baby when I bagged that buck. You embarrassed the hell out of me in front of Ben."

"I'm sorry." TH was trembling.

His father lowered himself so his face was level with TH's. "Sorry will not cut it. I didn't raise you to be a little pussy. We don't do pussy in this family. You got that, son?" The smell of whiskey was strong.

"Yes, sir," TH answered, tears welling in his eyes.

"That shit just won't go down around here."

Lying in the motel bed, TH felt his eyes glass over again. Over twenty years later and the scene still got him. That had been the beginning, he thought. That had been when TH had started to lose respect for his father and began to hate him.

· · ·

After failing to get back to sleep, TH decided to shower, get dressed and find something to eat. He ended up at the Start of the Day Café, an old place on 20. TH never ate that much breakfast, but he wasn't looking for quality. As it was, the coffee was lukewarm, and the pancakes were thick and too doughy. The salvation was the bacon; it was perfect.

He was looking deep into his second cup of coffee when he heard the little bell above the door ring. He looked up and saw the tall figure of Steve Marks enter the diner. Steve had been a classmate of TH's back in high school and a good friend. Now he was a detective on the police force. At first, TH thought the local cops might be tracking him, but Marks took a seat at the other end of the counter, unaware that TH was there.

TH had always liked Marks, so he picked up his coffee cup and strode around the corner. He was halfway to him when Marks spotted him coming. He got a big smile on his face.

"Look what the cat dragged in," Marks said. TH had forgotten how tall Marks was. He was well over six feet. He also forgot that Marks always dressed well.

"I thought you might have come in here to give me a hard time like some of your alumni did last night." TH took the stool next to Marks.

"What are you talking about?"

"Saw some of Milton's finest at Lifers last night."

"Don't tell me. Davis, Smith and Aft?"

"That would be the crew."

"Anything bad happen?"

"Ben and Jack were alright. Aft was an asshole, but I expected that."

Marks' coffee came, and TH noted that it was piping hot. "Aft is and can be a tremendous asshole."

"It was no big deal," TH said. "How is your artist girlfriend?"

"Her name is Tori, TH. She's fine. We're good." Marks took a sip of his own coffee. "TH, look I'm sorry about Melissa. I don't know what to say. It was a shock. I felt real bad for Booker. He looked like his life was over."

"It may be. I saw him last night, and he was pretty well into the bottle. He was having his daddy make all the arrangements for Melissa. Said he couldn't handle it."

"He couldn't find snow in a fucking blizzard."

TH laughed. "He was always a bit slow on the uptake," he said. "You guys don't know anything, do you?"

Marks shook his head. "About Melissa? Absolutely nothing. I was at home when the call came it. Case was ruled a suicide, and nobody has a clue why."

"Why it was ruled a suicide?"

"No. Why she did it. Everyone I talk to just shakes their head."

"I did too. Everyone coming out to the wake tonight?"

"I expect most of the town. Some out of respect for your father; a lot because they really liked Melissa. Teachers and students at the high school loved her. Town still loves your dad."

"Is Lou going to come out?" Lou Katz, another ex-schoolmate was the current Chief of Police. TH had once dated his wife, Mary.

"He'll be there. Mary, too."

"That was a long time ago, Steve."

The big detective ran his hand through his wavy, brown hair. "Anyway, I think just about everybody will be there."

The waitress did stop by and top off TH's cup with some of the hot coffee, and it tasted a lot better. "Ben Smith was telling me that Cindy Fuller finally got rid of Troy Stripling."

"That Stripling. He never grew up and just kept messing up. I don't know what Cindy saw in him, but he's gone. Left town."

"Cindy still a looker?"

"Looks the same TH, even after their daughter was born. She was no doubt the prettiest girl at that high school while we were there. Maybe a line or two in the face, but still gorgeous. Why don't you look her up?"

"I don't think so. I spent a good part of my high school years getting rejected by her and then seeing her end up with Stripling. My ego can't take anymore kicking in the teeth."

"Speaking of Cindy Fuller, you know they let Skitch Grayson out of prison."

TH was raising his cup to his lips but stopped. "They let him out?"

"He got lung cancer and it ain't good. Looks like maybe less than six months to go. He's in Marymore Nursing Home over in Platteville."

"No shit?"

"I still don't think he did it."

TH knew he was talking about killing Fatty Fuller. "You're not alone on that one, but we'll never know. I'm still surprised they let him out."

"The man's dying, TH. Sitting in a cage isn't going to make much difference at this point."

"I guess you're right. So how are things with my dad out and Lou running the ship? Same old Gestapo tactics?"

"Lou's a good man and runs it pretty tight. He's nothing like your dad and has a modern law enforcement approach to things. I think he's is going to be fine."

"He just doesn't like me."

"Well, you did sleep with his wife."

"That was a long time ago, as I said, and she wasn't his wife back then."

"That's just one of those things that guys don't forget."

TH looked at his watch and realized it was time for him to be heading over to pick up Rachel. "I've got to be going, Stevie. Off to see my old man."

Marks extended his hand and TH shook it. "I'd say something warm and fuzzy, but I know how much you two get along."

"Time heals all wounds."

"Yeah, in some cases. And TH, while you're in town, stay away from Aft. Since he retired he just drinks too much and seems to be all kinds of trouble."

"Where are the cops when this stuff happens?"

"Oh, we're around. It's just that those guys have a little bit of immunity around here. Just be careful."

TH nodded. "I will, Steve."

By the time TH got to Rachel's house, the sun had broken through some early clouds, but it was still cold. Most of the trees still had their leaves, but none were green. The browns, yellows, and reds of fall had taken over. As he pulled into Milton, TH reflected how pretty and peaceful a site it was. Much better than most of the day would be, he thought.

"Don't say a fucking word to dad until I get a chance to speak to him first," were the first words out of Rachel's mouth when she got in the car.

"I wasn't planning on saying very much, anyway."

She turned to him and patted his arm. "I'm sorry. I get so worked up over these visits. I never know how he is going to act. It's unnerving."

"I'll just follow your lead."

"Hopefully he's remotely human." She took out a pack of cigarettes and lit one. She quickly lowered her window. "This is what Melissa was really good at. When she'd go with me to see dad she could really get him to calm down."

TH was pretty sure that wouldn't be the case with his father seeing him. He just hoped he didn't rile him up too much.

Hillside Manor, where his father resided, was a combination of a nursing and rehabilitation center. It was north of Milton about fifteen miles. Most of the drive took them along the Mississippi, and then they followed a tree-lined road that took them up to a bluff that overlooked the river.

"Nice spot," TH said.

"Meeting with dad usually negates that feeling."

They were met in the lobby of the rehab portion of the building by a big, black woman, over six feet tall. Her name was Sheila Jones.

"Your dad is in his usual spot," Sheila said as she led them down a long hall. TH looked to Rachel for help.

"You'll see," she said.

They exited the building and walked along a tree covered path towards the river. It was still cold even though it had warmed up since early morning. They climbed another path of concrete that led them to a circular platform that gave them an excellent view of the river and the bluffs across from them. Towards the edge of the platform sat a hunched figure in a wheelchair.

"I'll let Teddy know that he has visitors," Sheila said.

They waited behind while the nurse approached the wheelchair.

"What's this?" TH said.

"This is where he sits. All day unless it's below freezing, snowing or raining. Sits here all day long, pissed at the world, and looking at the river."

"What about food?"

"Eats breakfast inside, they bring his lunch and dinner to him, weather permitting."

Sheila came back to them. "He said he didn't want any company, but I persuaded him to see you two. You know how he can be, Rachel."

Rachel smiled weakly.

"I'll leave you all alone. Just have reception find me when you leave." She turned and walked back the way they had come.

"Here we go," Rachel said. She stepped forward near her father; TH followed behind and out of sight.

"Hey dad," she said, coming around on the side to face her father. "It's me Rachel."

"I told that damn black nurse that I didn't want to see anyone," Teddy Brown blurted out.

"She told us you wouldn't mind seeing us for a bit. We'll only stay for a little while."

"Not too long," I hope, Teddy said.

"I brought someone here to see you."

"Where's Melissa?" Teddy asked. "She hasn't been to see me."

Rachel looked back at TH and then her father. "She's not here today, Dad. I brought someone else." Rachel waved TH forward. He moved along the edge of the platform noting that his father sat only about ten feet from the precipice of a cliff.

When he got close, Teddy Brown was staring straight ahead. His entire body was dressed in warm clothes, and there was also a thick blanket covering him. On his head was a wool cap that had been pulled down over his ears. The only thing TH could make out was his face. The old chiseled face had been replaced by one with lines, a side that drooped a bit and an eye that looked half closed. His nose was running a little, and there was dried residue around his mouth.

"Hello, dad," TH said.

The sickened face turned towards him. At first, there was no sign that his father recognized him. Both the good and bad eye perused for a moment. He brought the blanket up with his good hand and wiped his nose. "Well, if it isn't the son of a bitch son I have from California."

TH smiled. "I guess I have that coming. It's been a little long since I've been here."

"Well, what do you want?"

"I just wanted to stop by and see you and..."

"We have some news," Rachel said loudly.

"I hope it's better than the guest you brought to see me."

"It's not, dad," Rachel said, choking up. She wiped her eyes with a tissue. "It's about Melissa."

"What about Melissa?"

She wiped her eyes again. "Melissa died the night before last."

Teddy got a puzzled look on his face. He was trying hard to calculate something. "That can't be," he said. "She's only got to be like thirty years old."

"She was thirty-nine dad."

Teddy shook his head and his nose leaked. "People that are thirty-nine don't die."

Rachel was full out crying now; she had her chin down to her chest.

"Melissa killed herself, dad," TH said.

Teddy turned to look at TH and TH could see the anger that filled his eyes, but then they softened. "Why would she do something stupid like that?"

"Nobody knows," TH said. "The wake is tonight at seven. Ben Smith and Jack Davis are coming out to get you to bring you to Keifer's. Nurse Jones knows so she'll make sure you are ready."

Teddy was quiet for a moment, closed both eyes, and then nodded slowly. "I need you two to go now."

After walking back to the building and checking out, they were back in the car. Rachel was still crying, but not as much.

"He's a delightful fellow," TH said.

"A real peach."

"Seems pretty sharp."

"Sometimes, but the brain is only part of it. His legs don't work well, his left arm is dead, and he can't control his bodily functions. Sometimes I understand why he's a bit cranky."

"I'm sure seeing me didn't help."

She nodded and wiped away more tears. "That didn't seem to get things off to a great start."

•   •   •

Joseph Running Bear lived on fifty-five acres of wooded land near the town of Sterling. He did his own farming and raised cows, pigs and chickens. All of the vegetables that he ate were grown on his property. Any deer that were killed on his property he kept half the meat for himself. Joseph was a descendent of the Ottawa tribe; his family owned a large percentage of a casino near Minocqua, Wisconsin. He had a degree in Agriculture from Michigan State University. When he was twenty, he just missed qualifying for the United States Rifle Team. At twenty-three he was an Army Ranger Scout in Iraq. The following year he lost the lower part of his left leg to an IED. He had been on this land ever since he recovered from the injury.

TH drove the rental down the long drive that led to Joseph's house and office. He was glad when he got there that he only saw an old, beat-up Ford pickup in the lot. He knew it belonged to Joseph. He parked his car and stepped out into the bright sunshine. The air had warmed, but it was still cold. He thought of his father sitting out there under that blanket with his nose running.

"You're trespassing," said a voice in front of TH.

He looked to the front porch and saw the large figure of Joseph Running Bear looking at him. Joseph had graduated from the same high school class as TH. Even though they had drastically different circles of friends, they had always been close. "What do you do to trespassers, Joseph?"

The large Indian walked down the steps towards him. "On a day like this, with no one else around, I usually shoot them and feed them to the pigs."

"Usually?"

"I make exceptions, but rarely."

The two men hugged. "It's good to see you," TH said. Joseph was six-four, and he looked like he had put a little weight on.

"And you, my friend, but I am sorry that it is under these circumstances."

"You heard already?"

"I went to Sinclair's Hardware in Milton yesterday. It was all the old guys were talking about. When did you get in?"

"Last night. I saw Rachel and Booker last night. Saw my dad today."

"I heard he isn't doing so well."

"Mentally, he seemed okay; physically, he's still a mess."

"Treat you okay?"

"Probably not as well as you treat some of those pigs you've got."

"That bad, huh?"

"We're not real close. It's no secret."

"We have that in common. My dad still wants me to come up there and look over things around the casino. I always tell him no. I don't want to end up like all my relatives, doing nothing but getting drunk all day."

"Business good here?"

"There's always deer here, TH. We cull them every year, and every year there's more. Things are fine."

"You gonna make it to the wake?"

"I will. I hope the Three Amigos don't decide to pick me up for something." Joseph had gotten into a few altercations in town when he was younger. Logan Aft had arrested him twice. "That, and I hope my suit fits."

TH laughed. "I saw that fine group of gentlemen last night at Lifer's. Aft was his usual charming self."

Joseph's eyes narrowed. "Did he hassle you?"

TH shrugged. "More like telling me that I was a horrible son and then a pussy for not killing that deer back when I was twelve."

"He's just an asshole, TH, and a bigger one now as he gets older."

"Harder to get any worse."

"Don't know if you heard this or not, but Skitch Grayson got let out. Lung cancer."

"I ran into Marks. He told me."

Joseph nodded. "Stevie's a good one, but watch out for Lou. He doesn't like you. But anyway, I went and saw Skitch. He used to do some work for my mom when we moved down here. He was always real good to me."

TH's stomach tightened. Thoughts of the night that his father had told him that Fatty Fuller had been murdered crossed his mind. "So how is Skitch?"

"He wasn't so good, but good enough to tell me he had nothing to do with Fatty's murder. It was Aft and his buddies that set him up with that fishing gear story. He said they knew he used to fish along Whisper Creek all the time. That was his story."

TH remembered the day of the crime, the arrest of Skitch three days later, and then the quick trial and conviction. He never focused on whether Skitch Grayson was innocent or guilty. He only thought about his friend, Fatty Fuller, who he would never see again. The thoughts of Skitch's innocence came later.

"I was just getting ready to grill some burgers and have a beer," Joseph said. "You got a little time for lunch?"

TH's older brother Richie had told Rachel he'd be in town by four. The wake was scheduled to start at seven. "Sure, Joseph."

"If there's time after we eat, we can have a shooting contest."

"Why would I want to have a shooting contest with you?"

Joseph raised the titanium leg and smiled. "So I can tell people that a one-legged man beat you."

•   •   •

When he returned to his motel, there was a car with Missouri plates parked right in front of the stairs that led up to his room. When he got out of his car, TH saw the other car door open, and a man got out. TH recognized his brother, Richie. Where TH was a little shorter and stockier, Richie was taller and thinner. He hadn't seen Richie in over four years, and his brother looked older. His once full head of hair was going gray and wasn't as thick.

"You came all the way out here to greet me?" TH asked.

"Wasn't that far, and Rachel's kids were making enough noise to drive someone crazy."

They shook hands and looked at each other. At forty-one, Richie was eight years older than TH. He had left to fight in Iraq during Desert Storm and had then gone onto Kansas City and become a detective. TH had seen him four or five times in seventeen years.

"You look pretty good, little brother," Richie said.

TH held his finger and thumb about an inch apart. "I work out a little."

"Probably just getting chased by people who think you're stealing their cars."

"It is aerobic at times."

"Shall we get a beer or two before the wake begins?"

TH thought of the encounter at Lifers. "Let's stay out here. I don't need to go into town any more than I have to."

"Fine by me," Richie said.

They ended up at a little roadside bar called Johnny's that served burgers, Bud Light and Bud. Wine was red or white. The selection for hard liquor was more advanced. The two brothers settled on Bud Lights.

"Nice place," Richie said, looking around at the collection of mounted neon beer signs.

"Never been here, but the beer is cold."

Richie took a long swallow. "So what do you think?"

TH eyed him cautiously. "What do I think about what?"

"Don't answer a fucking question with one of your own. What do you think about Melissa?"

TH took a long drink of his own. "I don't know what to think. I got the impression that she had a pretty smooth, kind of organized life. If somebody asks you who you think is going to commit suicide her name isn't close to coming up for an answer."

"That's exactly right. I asked Rachel what she thought, but she didn't have any idea. She said you went and talked to Booker."

"The night I got here. He was in shock and very drunk. Genuine shock. I don't think he was capable of doing anything. His father was taking care of all the funeral and wake stuff."

"Bob Booker wasn't too capable on his best days."

TH laughed and raised his glass to toast Richie. "I saw dad this morning."

"Yeah. That's what Rachel told me. Said he got all emotional when he saw you."

"Something like that."

"Can you blame him, TH? The man had a stroke in March, and you wait until one of his daughters hangs herself to come see him. I don't care what kind of shitty relationship you have, that's pretty cold."

"How often do you come around?"

"Not that much, but I did come to see him after the stroke."

TH drained his first beer. "How does he treat you? You left home for the Marines and then went to KC to become a cop. Dad was pretty sure you'd be doing what Lou Katz is doing right now."

Richie waived to the waitress for two more beers. "Well, fuck that. I didn't want dad as my boss, didn't care for the way they managed Milton, and just didn't care for Milton."

"You always knew you weren't coming back here?"

The waitress came and smiled broadly at Richie. She was in her mid-thirties with dark hair, brown eyes, and a noticeable bosom. "She likes me, TH."

"You are a married man."

"On the road, little bro, and yes, I knew I was never coming back. One day we were fighting near Bagdad, and it hit me. I thought if I ever got out of that shithole, I'd never come back to this one. Just don't see the point in it."

"Why Kansas City?"

"Met a girl. She lived in KC. She became my wife."

TH had met Richie's wife Karen a couple of times. "That makes sense."

"How about you? You never wanted to come back?"

"Only when I feel guilty about missing something but other than that, no. I missed Rachel and Melissa, but still never thought I'd come back for good. Business is too good, anyway."

"You can make money stealing shit from people?"

"Pretty good money. And the shit I steal is not really owned by the people I steal it from."

"If you say so," Richie took another long swig of beer. "So is there any reason to be poking around to find out if there was anything wrong with Melissa? If the people who were closest to her don't know anything, I'm not sure we're going to find anything."

TH drank from his bottle. "You are probably right. You can go around asking everybody in town if they knew if something was bothering Melissa Brown and they'd all say no."

"Rachel was telling me that they let Skitch Grayson out of jail due to the fact that he's got lung cancer."

"I've heard that three times since I've been home. I guess the man is dying."

"People are just telling you because you were so close to Fatty."

"What do you think of that whole case?"

"A little rush to judgement for me. Skitch may have stolen the fishing gear, but to walk up behind Fatty and smash him in the head with a rock, I don't think so."

"You really don't believe he did it?"

"Skitch might have been a drunk, and once in a while he fell asleep in

Town Square, but that man wouldn't hurt a fly. There's no way he killed Fatty Fuller."

Milton has two funeral homes located within its city boundaries. Keifer's was the oldest, and it looked it according to TH. Everything about the place looked ancient. The Keifer family had been running the home for over a hundred years, and the current owners were old and dying out. They hadn't made any improvements to the home in years.

Keifer's had three parlors for wakes and Melissa was laid out in the largest. TH figured they were expecting a large crowd, but right now the place was quiet. The wake was to begin at seven, but he had arrived at six for a private viewing. Even as she lay there in her casket, Melissa looked so beautiful and so young. The only thing that seemed out of line was the scarf the home had arranged around her neck to hide the abuse the belt had done to her during the hanging.

TH's mother had died when he was four years old; his father was a workaholic. When he was younger, care at the Brown house was provided by hired help. As he got older, TH was raised by his brother and two sisters. Melissa, being the oldest girl, assumed the mother role. She always looked out for TH, especially when he began to argue with their father. She had always been a good sister, and now she was gone. TH had never thanked her, and now he couldn't say goodbye. Sitting in the row of chairs in front of the casket, he found himself sobbing and tears running down his face. As much as he hated his father, the reason that he seldom came home, he was mad at himself for ignoring his family. None of them had ever hurt TH.

When the wake began, TH found it funny how the members of his family positioned themselves. Bob Booker and the two boys sat on the couch directly in front of Melissa's casket. Teddy Brown and the Three Amigos set up shop just to the left of the casket. His father had been dressed in a dark suit with no tie. Even though he slumped a bit in his wheelchair, he looked better than he had out on the cold bluff. Rachel and her kids were standing to the side of Teddy. Richie was near the rear of the parlor, looking overly tense. Everybody had their own way of dealing with death, thought TH.

TH stood alone in the middle of the room on the opposite side of Rachel and Richie. He was nervous and edgy but composed. He was stunned at the number of people who came into the parlor at just past seven. It was like a starting gun had gone off. Most of the people were from town, and TH knew them all a little. There were some faces he didn't recognize and quite a few that he did. He smiled and shook hands, taking in all of the condolences. TH noticed that small groups of people were near Richie and Rachel, old friends. The largest group was by Teddy. There were twice as many people consoling Teddy as there were Booker and the boys. It was true that he was a town favorite.

He shook a woman's hand, forgetting her name, but remembering she had taught with Melissa at the school. He turned away as the woman approached the casket. When he turned back, he was looking into the beautiful face of Cindy Fuller. It had been years since he had seen her and not much had changed. There might be a couple of facial lines, but the green eyes still glowed and the red hair still shined. She smiled and gave TH a big hug.

"I thought I might see you at a wake or funeral someday," she said. "I thought it might be my dad or yours after his stroke. I never thought it would be Melissa."

"I never plan my trips to Milton, and I never thought my next one would be to bury one of my siblings."

Tears gathered at her eye's corners. One large one ran the length of her face. She reached up with a Kleenex to wipe it away. "I'm so sorry, TH. Melissa was such a good person. She was always nice to me and especially to Freddie. It just seems like such a waste." Freddie was Fatty Fuller's legal name.

TH fought to hold back his own emotions. "None of it makes any sense."

"It just brought back all of those old feelings when Freddie was murdered. Why was all I could think? Who would do something like that? Now it's why Melissa would do anything like that?"

"We may never know."

She took his hand in hers. "How long are you in town for?"

"Few days at least. I want to make sure everything is in as good a shape as can be before I leave."

"Come see me out at Ace's. I'm always on lunch at one. I'm sure there's a lot to talk about."

TH felt his chest swell. "I'll do that, Cindy. Before you go, is your dad doing okay?"

She shrugged. "Still fighting it, you know. He wanted to be here tonight, but I don't know if he'll show. It depends on what shape he's in." Fred Fuller, Cindy's father, had been an alcoholic for as long as TH could remember.

TH nodded. "I'll be sure to come see you."

She smiled and kissed him on the cheek. She started off towards the casket viewing line.

TH rubbed away a couple of tears and scanned the room. The group by his father had swelled, and both Richie and Rachel were talking with a number of people. He was never the family favorite with anyone, and many scorned him for leaving home and not returning very much. He was sure not coming back after his father's stroke had not helped people's opinion of him. Whatever opinions people had of him he had earned, he thought. He was ready to go outside and get a bit of fresh air when Steve Marks walked up to him.

"Twice in one day," TH joked.

"Sorry, it had to be at this venue."

"It's a sad one."

"I see your father is holding quite a grand court."

"He is. Forever the town hero."

"I guess I'll go give the ring a kiss after I see Melissa. Sorry, again, TH. I don't know what to say."

"There's nothing to say."

•   •   •

Across the room, Teddy Brown was greeting one visitor after another. Teddy, not much of a big talker anyway, said little. Most of the people shook his hand, asked how he was doing and thanked him for all of the service he had done for Milton. Teddy would nod once in a while, cracked a smile or two, but said nothing. When there was a break in visitors, Logan Aft idled up close to Teddy.

"I see your kid over there talking to that smart ass, Marks," Aft said. "Those two never got it right, Teddy."

Teddy lifted his head a little; there was a streak of drool running from his mouth. Jack Davis leaned in and wiped it for him with a handkerchief.

"We had a little run-in with TH at Lifers the other night. He was very disrespectful and made some half-assed comment about having to go and see you. I almost smacked the shit out of him right there. Isn't that the truth, boys?"

"He's never been very respectful," Jack Davis said.

"I didn't think it was a big deal," Ben Smith said.

Aft shot him a dirty look. "Don't be smart, Ben. The kid wasn't nice at all."

Ben Smith rolled his eyes and looked away.

"You want us to roust TH a little, boss. You always said that kid needed a good kick in the ass."

Teddy lifted his eyes toward Aft. He stared until Aft turned his eyes away. "I always said that TH needed a good kick in the ass from me. If the time comes that I for sure can't do it, I'll ask for help, Logan."

"Yes, sir," Aft said quietly. Ben Smith smiled.

•   •   •

TH finally got his chance to step outside and headed towards the exit. He was almost out of the parlor door when he nearly bumped into Mary Katz. She looked up in surprise as the two almost collided.

"Why hello, TH," she said. "Leaving already?"

Mary Katz was a little taller than TH and always wore flats when they went out. Tonight she wore a shorter heel but stood a couple of inches taller than him. She looked good in the navy dress she wore. TH knew they had three children, but her figure didn't show it. Except for a few grays showing in her long, dark hair, there were few signs of aging.

"I was just going to step out and get some air for a minute. It's very stuffy in here. Where's Lou?"

She pointed in the direction where Teddy and his crew were sitting. TH saw Lou Katz having a discussion with the four former cops. "He went in before me. I forgot something in the car."

"Does he know that he doesn't have to be that nice to my dad anymore?"

"Be nice, yourself. This is your sister's wake."

"I'm sorry," TH said. "Just been a lot going on the past few days."

"I know, and I'm sorry about Melissa. It was a shock to us all. Lou's people have been asking around, and a lot of people who knew Melissa said they knew nothing. It's a great mystery."

"Seems that way. Both Rachel and Bob Booker have the same story. The thing just blindsided them."

"Can we have lunch one day before you head back to California? I'd really like to catch up with you," she said.

For a moment he thought her eyes looked sad. Where Cindy Brown was the one that TH pined for, Mary Katz was the one that got away. "That would be nice," he said.

"This is what I forgot in the car." She handed TH a piece of folded paper and started off in the direction of her husband, still talking to Teddy's group.

When he stepped outside, he found that the night had clouded over. A dampness and chill had set in. It was only October, but it felt like snow. He lit a cigarette under a street light and opened the piece of paper Mary had given him. All it said was her name and a ten digit phone number. TH folded the paper and stuck it in his wallet. How harmful could a lunch be?

He was about to head back into the home when he heard his voice being called. He looked to his left, and a woman was walking up the sidewalk towards him.

"Is that you, TH?"

The woman had gotten closer and stepped into a patch of light. She was wearing a raincoat, but TH could make out the perfect hourglass figure under it. He could also see the bright, blonde hair being blown by the wind.

"It is, Tiffany. How are you?"

If there was a rebellious girl in TH's class, it was Tiffany Martin. She came from a broken family, and her mother was a partier and a gambler. Tiffany wore revealing clothes and make-up before they hit high school and she was always in trouble. TH had heard that in later years she had been picked up for solicitation.

"I'm good. I've been sober for a year, TH," she said proudly. "I've been really trying to get myself back in order."

"That's good, Tiff."

"I'm real sorry about your sister, and all. I didn't know her, but all I heard were good things."

"She was a real good person."

"I just wanted to stop by and see your dad and say I'm sorry. There were a bunch of times I got myself in trouble, and your dad helped me out. He's a good man."

TH smiled. Many in the Milton community revered his father.

"You steal repoing out in LA?"

"That's what I do."

"That's kind of funny. Your dad's this big cop, and you're kind of a thief."

TH nodded and let the remark go as Tiffany started towards the home entrance. He waited before she was inside before he headed back in.

•   •   •

Inside of the parlor, TH found Richie and Rachel talking in one of the corners of the room. No one else was with them at the moment.

"Saw a couple of your old lady friends stop by and see you," Rachel said. She wore a big smile, but TH noticed the heavy dark shadows under each eye.

"Guess I was popular once in this town."

"Once is the operative word," Richie said. "Mary Katz and Cindy Brown both still look pretty good."

"You men are pigs," Rachel said.

"That's nothing," TH said. "Tiffany Martin stopped by to say hello outside. She still looks pretty good, too."

"That one's trouble," Rachel said, "and her name isn't Martin anymore. Now she goes by Tiffany Gold. She got busted several years back for hooking, but dad got her off. Now I guess she makes an honest living as a dancer at The Heavenly Palace."

The Heavenly Palace was a strip club on Brewster. "I guess that's legal," TH said. He noticed that Tiffany was talking with his father and the Three Amigos. They all seemed to be laughing.

"From what I hear, if you pay for a couple of table dances that will get you admitted to the back room where you can get a BJ if you want," she said. "I don't think Tiffany has gone totally legal yet."

Richie was smiling. "She had a tough life with her dad gone and the mother drinking and gambling all the time."

"We didn't have the greatest life," Rachel said. "Our mom was gone, and we didn't end up hooking or dealing drugs."

"What was so wrong with our lives?" Richie said.

Rachel pointed to the other end of the room. "He's sitting over there in that fucking wheel chair."

Before Richie could respond, a middle-aged woman, in a rumpled dress came up to them. Her hair was severely windblown, and her mascara told you she had been crying a lot. In her hand, she carried a soggy handkerchief.

"Hello, Margaret," Rachel said. "Richie, TH, this is Margaret Hatch. She's one of the teachers at the high school."

"Nice to meet you," Richie said.

"Don't sweet talk me," Margaret said. She looked like she was gritting her teeth. "You Brown's, every last one of you, from your father down to TH, should be ashamed of yourselves. The way you act all high and mighty around here and have no respect for each other. You are the ones that are ultimately responsible for what happened to Melissa. Such a warm and good person and now she is gone. Go home, all of you, take a look in the mirror and you'll see the reason she is no longer here." With that, Margaret turned and marched away from them towards the exit.

"What the hell was that about?" TH asked.

"She doesn't seem to like us very much," Richie said.

"She's just a lonely old curmudgeon of a woman," Rachel said.

•   •   •

While they were talking to Margaret Hatch, Joseph Running Bear entered the parlor on the other side of the room. In most social settings he felt uncomfortable. In this one, where he felt he should put on a suit and tie he felt totally out of place. The suit he wore didn't fit well, and the dress shoes hurt his feet. He was there to pay respects to TH and then he would be gone. He was waiting for the Browns to finish with Margaret Hatch before he went over there.

From all the way in the front of the parlor, Logan Aft saw Joseph standing all alone in the corner. He nudged Jack Davis. "Look who decided to pay a visit to Milton tonight."

"Tonight of all nights," Jack said.

"Must have forgot what the rules were." Aft hitched up his pants and with Davis behind him headed toward Joseph. They walked along the wall opposite of where TH stood with his brother and sister, but he saw what was happening.

"Oh shit," TH said. "He grabbed Richie's arm and pointed at the duo moving swiftly towards the rear of the parlor.

"Look at who decided to pay us all a visit," Aft said when he got to Joseph. Joseph was almost a full foot taller than Aft.

"Good evening, Mr. Aft, "Joseph said quietly.

"What are you doing here, Injun Joe?" Aft said.

Joseph looked straight ahead. "I have come to pay respect to the Brown family for the loss of their daughter and sister."

"Well, I think you have paid enough respect. Time to head back to the reservation."

"When I have spoken to TH, I will leave," Joseph said.

"What's going on here?" Ben Smith said. He had come up behind Jack.

"Injun Joe knows he ain't supposed to be inside the town limits," Aft said. "I was just reminding him."

Jack Davis unbuttoned his suit jacket, revealing a holstered forty-five. "Time to leave, Joe."

"Hold on a minute," TH said, coming up to the group. Richie was right behind him. "Joe's just here to see me. That's all. This is my sister's wake."

"You don't think we are going to listen to you, TH, do you?" Aft said.

There was a brief moment of silence where all of the parties could feel the tension rising. Aft wore his snarling face, Jack Davis had his gun ready, and Ben Smith wasn't sure what he was supposed to do. Joseph looked calm while TH and Richie looked tense.

"Stop it! Stop it right now." The voice came from behind them all, and they all turned to see the tall, skinny figure of Lou Katz. Steve Marks trailed behind him. "What the hell is going on here?"

Logan Aft smiled. "Well, Chief Katz, Injun Joe here knows he's not supposed to be inside of the town limits."

"Logan, you know that there are no restraining orders in place to keep Joseph out of the town," Lou said. "If he's not breaking any laws, there's no reason why he can't be in town."

Again that big Aft smile. "It's an understanding with Joseph that we've had for quite a few years."

Lou Katz shook his head. "Not tonight, Logan. Joseph can pay his respects. You boys should head out and go get a beer."

Aft stopped smiling and looked at Joseph. "Don't fuck up, Injun Joe, cause we know where you live."

Aft stepped to the side and deliberately banged into TH as he tried to get out of the exit. He backed up a bit as Jack Davis appeared behind him, coat open, showing the revolver. "You watch it too, TH. We don't need any shit from you while you're in town."

"Sure thing, Mr. Aft," TH said as Aft, Jack Davis, and Ben Smith walked out of the room.

Lou Katz shook his head and headed back to where his wife was still keeping Teddy company.

"Some things never fucking change," Steve Marks said. He turned to go back towards Lou.

TH walked out onto the porch in front of the home and watched as the Three Amigos headed for the parking lot. Joseph Running Bear came out after him.

"Not the friendliest group of people in town," Joseph said.

"It's Aft. He's the one always looking for trouble. Davis just follows him, and Ben Smith is somewhere in the middle."

"At least Lou stuck up for us."

"Lou couldn't have a fight break out in a funeral home while the Chief of Police and his top Deputy are standing there. Watch out for Aft. He's itching for some type of trouble. Why'd you come here anyway?"

"Like I told Aft, to pay my respects."

"You paid your respects when I saw you and, anyway, you look silly in that suit and tie."

Joseph smiled. "I tried. My feet are very sore. At least, one foot."

TH smiled. "Just look out for Aft."

"I won't be coming into Milton for a while. If he wants me that bad, he'd have to come out to the preserve, and that would be a serious mistake."

The door opened behind them, and Lou and Mary Katz stepped out onto the porch. Mary smiled weakly. Lou looked disgusted.

"Thanks for stepping in, Lou," TH said. "If you hadn't it might have gotten ugly. You never know with Aft."

"I'm sorry, Joseph," Lou said. "Sometimes Aft thinks he's still active duty and their word is what matters in the town."

"I'm used to Aft giving me a bad time, Lou. I just thought he'd be a little better behaved inside of a funeral home," Joseph said.

"Might as well have been Lifers," TH said.

Lou nodded. "TH, I'm very sorry about Melissa. We all knew her, and it's a great loss for everyone. I just wish I had more to tell you about why she did what she did. We've asked around, and no one knows anything."

"It's the great mystery," TH said.

"I was talking with your dad, and he told me how happy he was that you came by to see him. Said he was glad you set yourself up out in California. I think he actually said he was proud of you."

"Doesn't sound like my dad."

"I heard him say it," Mary said. She was smiling broadly.

All for show, thought TH. "I guess I'll have to take that as a minor victory."

•   •   •

Behind the home that the Fullers lived in on Maple Street was a small shed that was used for storing gardening tools and a myriad of junk that accumulated dust and rust. When Freddie "Fatty" Fuller was nine years old, he began an immense interest in animals. His interest was at such a high level that he began capturing a number of these animals and house them in the shed that eventually became a menagerie. All of the tools and junk were cleared out of the shed, Fatty's father installed shelves, lighting, and heat, and the small zoo grew. The shelves became crowded with cages, tanks, and bowls housing mice, a rat, a hamster, a guinea pig, two rabbits, turtles, newts, frogs, fish and even a couple of birds that Fatty had found injured and nurtured back to health. Sometimes there were mishaps when the electricity that was running to the shed went out. This caused the heating to be sporadic in the winter, and a few of the creatures suffered, but under Fatty's careful eye most of the animals did pretty well. Other than fishing, which allowed Fatty to peruse the banks of Whisper Creek for new additions to the zoo, the animals were Fatty's biggest interest. On the door, a sign proudly read, "Freddie Fuller's Zoo".

It was almost understood that if you visited the Fuller home, you would be invited by Fatty to come and see his zoo. Only the rude, or those that had seen it many times, begged off on the invitation. TH had seen it so many times that he could recite exactly what animals were present in the zoo. He had witnessed the highs of Fatty acquiring a new animal and also the lows of watching Fatty's distress at one of the critter's passing. TH never said no when Fatty asked him to see the zoo. He knew how much it meant to him. TH began to understand what a special person Fatty was by exhibiting the care he provided to the animals that resided in the zoo. TH hoped he would find a passion one day that would match that of Fatty's.

In the summer, before TH's sophomore year in high school, July had been an oppressive month. The temperature hit a hundred degrees on several occasions, and it didn't rain for five weeks. Milton and the surrounding areas were parched in the midst of a full-fledged drought. The baseball diamonds that TH spent most of his days on were rock hard. The town's fire department issued several warnings. Anything in the area that was made of wood was close to being kindling. Fires would be imminent and dangerous.

On the night of July eleventh the phone rang in the Brown home. TH was still in his baseball uniform, sitting in the kitchen eating a leftover meal of meatloaf and mashed potatoes. His sister Rachel answered the phone and quickly called for their father. Teddy Brown had been in the living room, and TH heard him pick up the phone.

"Oh shit," Teddy said loudly. "Let me get my things, and I'll be right over."

"What is it, dad?" Rachel said.

"Somebody torched that little zoo that Fatty had in their back yard. I guess the thing just about burned to the ground."

"Oh my god," Rachel said.

TH got up from his chair in the kitchen and raced into the living room where his father was gathering his things. "I'm going with you," he said.

His father looked him up and down, standing there in his dirty uniform. "Your job is to settle Fatty down. I guess he's pretty upset."

It was only a block and a half walk to the Fuller's house, and even in the dark, they could see smoke rising from the back of the house. When they got to the back yard, the fire department was done. Where Fatty's zoo had been was now a pile of smoking rubble. TH could make out Cindy Fuller and her father and Ben Smith with Jack Davis.

"It's totally gone, Chief," Ben Smith said.

"The fire department said gasoline was used to start the fire and with the wood being so dry it went up like hay," Jack Davis said.

"Jesus Christ," Teddy Brown said.

TH walked over to Cindy. He could see the tears streaming from her eyes. "Where's Freddie," he asked.

She turned to him. "He's in the house. He couldn't look at it any longer."

One of the things Fatty did was take a Polaroid of every animal in the zoo and give it a name. The pictures were then posted in a photo album with the animals' name and date it entered the zoo written below it. TH found Fatty on their living room floor looking over his picture album. TH sat down next to him.

"You okay, Freddie?"

Fatty looked at TH with red eyes and crusting around his nose where it had run and dried. "Remember Herman, TH?" he said. He was pointing at a picture of a light brown mouse, one of the zoo's first residents. TH was quickly reminded of how young Fatty acted.

"I do."

"And Jimmy?" Fatty was pointing at a cricket that had lived a lot longer than TH would have imagined.

"They're all gone now, but I have my pictures to remember them TH. I can remember them."

"Freddie, as soon as we can, we'll get started on building you another shed, and you can start the zoo back up."

Fatty was looking intently at the pictures and TH wasn't sure he had heard him. "We'll get the zoo started up as quickly as we can," he said again.

"No. No more zoo." He held up the album. "This was Freddie's Zoo, and now it's gone. I don't want to build it up again. I don't want to go into that yard anymore."

TH wiped away a lone tear. "That's fine Freddie, whatever it is that you decide to do."

Fatty looked right at TH. "Why'd somebody do this, TH?"

Word got around pretty quickly who had done it. The boy's name was Lenny Granier. He had asked Cindy Brown out so many times she had forgotten the number. Every time he asked she had said no. The last time she had said no she had told Lenny that she would never go out with him.

It wasn't that Lenny was a real bad kid. He was a nice looking kid whose father owned an auto mechanic's shop. The thing with Lenny was that he got caught smoking dope more than once and had also been in a number of fights on school property. He was lucky to have graduated that past May. Now he worked in his father's shop and harassed Cindy. Word of the harassment and her rebukes got around town.

At twelve-fifteen on the night of the fire, Logan Aft and Jack Davis found Lenny's car parked in the rear lot of the Trips Aces Casino. Lenny was clearly drunk and passed out. In his trunk, the two cops found two empty gas cans. Lenny had the motive, and now the cops had the evidence. Lenny was arrested and charged with arson. His family used all of their savings and then mortgaged part of their house and business to hire proper legal representation for him, but it wasn't enough. Even though he said he had nothing to do with the fire, he was found guilty and given two years imprisonment. If he was a good boy, he could be out in nine months. The harassment of Cindy Fuller was over, the rubble where Freddie's Zoo had been was cleared, and grass was quickly planted over the spot.

The Three Amigos

The following morning was cold, wet and dreary. Low clouds left the town covered in a dense fog. The temperature was in the low forties and came with a mist that swirled with the blowing wind. It had originally been planned to have the final prayers for Melissa said at the gravesite, but the awful weather dictated that everything be done inside.

The little room they were all crammed in got TH a little closer to his family and the Three Amigos then he would have liked. After the wake, he had gone to Aces and played video poker and drank whiskey until one o'clock. His head still hurt, and the sight of Logan Aft standing near his father made his stomach roil. He was trying to pay attention to what the pastor was saying, but he kept looking over at his father and his entourage.

"James Booker," the pastor said, "Melissa's father in law, has invited everyone back to their home for a light lunch and refreshments. There are maps at the front of the room to show you how to get there."

When TH stepped back outside his phone rang. He looked down and didn't recognize the number, but saw that it was local. "Hello," he said.

"TH, it's Mary." Mary Katz, Lou's wife.

"I thought I was supposed to call you," he said.

"Yeah, I know. I just didn't want you to leave without us talking."

"I wouldn't have done that. We were just finishing up with the funeral. Booker, Senior, has invited everyone to his place, but I've had enough for a bit."

"Ben Franklin once said that relatives are like fish. After three days they start to smell."

"It is the third day."

"You want some company?"

"Sure."

"Caliendo's?" Caliendo's was an Italian place on the west end of

Dubuque.

"Cheap food and cheap wine."

"It used to work for us."

"It did."

"Say one o'clock?"

"That will work."

When he hung up, Richie and Rachel were standing there. Rachel had been crying, and her mascara was running terribly down her face.

"Coming to lunch, little brother?" Richie asked.

"Going to pass."

Rachel's head jerked up. "You're not leaving yet? You haven't spent any time with my kids."

"I'm not leaving. I just can't do the lunch thing with the Bookers."

"I'm going to go see Billy Tasker after lunch," Richie said. "He's got some shotguns he wants to get rid of."

Rachel excused herself because one of her boys was calling her name.

"How long you sticking around, Richie?"

Richie looked out across the cemetery. "Karen took the kids to her mom's for a few days, so I'm in no great rush to get back."

"I thought I'd run out and see Skitch Grayson tomorrow and ask him about the Fatty Fuller murder. Thought you might want to tag along."

Richie smiled. "Don't think he did it?"

"Don't know, but based on what you said, I've got some questions. Why not ask him?"

"Sure, I'll go."

"I'll call you in the morning."

• • •

Mary was sitting in a corner booth of Caliendo's near the rear exit. The restaurant had been there for over fifty years in a converted house on the western edge of Dubuque. They were proud of their dimly lit atmosphere and checkered tablecloths. As teenagers, TH and Mary had snuck out here a few times to get away from Milton. They could eat dinner and visit a small motel for not much money. TH remembered those as good times.

She was wearing a cream colored sweater and jeans with her dark hair pulled back into a ponytail. On her lips was a red shade of lipstick that TH had once told her he really liked. She stood and gave him a quick peck on the cheek when he got to the booth.

"Funeral go okay?"

"Sad funeral on a dreary day."

"I'm glad that you came to see me."

"Been here long?" he asked.

She pointed to an empty wine glass. "Long enough to be ready for round two."

He squeezed into the booth and looked around the old restaurant. "Nothing seems to have changed very much."

"Nothing in Dubuque, or Milton, ever changes very much."

"You sound a little down."

"Not down, TH. Just being realistic. Once you get married and have kids and settle in, there's not a whole lot of change."

He laughed. "I don't know about the marriage or kids, but I'm pretty sure life kind of settles down for everyone. Ted Turner once said the last interesting thing he did was when he was sixteen."

"We did a few interesting things at sixteen." Now she smiled.

"Some were very interesting."

A waiter stopped by, and TH ordered a glass of the house red and Mary ordered a refill.

"Other than what happened to Melissa, are things okay with you?" She looked concerned.

"Like everybody, I get up, go to work, come home, pay my bills and go to sleep."

"No girlfriends, TH?"

"Nothing currently."

"And you still like the repo-man thing?"

"It's a requisition firm. If somebody's stuff gets stolen, and they know where it is, I'll go get it. We also will get back stuff, like boats and cars that people forget to pay for."

"The stolen stuff, it's not easier to call the cops?"

"Some of the stolen stuff might have been stolen before. It's a sticky wicket."

The waiter came with the wine, and they each took a sip.

"A recent vintage," TH said.

"Like last week."

"Or yesterday."

"So you like LA?"

"I'm not in LA. I'm in Costa Mesa."

"You know what I mean."

"Sure. What's not to like? Nice weather. The ocean's fifteen minutes away. It's all pretty good."

"Never coming back to Milton?"

"Never for longer than I have to. The things I come back here for are dwindling."

She took a sip. "That's a little hurtful."

"Sorry, but you're taken, my father and I don't get along, and my surviving sister is a nut job. Steve Marks, I guess he still dates the artist?"

"Tori Rooks. He lives with her."

TH rolled his shoulders. "I guess I can hang around with Joseph Running Bear."

"That would only get you into trouble. Logan Aft is out for Joseph. I don't advise hanging around anywhere near Joseph."

"Aft is crazy. Hassling Joseph for something that happened years ago. Why doesn't Lou put an end to all of that stuff? My dad and his team are no longer running the Milton PD."

"Part of the deal."

TH stopped his glass midway to his lips. "What deal?"

"It's kind of unofficial, but it's tied into the pensions they all get from the department. When Lou took over for your dad, after the stroke, he was put on sort of a probation period. Part of the probation was that the Three Amigos are quasi deputies for the department. Technically, not a whole lot Lou can do to those three. Plus, Lou still defers to your father for a lot of answers."

"Jesus! That's about as scary as you can get."

"There's a lot of scary stuff out there that you would probably be better off not knowing."

"But Lou knows about it?"

She shrugged. "I've probably said a little too much."

"Come on, Mary. You can't lead me along like that."

The waiter came by and asked if they were ready to order, but Mary shooed him away with her hand.

"It's all about control," Mary said. "Your father and the Three Amigos control Milton. There's not much more to say."

"You mean they controlled Milton, past tense?"

"No. I mean they control it. They hold the cards on a lot of prominent people. Mayor Garrett is one of them. As long as he's in office, your father and the Amigos run this town, period."

Wilson Garrett had been the mayor of Milton for over twenty-five years. He was a short man, about five-four, with a frumpy, little plump wife and a flock of kids that were all overweight. They all went to church every Sunday at St. John's Lutheran.

"What cards could he hold on Wilson Garrett?"

"Not sure, and Lou won't tell me, even if he knows, but it's there. Garrett controls the town council and anything to do with Teddy and the Amigos gets passed."

TH picked up his glass, swirled it around a bit, and finished it. He pictured Wilson Garrett wearing his ill-fitting suits, bow ties, and round-framed glasses. Seemed like a very harmless, small-town politician. What had he ever done that would allow his father to gain some sort of edge over him?

"You went away somewhere?" Mary said.

He wished he was far away. "You want to order some food?"

"I'm starving."

TH had lost his appetite, but they each ordered lunch anyway. TH picked at his pasta, but the red wine went down easily.

* * *

On the way back into Illinois, TH stopped at the Trips Aces Casino. Even at mid-day, the place was jumping with all of the people trying to hit the big one. The blackjack and poker tables were teeming with players. The electronic sound of the slot machines was drumming out the sixties music being piped into the gaming floor. TH noticed that most of the people looked like retirees, but many looked like they couldn't find two nickels to rub together.

He wandered around the table games section until he saw Cindy Fuller dealing blackjack at one of the tables. She, like all of the dealers, was wearing black slacks, a white ruffled shirt, and a red bow tie. Her red hair hung loosely on her shoulders as she dealt cards to the players. Even as pretty as she looked, she looked tired. TH wandered by her table, caught her attention, and asked if she could come down to the lounge.

"About fifteen minutes," she said. "I've got a break then."

TH entered the lounge and found a counter that had a video poker game. After the other night's losses, he decided to be conservative. He only put a fifty into the cash slot. A waitress came by, and he ordered a diet Coke.

Like the other night, the machine was not cooperating with him, and he was losing hand after hand. He was happy when he saw Cindy enter the lounge and he cashed out. They found a booth away from the noise of the slots. He ordered another soft drink; she just had water.

"I was in the neighborhood and thought I'd stop by," he said.

"That's okay. I've only got twenty minutes, but we can talk."

Again he noticed how tired she looked, almost sad. "You doing okay?"

"Me? I should be asking you that with the week you've had."

"It hasn't been a great one."

"Everything go okay with the wake and funeral?"

"About as well as can be expected. A lot of people came out and paid their respects. That was good to see. My dad behaved himself, and Logan Aft tried to get into it with Joseph."

"Logan Aft is an idiot," she said loudly. "He is as bigoted a man as you'll ever find. He is everything a cop shouldn't be."

"He used to hassle Troy?" TH asked of her ex-husband.

"All the time. Troy wasn't any trouble. He was just an enormous fuck up. He was also my biggest mistake, but he is my daughter's father."

"Something about who is your father around good old Milton."

"That's the thing, TH. I never understood what was going on with you and your dad. Everybody in town loved him. You were the only one that I knew who actually despised him."

TH sipped the soda. "He wanted me to be like him. I wasn't. It led to conflicts, one right after the other."

"It seemed like it got really bad after Freddie was killed."

"For some reason, after that, my dislike for him seemed to heighten. I don't know what it was. I was supposed to go to school out west and play ball. Well, I went west, never played ball, and the rest is history."

"You know, after my mom left, when Freddie was a little guy, your dad used to stop by the house about once a week. He'd chat with my dad, make sure I was alright, and always have some sort of gift for Freddie. This went on until the day Freddie died. Then it stopped, just like that."

TH felt a little envious. "Why do you think that was?"

"I think he felt bad for us. Freddie had his issues, my mom split, and my dad was struggling to make everything work. Your dad was just trying to help."

"But after Freddie died, it all stopped?"

"Pretty much. He stopped coming by the house and didn't have much to do with my father. That was when dad really started to drink. When Freddie died, my father viewed his life as an epic failure. I think he thought your father thought the same thing. That was why he stopped coming by."

"He stopped talking to you?"

"I'd see him now and then, he'd say hello, and that was about it. Once, he must have heard I was seeing Troy, he told me to watch out for him. Maybe I should have listened."

"That bad?"

She smiled. "He was always such a fun guy to be around, but that was his best trait. He would work for a while and then not. He would always drink too much, but never hurt anyone. He liked to gamble, badly, with money we didn't have. Lastly, he never found a woman he didn't think he could get into bed, and he tried an awful lot."

"How's life without him?"

"It's quiet. I make ends meet, but it gets a little lonely."

"Looking for a little company? I'm going to be around a while."

Again, she smiled. "I've got to get back, TH. They get pissed if you're late coming back from breaks. I get off the next two nights at eight. I've got a lady that looks after Susie when I'm out. Maybe I can get her to work late one night."

TH scribbled his cell number on a napkin. "If it works out, call me."

"Another thing I should have listened to," she said.

"What's that?"

"You asking me out all those times. I always liked you, but just not that way. I don't know why, but after seeing the fucking mess my life turned into, I should have said yes at least once."

She patted his hand and got up to go back to her blackjack table. It was just past four and still gloomy outside. The waitress came by, and TH ordered a bourbon. He also spotted an ATM in the corner of the lounge. He didn't have enough cash on him to attack the video poker game properly.

Skitch Grayson

The drive to Platteville, Wisconsin took forty-five minutes the next morning. Even though TH had stayed at Aces for a few hours and drank quite a bit of bourbon, he didn't feel that bad. Looking at Richie next to him in the rental, TH got the feeling his older brother hadn't faired so well. Richie was wearing sunglasses on a cloudy day and reeked of alcohol. He hadn't said much, until they were driving along a country road and Richie spotted a gas station.

"Stop here, TH," Richie commanded.

"Need something?"

"Got to pee and get a coffee." Richie was almost out of the car before it stopped rolling. TH used the opportunity to fill up the car. The gas was easily twenty percent cheaper than in Orange County.

"You feeling okay?" TH asked when Richie got back in the car.

"Maybe overdid it a bit, but I'll be okay. This coffee is strong."

"Buy any shotguns?"

Richie looked at him strangely and laughed. "I don't think we ever got around to talking about shotguns. We were just shooting the breeze, and the vodka came out."

"How was the luncheon at the Booker's?"

"Bad. Bob and his mother and father all started crying, and pretty soon a bunch of people were crying. It was tough."

"Dad make out okay?"

"He was huddled with those three idiots of his and seemed kind of oblivious to what was going on. I think after the two days he was kind of worn out. I went over to talk to him once, and he didn't seem to know who I was."

"And Rachel?"

"Fucking basket case. When the Bookers started crying, she joined right in. I gave her and her kids a ride home. I didn't think she could drive."

Richie took the plastic top off of the coffee and took a big drink. He moaned as if the coffee were putting blood back into his veins.

"I was thinking, you and I both left Milton about the same time. I was supposed to go play ball in California. You went to Iraq," TH said.

"So?"

"Well, I didn't come back because I really didn't like Milton and dad really didn't like me. Why'd you end up in KC?"

Richie took another drink and turned to look out his window at some cows that were grazing in a field. After a moment, he looked at TH. "After Desert Storm, I was wondering what to do. I even thought I'd go back in the Marines. Somebody told me the KC Police Department was hiring and liked veterans. I went down there, applied, got hired and not more than a month later I met Karen. That's kind of how the whole thing played out."

TH looked closely at his older brother. He had seen war in Iraq and was now a homicide investigator in Kansas City. Where TH's hair was still thick and dark, Richie's showed that it was receding and getting some gray to it. "You were supposed to come back to Milton and work with dad on the force here. He would have made it easy for you. Whatever happened to that?"

Richie laughed. "Where you had your little issues with dad on just about everything, I had some major issues on how he ran the force and policed Milton. I didn't like it. I wouldn't have fit in at all. It was just better not to come back home."

"So how are you and dad these days?"

He sipped his coffee. "We're good. I'm sure he wishes I'd come home to work with him, but at least I became a cop. You left, never came home, and became a repo man. Some of the stories I had heard, true or not, were that you were doing some things that were a little on the fringe of the law."

TH couldn't argue with that. "Let's just leave it at dad and I could never get along, not even for an hour."

Richie tipped his cup at TH. "Fair enough, little bro."

•   •   •

Platteville, Wisconsin fit the billing of the sign that stood on the outskirts of town that read, *Platteville, a Community in a Small Town.* The town was small and was lined by all it's boundaries with fields of corn. One of the town's only unique distinctions was that the Chicago Bears had used it for their summer camp for many years. TH and his father had made the trek to see the Bears practice one day. It was almost ninety that day, and TH found out that NFL teams don't do that many interesting things while practicing, like hitting each other.

Unlike Hillside Manor, where Teddy Brown was living, Marymore Nursing Home was not on a bluff overlooking the river. Instead, it was located in the middle of town and was surrounded on all sides by residential properties. The place looked a little run down and forlorn. The building, a one-story frame structure, needed a fresh coat of paint. The lone oak tree on the front lawn had lost all of its leaves. Even the drive that led to the parking in the rear of the building was cracked and had many holes. TH wondered how anyone could end up in a place like this, even somebody like Skitch Grayson.

A mix of smells greeted TH and Richie as they made their way to the lobby desk to ask to see Skitch. There was a hint of medicine, urine and musty. The inside wasn't much better than out. The place needed decorating and new furniture.

"Nice fucking place," Richie said.

"Shoot me before I end up in a place like this."

"I'll probably go first so please do the honors."

They had called ahead and found that Skitch was having a good day. He was awake and alert. When the nurse told him some visitors from Milton wanted to come up and see him, he was very happy. Skitch hadn't had many visitors since he became a resident at Marymore.

Skitch was in a small room that held two beds, but his was the only one occupied. TH was surprised that he was not hooked up to a heart monitor or an IV of some sort. He was just laying back on a stack of pillows watching *The View* on the TV. TH remembered a much bigger man with a big gut. Now he saw a skinny figure, no gut, gray hair, gray skin and beady, black eyes that turned on him and Richie when they entered the room.

"You must be the two from Milton," Skitch said quietly but clearly.

"We are," TH said. "I'm TH Brown and this is my brother, Richie."

Skitch squinted, the black balls now peeking through thin slits. "The two Brown boys," he said. "Bring me good news like your daddy died?"

"Nothing like that," Richie said.

"Maybe Logan Aft? Somebody blow his fucking head off?"

This brought a smile to TH's face. "Not that lucky either, Skitch."

Skitch closed his eyes. He quickly opened them. "Well, as you can see, I'm dying. Not in too much pain, but the morphine helps with that. So not too much good news here. When I heard you were from Milton, I thought you might bring good news, but my only two wishes weren't answered."

"Sorry to disappoint you," Richie said.

"So what do you two want?"

TH cleared his throat. The smells in the little room were worse than in the lobby. "We wanted to talk with you about Fatty Fuller."

"You mean the retarded kid that I spent fourteen years in jail for smashing his head in with a rock?"

"Jesus," Richie said.

"Jesus, God and the Holy Ghost weren't there when I asked them for help," Skitch said. "I asked and asked and asked. Nobody helped me. Nobody wanted to help me. I had killed some poor innocent kid, and I would have been executed, but they couldn't find any real evidence that I had killed Fatty. Just that fishing gear in my shed."

"Why did they never find any evidence that you killed Fatty?" Richie asked.

Skitch smiled. "Most amazing reason ever. Cause I didn't kill the boy."

The boys looked at each other. Of course, they both expected that Skitch would say this.

"Look Skitch," TH said, "we're all sorry you went through that trial and jail time, and now you've got cancer. Life hasn't been great to you for some time, but why should we believe you?"

Skitch groaned and shifted on his pillows, searching for comfort. "Sometimes not even the drugs work."

"You want anything?" TH asked.

He shook his head. "I used to see Fatty fishing along Whisper Creek. I'd see him down there a lot. He was a real good kid, real friendly. That kid was always smiling. I called him Freddie, his name. Only mean or ignorant people called him Fatty. I wouldn't say we were friends, but we'd say hello, and he'd show me what he caught, but it didn't matter. If he caught nothing, he'd still smile and be friendly. He may have been the happiest kid I'd ever seen."

TH found himself nodding, Richie was looking down at the floor, shuffling his feet.

"I liked Freddie. I liked him a lot," Skitch said. "I never would have killed him. But why did they say I killed him? They said to steal his fishing gear. I stole all of his tackle and stuck it in my shed where any idiot could find it, and that's what happened. Logan Aft found it all back there, and I was arrested.

"Amazing how I took Freddie's three poles and tackle box and added it to my twenty or so poles and all the tackle I had. I really needed Freddie's."

"So what happened?" Richie said.

Skitch pointed to a cup on his bedside table that had a straw in it. TH grabbed the cup, which held water, and put the straw near Skitch's lips. The old man took a couple of swallows, a good portion of the water running down his chin.

"The night I was arrested, they came pounding on my door. It was Aft, Jack Davis, and Ben Smith. They had to pound quite a bit because I'd been drinking. Aft was the one who did all the talking. Mostly it was yelling. Jack and Ben were holding Freddie's fishing poles and tackle box. Aft said they found it in my shed and could I explain myself. I think my only response was how did it get in my shed? That was enough for Aft. He punched me so hard in the gut that it knocked me down. They cuffed me and the next thing I know I'm in the Milton jail."

TH held the water up for him, and he took another drink. Most of this stayed in his mouth.

"It all happened so fast," Skitch continued. "I was arraigned and given this young kid to represent me. He did the best he could and got the trial moved to the next county, but it didn't matter. I was the guy who murdered the retarded kid. I knew he was always along that river near nightfall. I knew he'd be alone. I killed him like a coward with a rock from behind so I could steal his fishing gear. I kept saying I didn't do it, but it took that jury about an hour to reach their guilty verdict."

TH was shaking his head. "No alibi of any kind, Skitch?"

Skitch laughed. "Sure. Homer Penn."

"Who the hell is Homer Penn?" TH said.

"Is he that old coot that used to run the fishing charter along the Mississippi?" Richie asked.

"That's him. He and I were drinking out at The Lighthouse the night Freddie was murdered. I drove myself home that night. I had my truck. I was never anywhere near Whisper Creek that day."

"Wait a minute," TH said. "If you were with this Homer Penn why not get him to testify?"

"Easy. He didn't want anything to do with the case. Said we were drinking, a lot, but didn't know where I'd gone after I left him. Couldn't recall what time I left the bar. He wasn't clear on anything. I know I left the bar after the time Freddie was killed."

"That's ridiculous," Richie said.

"Not so much," Skitch said. "Homer could see what I was going through and he didn't want any part of it. He figured if he testified for me people like your father and Logan Aft would be out to his place in a hurry. He just didn't want the trouble. I can't really blame Homer."

"Do you think he would talk to us now?" TH said.

"Doubt it," Skitch said, smiling. "Hear he's been dead about ten years. Why you two poking around about this now?"

"There's a couple of people down in Milton who don't think you killed Freddie. We just thought we'd look into it."

"That's nice to hear, but it's a little late. There might be one more thing that might make people think that I didn't kill Freddie."

"What would that be?"

He pointed his finger at a tall dresser in the corner of the room. "Go into the top drawer. There's a bible in there."

Richie moved to the dresser and took an old bible out of the drawer. "This help you much?" he asked.

"A lot of things help in prison."

"So what does this bible tell us about the murder?" TH asked.

"Not the bible. The letter inside the top cover."

Richie opened the book and took out an old piece of paper that had been folded into quarters. He opened the paper and read it. He handed it to TH.

Dear Mr. Grayson

I am writing to you at this time to express my sorrow at your imprisonment. I am quite aware of the investigation that took place after the crime was committed. I am sure that this investigation was not done according to normal procedures. I am also quite convinced that you did not kill the Fuller boy.

I'm not sure what my writing to you at this late date does for you, but I wanted you to know that I am sorry.

Sincerely,
Marilyn Aft
October 3, 2011

TH finished reading the letter, refolded it, and handed it back to Richie who put it back in the bible.

"How do you know Marilyn Aft?" TH said.

"I used to do a bunch of chores around their place. She was a real nice lady, and she always paid with cash and on time. I got the letter six years ago. I thought about showing it to my attorney, but he moved onto Wisconsin. I also wondered what good it would do and how much hell Mrs. Aft would go through if I dragged her into the whole thing. I decided to let it go."

"Did you know Logan Aft very well?"

"Well enough to know what an asshole he is. I had a few run-ins with him, but nothing serious. I kind of knew they were having some marital problems. They broke up the same year as the murder."

"So, Skitch," Richie said. "Who killed Fatty Fuller?"

Skitch looked toward the lone window in the room. "I don't know," he said. "I just know they wanted to arrest somebody for the crime so the town would stop talking about it. That somebody was me."

"So what do you think, TH?" They were on their way back to Milton. The clouds had parted, and the sun was coming out.

"Don't know what to think. Says he was with Homer Penn at the time of the murder, but Penn is dead, so nobody can corroborate that."

"What about the Marilyn Aft letter?"

Richie laughed. "In our business that's called conjecture. It's not evidence. She says she thinks the investigation was a little hinky and that she's convinced that Skitch wasn't the killer. Both of those add up to jack shit. They don't mean much. Unless Marilyn Aft can point us at some evidence, there's nothing there."

"But it might be worth talking to her?"

"Leave no rock unturned."

•   •   •

TH dropped Richie by Rachel's house and said he'd get to him later; Richie said he needed a nap. On the way back to motel, TH stopped and grabbed a burger and fries from a local fast food place. He'd just finished the last fry when he pulled in to the motel parking lot. Parked in the spot right under his room was Joseph Running Bear's truck. As TH got closer, Joseph got out of his truck.

"I didn't think I'd see you here today," TH said.

"There is something I'd like to show you. Have you got time? It's out at my place."

TH was going to call Steve Marks, but that was it. "I'm free. What is it?"

"I want you to see it."

They both climbed into Joseph's truck and were soon barreling eastward on Route 20 towards Sterling. When they got to the road that led up to Joseph's property, Joseph had said nothing else about what he wanted TH to see. TH could tell by the clenching of Joseph's jaws that the big Indian was upset about something.

When they reached the property, Joseph pulled up to his normal spot and parked. Both men got out of the truck. Joseph reached back and took a shotgun from behind the seat. TH looked over the house and office. Nothing seemed out of place.

"Follow me," Joseph said.

They walked around the rock path that led to the back of the building. From here you could see the areas that housed the cows, pigs, and the chicken coop. Joseph first walked into the cow barn. It didn't take long for TH to see what he wanted him to see. About ten feet inside the door was a large male cow lying on the floor of the barn, dead. TH could see the large pool of blood that ran mostly from the cow's head.

"Jesus," he said.

Joseph bent over and grabbed the cow's head. He pulled it up only slightly, and it almost came off of the rest of the body. Joseph slowly lowered the head and went deeper into the barn. There were sixteen stalls. In fourteen they found other cows with their throats cut.

They walked back out in the sun and TH could see tears running from Joseph's eyes. They crossed the yard to the pens that held the pigs. Inside was no different from the cow barn. Over twenty pigs lay in the slop, throats cut from ear to ear.

Joseph walked back outside and used his sleeve to wipe his eyes. He took several deep breaths to calm himself. "I'd show you the chickens, but it's close to the same except they shot them all. It's tough to cut a bunch of chicken's throats."

"Who?" TH asked.

"TH, do not embarrass yourself or hurt our friendship by asking stupid questions. You know who."

"But why would Aft and his men do this?"

Joseph wiped away more tears. "Aft doesn't like anyone who isn't white. He especially doesn't like them if he thinks they got the best of him at one time. That fits me."

"When could they do all of this?"

"Yesterday. I was in Rockford for most of the day and got home late. I didn't even check on the animals until this morning. I came by your motel and waited for you. I wanted you to see what your father's men did."

"Wait, Joseph. You of all people know how I get along with my father."

Joseph shook his head. "I don't mean that. I just wanted you to see how mean and unlawful they can be."

"Who knew you'd be gone?"

"Only the people I was going to see in Rockford. Aft and his crew must have come here looking for me. When I wasn't home, they took it out on the animals."

"We've got to tell Lou and Marks. This is unbelievable."

"It's also in an unincorporated area. Lou and Marks have no jurisdiction here. Have to call the County Sherriff. Who knows what they'd do. Aft and his buddies already have ten alibis."

"So what do you want to do?"

"I want to stay quiet and wait. I want to wait for the proper time to hit back at them. That time is not now, but it will come soon."

•   •   •

"Detective Marks," Steve answered after one ring.

"This is TH. I need to talk with you."

"Urgent like?"

"Pretty much so."

"Don't suppose you want to give me a clue over the phone?"

TH thought of Joseph and all of the dead animals on his property. "Let's hold off until we get together."

"I can meet you at the bowling alley in about an hour. I've got a few things I need to wrap up."

"Does Lou need to know that you are meeting with me?"

"Not if I don't tell him."

"Don't tell him."

"One hour, TH."

•   •   •

The Milton Bowl stood on the south side of town near Main Street. This is the area of town where the grocery store, retail shops and most of the services for the town were housed. When Brewster Way became popular, the townspeople wanted an area where they could shop, eat and bowl in without dealing with drunks, gamblers and exotic dancers. It was far enough away from the nightlife that you didn't know the casino and strip joints were there. The bowling alley had twelve lanes, a video game room, and a small bar. Steve Marks knew that at this time of day no one would be in the bar. He parked behind the alley and entered at the rear entrance. He saw TH sitting at the bar looking at his cell phone.

"Checking out the news or are you a big social media guy?" Marks said.

TH looked up from his phone. He hadn't seen Marks enter the bar. As always, Marks was dressed impeccably in a fine suit. Living with a successful artist must help in the clothing budget. "Just checking out what few investments I have."

The bartender, a short, fat guy who also served as the afternoon cook came by. Marks ordered a Coke; TH was already working on a whiskey and water.

"You said you had something that you wanted to talk with me about. Something that I couldn't share with Lou."

"A couple of things."

"Okay. A couple of things. What do you want to start with?"

"I just left Joseph a little bit ago. There's been some trouble out at his place."

"Trouble with a hunter?"

"No. Trouble with somebody coming out there and slaughtering all of his cows, pigs, and chickens."

Marks took a sip of the Coke. "When did this happen?"

"Sometime yesterday. Joseph was down in Rockford. Somebody showed up and cut the cow's and pig's throats. Then they shot all of the chickens."

Marks was thinking. "That's awful, but I'm not sure what I can do. It's out of my jurisdiction."

"Sure it is, Steve, but we're pretty sure it was Aft, Davis and Ben Smith."

"Do you have proof of this, TH? You just can't go around charging people with stuff like that."

"No proof, Steve. Just that it happened the day after the altercation at Melissa's wake."

"So what would you like me to do?"

TH knew Marks' hands were tied. "Nothing. If Joseph does anything legally, it's going to have to be with the county police."

"So is this what you didn't want me to tell Lou?"

"Actually, that is something I'd like you to tell him. What those three guys are allowed to get away with is ridiculous. They are the town's vigilante service."

Marks winced. "Part of their pension is geared towards them being deputies for the department. Not really cops, but still able to get involved."

TH thought of what Mary Katz had told him. "That's absurd. What does Lou think of that?"

"When Lou took over after your father's stroke he inherited that deal so you can't punish him for that."

TH took a sip of his drink and signaled to the bartender for another. "I heard that my father got help from the mayor pushing this through the city council."

"I'm sure that's probably true."

"Do you know of anything that my father has on the mayor to always get this unflinching support?"

Marks laughed. "Why does there have to be this grand conspiracy? The mayor and the police department have always had an excellent relationship. The mayor is our strongest opponent for the way we handle things in the city."

TH knew he wasn't going to get anything more out of Marks on that topic. "Richie and I saw Skitch Grayson. He said he didn't kill Freddie Fuller."

Marks shrugged. "That's not news and, anyway, I don't think he did it either."

"Says he was with Homer Penn at the time of the murder, drinking. Homer couldn't remember much about the night because he was afraid of

Logan Aft and his crew."

"Could also be true."

"Skitch showed us a letter he got from Marilyn Aft. She said she thought the investigation was suspicious and that she was convinced that Skitch hadn't committed the murder."

"You don't say."

"I saw the letter. Of course, Skitch got it something like eight years after the crime."

"Look, TH, I don't think Skitch killed Fatty. I also have no idea who did. What I do know is that Marilyn Aft is crazy. Has been for quite some time. She would call the department regularly after they got divorced to tell us to keep an eye on Logan. She was always saying Logan was going to come for her. Logan just told us she was nuts."

"When did they get divorced?"

"Probably around the time Fatty was murdered."

"She still live in town?"

"Nope. She moved over to Cook. Lives on a quiet little street not far from the river."

"Think she'll talk to me?"

"She'll talk to anybody, TH. Like I said, she's a little crazy."

"I think I'll go see her. I'm interested in why she thought the investigation into the murder was not handled correctly. Also her reasoning behind Skitch not being the killer."

"You're not a cop, TH."

"Richie is."

"He's a KC cop, a little far from home."

"We're just asking questions."

"Just watch it. Aft hears you're talking to his wife might not go over so well. And another thing. Keep my name out of all of your investigations. I happen to need and like my job."

TH smiled. "Tori not taking good enough care of you." Tori Rooks was the artist that Marks lived with.

"Fuck you, TH."

"You ever going to marry that nice woman?"

"I've asked. She says no."

"How long have you been together?"

"Going on five years. We have a good thing. I think Tori believes marriage will ruin it all. I don't bring it up anymore."

"I don't get it. She's a beautiful, highly successful artist. How did she end up with you?"

"If you take a look around Milton it's very hard to find anyone who has as much smooth as I do. Plus she knows no one will try to steal her stuff if they know an armed man lives with her."

TH laughed. "Second part, I get. First part is all shit."

"Believe what you want, but do listen when I tell you to watch out for Marilyn Aft. Anything to do with Aft can be destructive."

TH sipped his drink. That he believed.

•　　　•　　　•

The last thoughts that TH had before he fell asleep were of Marilyn Aft. He remembered her as a nice looking lady who wore skirts that were a bit too short and glasses which made her look smart. He remembered asking himself, even as a kid, why such a woman would be married to a guy like Logan Aft. TH could never remember a time when he didn't think of Aft as an unpleasant, mean man.

What plagued his thoughts about Marilyn Aft was the letter she had mailed to Skitch Grayson, years after the Fatty Fuller murder. Why was she so sure that the investigation hadn't been a normal one, and what convinced her that Skitch wasn't the killer? These thoughts stuck with him until he finally fell asleep.

When he first heard the pounding on his door, he was sure it was part of a dream. As the pounding persisted and his eyes opened, he realized this was no dream. He got out from under the covers, found the light and opened the door. When he opened it, he found Cindy Fuller standing in his doorway.

"Nice look," she said, referring to just the boxers that TH wore.

"Did I miss a date?"

She rested her hand on TH's chest and slowly pushed him back into the room and towards the bed, closing the door behind her. "No. The date is just beginning."

She continued to push until TH was back on the bed and she was straddling him. It wasn't long before she'd lost the ruffled shirt and black slacks she wore. Soon, TH was no longer wearing the boxers.

"Those years out in California helped you," she said when they were done.

"How so?"

"You actually seemed like you cared about what was going on with me. Most of the men in Milton think it's okay to be done in like forty-five seconds."

TH laughed. "I tried to give you enough opportunities, but you wouldn't bite."

She snuggled close to him. "As I said earlier, I made a few mistakes along the way."

"Well, I'm glad you came by."

"I am, too."

They lay there quietly for some time. The only sounds were noises the wind outside made or the creaking of the old motel building. TH was thinking Cindy had fallen asleep.

"How long are you staying?" she asked suddenly.

"I'm not sure. Richie and I are looking into a couple of things."

She propped herself up onto one elbow. "What kind of things are you looking into?"

"Freddie's murder for one thing. We went out and saw Skitch Grayson."

Now she sat up in the bed, the covers falling from her. "Why in God's name would you go out and talk with Skitch Grayson?"

He couldn't see her eyes, but he could feel the green of them lighting up. "A number of people mentioned to me that they didn't think Skitch had killed Freddie."

"A number of people? Who?"

"Richie for one, Joseph and Steve Marks."

"Why would they say that after all of these years?"

"I don't know. Maybe because I left soon after the murder and they felt they wanted to share their thoughts with me."

"I wish people would just leave all of that alone. That was over fifteen years ago, and Skitch Grayson was the killer. The jury found him guilty, and he did his time. Sorry, he's got cancer, but they should have executed him a long time ago. All of this talk, so many years later, drives me nuts and I know it eats at my father."

"I don't think he did it."

"You're starting to piss me off, TH."

"He said he was drinking with Homer Penn at the time of the murder, but Penn had a convenient lapse of memory for fear of what Logan Aft would do to him."

"That is the flimsiest excuse I've ever heard."

"Maybe, but then he got a curious letter from a surprising person."

"Skitch got a letter?"

"Yes, he got a letter from Marilyn Aft that said she didn't think Freddie's investigation had been handled properly and that she was convinced that Skitch hadn't killed him."

"Marilyn Aft? Crazy Marilyn Aft?"

"That's the only one I know."

"And when did Skitch get this "curious" letter?"

"About six years ago."

"Let me see, years after the murder, crazy Marilyn Aft sends Skitch Grayson a letter saying the murder investigation wasn't handled properly and that she didn't think that Skitch had killed Freddie. Am I following?"

"That's it in a nutshell."

"It's a damn good thing you didn't become a cop, TH, because that is the biggest bunch of crap I've ever heard. That and your buddies telling you that Skitch didn't do it."

"I guess it's more like a feeling."

"A feeling," she yelled. "I'll tell you about feelings. Freddie was born with Down Syndrome. That had to demoralize my parents. I know it did because four years later my mom took off. That pretty much meant that my dad, and whatever I could do, were stuck raising him. This was all real tough on my dad and led him to drink a lot more than he should. So there was a lot of stress. And then when Freddie was killed, dad and I both thought we had let him down.

"When Skitch Grayson was convicted, some of the guilt went away. Eventually, all of those feelings faded with time, kind of like the print on Freddie's gravestone. Now, for some reason, years later, people are talking about Freddie's murder. People are saying maybe Skitch didn't do it. I've heard these things, and I'm sure my dad has. Do you know what that does TH?"

"I can't imagine," he said sheepishly.

"I'll tell you what it does. It's like somebody's picking at an old sore, one that's almost healed, picking at it so much that the wound starts to bleed again. Do you understand that?"

"Yes," he mumbled. "I guess I wasn't thinking."

Cindy got out of the bed and turned on a table light. She found her clothes and quickly got dressed. "You weren't thinking. Anybody who starts these rumors forgets that there were other victims that night and that they have feelings. Some things, regardless of how shitty they are or what you may or may not think, are better off left alone."

With that, Cindy stormed out of the room, slamming the door behind her. What had been a rather fantastic hour had turned into an awful five minutes. From Cindy's perspective, Skitch Grayson was the killer. His conviction had brought some closure to the case and had let the healing begin. Now TH was out there poking around, and some of the wound reopened. Maybe he was stupid for asking around. Maybe he should stop. First, he would listen to what "crazy" Marilyn Aft had to say. What could it hurt?

·   ·   ·

Across town, on the balcony of a tenth-floor condo, Steve Marks leaned against the edge of the hot tub and looked out over the Mississippi. Even on this cold October night, the warm water in the tub was soothing his body. The beer he had been drinking was almost gone, and he was dreading getting out of the water to get another. He looked over at Tori Rooks's glass of chardonnay, but it was almost full. She would not be getting out of the water to get another drink soon. Steve sighed loudly.

"Did I lose you somewhere?" Tori said.

He looked over at her and in the moonlit night she looked more beautiful than ever. The gleam from the moon was catching her face and auburn hair perfectly. "Just thinking that I had to get out of the water to get another beer."

"That would be awful."

"A real travesty."

"But that's not what I lost you too. I know that look that you get when something is bothering you."

"Yeah. My beer is almost gone."

"Steve, don't bullshit me."

He took the bottle of beer and drained the remaining liquid. The cooler was about ten feet away. "A long time ago, about six or seven years before you got here, there was a murder near town. A kid by the name of Freddie Fuller, everybody called him Fatty, was killed down by Whisper Creek. Somebody bashed him in the back of the head with a rock, and he fell into the creek and drowned."

"That's awful."

"The real awful part was that Freddie had Down Syndrome. He used to fish by the creek a lot, and somebody killed him and stole all of his fishing gear."

Tori took a drink of her wine. "Never solved, I take it?"

"Oh, it was solved and quickly. Guy was convicted and sent away for life. He recently got cancer and is living in a home in Platteville. Not long to go."

Steve watched as Tori moved to the edge of the tub and climbed out. Even in the short steps to the cooler, he was amazed by her graceful walk. She grabbed a beer from the ice and took the top off the bottle. She handed it to Steve and got back in the water. He took a sip of the fresh beer.

"So there was an awful murder," she said, "the killer was caught, convicted and got cancer. What am I missing here?"

"The murder happened before my senior year in high school. Everybody knew Fatty; everybody like him. He was going to be the manager of our school baseball team. When he was murdered, the whole town was bummed out."

"Well, what you've said doesn't exactly sound like a very cheerful tale."

"If you ask people what the biggest crime to ever occur in Milton was they will tell you it was the murder of Fatty Fuller."

"So why is this bothering you tonight?"

"It might be a bit of an urban myth, but I have been hearing about it forever, maybe right after the killer, Skitch Grayson, was convicted."

"Hearing what?"

"That Skitch didn't do it. A lot of people think he was framed. Many people think evidence was planted on him. One of the investigating officer's wives sent Skitch a letter saying she didn't think he did it and that the investigation wasn't run properly. That and something my good friend, TH Brown, said to me."

"The thief?"

"He's a professional repo man, not a thief."

"I don't see the difference, but I'm just a simple sculptor. What did TH Brown say to you that got that motor in your head whirring?"

"You know the Three Amigos, the cops that make up former Chief Brown's entourage?"

"I've seen them. If you hang out with a Milton cop, you can't miss them."

"Right, well when they retired the mayor got a deal approved for them where they were designated deputies for life in Milton as part of their retirement. They almost have as much street power as I do."

"Sounds a little weird."

"Especially since these guys are a little crazy."

"Where's all this leading?"

"It's what TH said. He wanted to know why the mayor would get such a deal passed. He wanted to know what his father and the Three Amigos had on Mayor Garrett to get him to agree to that deal. It got me thinking."

"Don't tell me. You think that Wilson Garrett somehow murdered Fatty Fuller and Chief Brown covered it up in exchange for the great pension deal for his buddies?"

"Something like that, but one thing I can't figure out."

"Like why would Wilson Garrett hit a kid with Down Syndrome in the back of the head with a rock and leave him in Whisper Creek to drown?"

"That part doesn't seem to fit my little puzzle."

"Maybe your puzzle is fucked up."

Steve smiled and moved close to Tori and put his arms around her. "Could be, but the whole Skitch Grayson as the murderer and the Three Amigos' pension deal has me thinking."

She placed a hand on his chest and let it slide all the way down to the top of his swim trunks. Steve tensed under her touch. "Think you can hold off on solving this great mystery until tomorrow. I leave for Minneapolis in the morning." She lightly kissed his cheek.

"Yeah, I think so," Steve said.

Tori took his hand and led him out of the hot tub and towards the room through the sliding doors.

Steve was distracted, there was no doubt, but the letter Marilyn Aft had sent to Skitch Grayson and the Three Amigos pension deal signed by Wilson Garrett, had all of his attention.

•　　　•　　　•

Maggie Brown, TH's mom, died of breast cancer when TH was four years old. As tough as it was, Teddy Brown did everything to make sure that the family life stayed the way it had been when Maggie was alive. Teddy was a great provider; money was never an object, so the Brown family didn't go without much. There was always a lot of help from the neighbors, especially with watching the children while Teddy was off working, which sometimes ran into late hours.

The one thing that Teddy liked to make sure of was that holidays were always special and he went out of his way to secure this. Every year on the Fourth of July Teddy hosted a massive barbeque in their back yard. In Milton, this was one of the top events of the summer. On Easter Sunday, Teddy went out of his way to hide the baskets in unique spots for the kids to find. The baskets were always loaded with candy and at least one special gift for each child. The one holiday that seemed to bring out the best of Teddy's holiday parenting was Christmas.

Each year, right after Thanksgiving, the Brown family would make a trek into the woods to find the perfect tree. The tree would be cut down and loaded into Teddy's truck. When they got the tree home it was erected, the fireplace would be lit, hot cocoa would be made, and Christmas carols filled the house. The rest of the day would be filled with the family unpacking all of the decorations that Maggie Brown have saved over the years and decorating the tree and the remainder of the house. Teddy and the boys would do the outside lights, sometimes in the bitter cold. At the end of the day, the house and the tree would look like something off of a Currier and Ives picture.

Christmas Eve was for family only. On Christmas Day, after church, a number of Teddy's cronies from the force would drop by the house and have a drink or two with their boss. Later in the day friends, the mayor and other city council members would stop by. The house bustled until late in the day. Christmas Eve was different.

On Christmas Eve, Teddy would rise early and prepare the turkey, stuffing, sweet potatoes, mashed potatoes, vegetables, and fresh bread. Each year he would come up with a new soup recipe, and this would be for their lunch. Dinner would always be at six o'clock, followed by desert, table games and opening the gifts. Teddy would never tell the kids when the gifts would be opened. This was his surprise. He would always spring it on them at any given time. TH remembered that Christmas had always been a great time, at least up until he became nine years old. Something that Christmas changed.

That Christmas Eve was much like they'd always been. Teddy cooked, carols were playing, and Christmas movies were running on the VCR. Log after log burned in the fireplace. The house smelled like Christmas. Nothing was out of place until they sat down for dinner in the dining room.

Teddy said grace and then began to dish out large helpings of sliced turkey. The smells from the food were overwhelming. Teddy served the two girls first and then Richie, TH and himself. All of the plates were piled high with food. Everyone was ready to eat. It was at this time that Melissa started to cry.

TH thought he was the first one to notice. At first, Melissa sniffled a few times and then she would let out a sob or two. She was trying hard not to make any noise and desperately wiped away loose tears. With each passing moment, her actions were more noticeable. Soon she was sobbing uncontrollably, and tears were running down her face.

"Melissa," Teddy said from the head of the table, "what is wrong with you."

She tried to quiet herself, tried hard to stop the sobs and the tears, but it was no use. She was out of control.

"Melissa Brown," Teddy said loudly, "look at me."

Melissa lifted her eyes towards him; they were already red from the crying.

"It's Christmas Eve, child. The most wonderful day on the planet. What on earth are you carrying on so much about?"

Melissa shook her head. "Nothing, sir."

"Nothing, sir," Teddy repeated. "It's Christmas, and you are balling your eyes out at the dinner table, and you tell me it's nothing?"

All Melissa did was shake her head.

Teddy looked for a minute at his fifteen-year-old daughter and then slammed his hand down on the table. His glass of red wine went flying. TH and Richie jumped in their seats; Rachel started to cry as well. "God damn it," Teddy roared. "You tell me right now what made you cry so much that you had to ruin our Christmas dinner."

Melissa kept her head down, but managed an answer, barely at a whisper. "I miss momma."

Teddy cocked his head to one side. "You miss momma?"

Melissa nodded. "Yes."

"Don't you think we all miss momma?"

Tears ran down her face, snot bubbles from her nose. "Yes."

"Well, I don't think your momma would approve of you acting up in front of the whole family and ruining our Christmas dinner. Do you?

"I suggest that you pick yourself up from this table and go into your room. You can come back out when you decide that you can act properly."

Melissa got up quickly and bolted out of the room and up the stairs to her bedroom. Teddy pointed a carving fork at the other three children. "I would suggest that the remainder of the evening move along without any further problems."

And the night did go along as Teddy prescribed. The dinner was finished. Desert was served, games were played, and all of the gifts under the tree were opened, except Melissa's. It was past midnight when TH finally climbed up to his bedroom. TH didn't see Melissa the rest of the night. In the morning, he was the first one downstairs. He looked under the tree where Melissa's unopened gifts had been. None of them were remaining under the tree.

Mrs. Aft

The following day brought bright sunshine and a stiff, cold wind out of the north. TH had called Richie first thing in the morning, and his older brother was eager to get going and out of Rachel's noisy house.

"Don't the kids go to school?" TH asked.

"Who said anything about the kids?" Richie said. "Rachel has a few days off, and she sits in the kitchen and drinks coffee with both the TV and radio on. The only place I can get any quiet is up in the little room I'm using. That would be okay, but it's cold and claustrophobic up there."

"Should have gone the motel route. It's quiet, and you get some interesting guests."

Richie turned in the car to face TH. "Like who?"

"Joseph Running Bear came by. He picked me up and took me out to his place and showed me what somebody had done to his livestock and chickens."

Richie groaned. "Is there a short version?"

TH told him about the slaughter at Joseph's house and about his trip to Rockford.

"Doesn't recall telling anyone he was going down there?"

"No, but does it matter. Somehow Aft found out and paid Joseph a visit."

"You don't know it was Aft."

"No proof, but let's not be ignorant."

Richie coughed hard into his sleeve. "Any other visitors?"

"Cindy Fuller stopped by."

Richie smiled. "She bring you cookies?"

"Funny, but no. I told her that a number of people had questioned whether Skitch Grayson had killed Freddie and that we had gone and paid him a visit."

"How'd she take it?"

"Not well. That's why I'm running it by you. She seemed to be telling me we should leave everything alone and that we were opening an old wound by poking around."

"I've seen this a lot," Richie said. "As cops, we deal with murder in kind of a disconnected fashion. We feel sorry for the victims, and we feel sorry for their families, but the murder doesn't drive a stake thru our hearts. If it did, we couldn't do our jobs. When you have a loved one die, you feel awful for a while, but then the pain eases. When you have a loved one murdered you always feel awful, and the biggest reason for this is you can never answer the question why. Why would someone kill your loved one?"

"I'm sure that's what it is with Cindy and her father. Why would someone kill Fatty who was probably the sweetest person in Milton? I'm sure that question eats at them every day even though it's been fifteen years since the murder. Yeah, if people bring up the murder or question whether Skitch Grayson killed Fatty, I'm sure it eats at them."

"So we should stop?"

"I didn't say that. If Skitch didn't do it and got railroaded, I think we should find the truth. Maybe you shouldn't update Cindy on what we're doing. That's all."

TH looked off to his left at a pond with steam rising off the water. "Cindy also told me that dad used to come visit their house after Mrs. Fuller took off. She said he felt bad for them and he used to bring Freddie little gifts. Stuff like that."

Richie rolled his shoulders to relieve tension. "It probably seemed like it wasn't possible, but to a lot of people in this town, dad had a big heart. I know he liked Fred Fuller. I know he felt bad when Mrs. Fuller left them. Here were Fred and Cindy stuck with a four-year-old with Down Syndrome. I know this is when Fred really started to hit the bottle. I know it all bothered dad, so he probably was just trying to help out."

TH wondered why his father couldn't show a little more love around his own family. Most things weren't bad, but with the things you didn't see, like love, they were lacking.

"Marilyn Aft's house should be just down here on the left," Richie said, checking the GPS on his phone."

"Steve Marks says she's fucking crazy."

"And Steve Marks works for Lou Katz, who took over for our father and his Fascist regime."

"What does that mean?"

"Let's ask Marilyn Aft our own questions, and we'll decide whether what she tells us is any good or whether she's crazy."

"Always the cop."

Richie smiled. "It's what I do for a living."

Marilyn Aft lived in a small, ranch style home at the end of a long street. Her house, a sickly, pale yellow building, was surrounded by a wooden fence. The drive that led up to the side of the house was gravel and TH's car kicked up dust as they drove up to the house. On this bright fall morning, the house projected a good share of gloom. Maybe it was time after talking to her to let this thing go, TH thought. Freddie was long gone, and Skitch Grayson would be dead soon. Did any of this matter?

●　　　　●　　　　●

Marilyn Aft looked anything but crazy when she answered her door for TH and Richie. She was a petite woman of about sixty whose dark hair had started to turn more to gray. She had an attractive, line free face that smiled at her two visitors. Her blue eyes were alert and looked from one man to the next. She wore navy slacks with a light gray, thin sweater.

"How can I help you gentlemen?" she asked.

"Good morning, Mrs. Aft," TH said. "We were wondering if we could have a word with you."

The smile that she wore left her face. Her eyes went from alert to concern. "You're the two Brown boys," she said.

TH smiled. "We are. I'm TH, and this is my older brother Richie."

"I know who you both are. I'd seen you grow up for years. You look like your dad, TH."

TH wasn't sure how to take this, but it was true. Subtract the age difference, and they closely resembled each other. "Like I said, we were wondering if we could have a word with you. It shouldn't take long."

"I'm very sorry to hear about your sister. I'm sure that was very tough for all of you to deal with. Your mother, I think it's a good thing that she's gone. Losing a child before you go is extremely difficult."

"It's been a tough week," TH said, "but thank you for the kind words."

"But you didn't come out here to talk about your sister, did you? I'm not sure what else I can talk to you about. I've been out of Milton for quite some time. I don't miss it, and I certainly don't talk about it."

"Skitch Grayson, Mrs. Aft," Richie said. "We'd like to talk to you about Skitch Grayson and the Fatty Fuller murder."

The smile came back again, but this time it was a wry one. "That I can talk about. Why don't you boys come in out of the cold?"

"That was subtle," TH said to Richie as they entered the house.

"If I had to listen to you, we'd still be out there."

The interior of the house was small and tight, but clean and nicely decorated. Marilyn led them into a small living room that looked out over a farmer's field in the back. TH thought the view was forlorn, especially now with the corn stalks all brown and about to be plowed under.

"Can I offer either one of you anything to drink?" she asked.

They looked at her and simultaneously shook their heads. They had both taken a seat on a large, leather couch. Marilyn sat down in an armchair across from them.

"We went and saw Skitch the other day," Richie said. "He's in a home up in Wisconsin. He's got lung cancer."

She shook her head slowly. "That's terrible," she said. "First prison and now cancer. How cruel can life be to one person?"

Richie shifted on the couch. "Why is that cruel? I mean, he was convicted and was sent to prison for a crime he committed. Unfortunately, many years later he got lung cancer. You can't smoke unfiltered Camels most of your life and not expect something bad to happen."

She nodded. "That's true," but then her eyes narrowed. "What exactly is your interest in Skitch Grayson? That murder is fifteen years old, and now you want to talk about it. The other thing is your father's people were in charge of that investigation. I understand he can still talk and knows what's going on. Why don't you talk to him?"

"Our father," TH answered, "and his people might not agree with some of our views of the murder or the way the investigation was handled."

Another small smile. "What are those views?"

TH exhaled loudly. "We don't think that Skitch Grayson killed Freddie."

She leaned back against the back of her chair and crossed her arms. "You said you went to see Skitch. What did he have to say?"

"He said he didn't do it," Richie said. "Also showed us a letter that you sent him that said you didn't think he did it and that the investigation was poorly run."

"I don't think he did it, and as for the investigation, I think it was a total farce."

"Why don't you tell us why you believe all of that?"

She uncrossed her arms and put them on the armrests. "For one thing, Skitch Grayson was not a murderer. He wouldn't hurt a flea, especially someone like the Fuller boy. It's absurd for anyone to think that he could walk up behind that boy, bash him on the head with a rock and leave him to drown in that creek."

"I work homicide in Kansas City, Mrs. Aft, and I have seen a lot of murderers who were more mild-mannered than Skitch."

"That may be, Richard, but what motive did Skitch have to kill Freddie? To steal a few fishing poles and some tackle. That's ridiculous."

TH saw that Richie's face was getting a little red. "Look, we all believe that Skitch didn't kill Freddie, but regardless of what any of us say here today, we can't prove a thing. In order to help Skitch out, if that's possible, we have to find something that exonerates him. We think that maybe you know something about the investigation and the arrest that might help us out."

Marilyn stood and walked to a small table near a large bookshelf. The table had two decanters that held liquor in them. She took the one that held scotch and poured herself a small glass. She took a sip and returned to her chair. "I'm not sure I can give you anything that proves much. This is all conjecture on my part."

TH looked at Richie. "There's your word."

"Mrs. Aft," Richie said. "Why don't you tell us about the investigation? Maybe there's something there that can help us."

She looked out the windows towards the corn fields and shook her head. "That was kind of the beginning of the end for Logan and me, not that we had that great of a relationship anyway."

"So what happened?" TH asked.

"We were both home the night of the murder which was a rarity. Most of the time Logan went out to Lifers, but that night we were home watching television. I even remember Logan saying something about it being good to have a night where he could relax and not have to do anything.

"It was a quiet night. We had the windows open, and all you could hear was the occasional buzzing of a cicada. It was around ten o'clock and were about to go to bed when we saw the headlights of a car pull into the drive.

Logan got up from his chair and looked out of the window. 'It's Chief Brown', he said."

She stopped and took a sip of the whiskey, closing her eyes at the same time. "I knew something pretty bad had happened if your father came out to the house to tell Logan. He didn't come around our house that much."

"What did our father say?" TH said.

"When he came into the house he looked awful. I could tell he was down about something. His hands even shook a little. He told Logan and me what had happened to the Fuller boy. He told us it was the worst crime that had occurred since he had been the chief. He couldn't understand how or why anyone would do anything like that to a kid like Fatty Fuller. You sure you two don't want something to drink?"

TH and Richie both said they were good.

"You may not be when this story is over," she said. "Logan asked Chief Brown if he wanted him to spearhead the investigation. Your father said, 'why the fuck do you think I'm here Logan?' Those were his exact words. Logan turned a little white when the chief said that. Those guys might have been police officers, but they weren't homicide people. I'm sure Logan was thinking he had no idea what to do."

"Did Logan say anything to my father about this?" Richie asked.

Marilyn laughed. "If you think that any of those men, Logan, Jack or Ben, questioned your father very much, you're crazy."

"So far all you've told us is our dad told Logan to take over the investigation. Nothing strange there. What got you thinking that the investigation was handled improperly?"

"You didn't let me finish? Logan was standing there nodding his head up and down as your father spoke. The look he wore was somewhere between dumbfounded and stupid. As your dad talked, he seemed to be getting more agitated. He finally grabbed Logan by the shirt and asked him if he was hearing all of this. Logan said yes, sir, very smartly. Your dad said, 'Make sure you understand, Logan. I don't want the whole town talking about this murder for weeks and weeks. I want this case taken care of pronto' "

TH and Richie looked at each other. Pronto was a phrase that Teddy used a lot when talking to them at home.

"So Logan was under immediate pressure right away to get something done in a hurry. I don't think he slept a wink that night."

"What happened next?" Richie asked.

"A couple of days later, I got a call from Logan. He said they received a tip that Skitch Grayson had some of Fatty Fuller's fishing tackle in this old shed in the back of his yard. They went out there and found the gear and arrested Skitch."

"Any idea where this tip came from?" TH said.

"No. I never heard that."

"Skitch used to do some work for you guys around the old house. You knew him pretty well," Richie said. "What did you think when Logan told you they had arrested Skitch?"

"I told him they were crazy. I told him Skitch wouldn't hurt anyone and that they had made a big mistake."

"Logan doesn't seem like the type to take those words lightly," TH said.

"That's putting it mildly. What he said was in a case as important as this one it would be a lot better for everyone, especially me, to shut my mouth and keep their opinions quiet."

Richie let out a large burst of air. "No offense, but what you're saying is that our dad came to your house and pretty much told Logan to solve this murder one way or another and to make sure it was done quickly."

"That's exactly what happened."

"But how did Fatty's fishing gear end up in that shed?"

"That's one I can't answer for you. My thought is that somebody knew who had the gear and somehow got it into Logan's hands and he planted it."

Now Richie laughed. "I can understand that my father wanted a fast conclusion to the case. That much I can believe, but it's the part about Logan securing evidence and then planting it on Skitch's property to frame him that has me going a little bit. You're telling us that my father had this much control over Logan."

"The men that worked for your father feared him. They did what they were told, or they knew they would suffer the consequences."

"Even a guy like Ben Smith?" TH said.

"Those three, Logan, Jack Davis, and Ben. If your dad said to do it, it got done, and it's not the first case of murder that ended a little suspiciously. Do your research on the history of murders in Milton, and you'll find some interesting stuff."

Richie was shaking his head. "I just can't believe that our father could control those men so much."

"You're shaking your head, Richard, but it wasn't just the men he controlled. It was the wives and families of those men."

"What are you talking about, Mrs. Aft?"

She took a sip of her whiskey. "Teddy tried to control us all, including the wives. He tried to control me, Grace Davis and Ann Smith."

"What do you mean control?" TH said.

She smiled. "Teddy had full control of those three men. Their futures were in his hands. If he wanted things done, they did it, or their careers would suffer. They all knew this. Teddy was also able to control how they advanced or progressed in the department; sometimes this was based on the way the wives treated Teddy. He used them all."

"When you say the way the wives treated Teddy, what exactly do you mean?" Richie asked. His face was still red and appeared close to losing his temper.

"You're a detective somewhere, aren't you, Richard?" she asked.

"Kansas City."

"What do you think I mean, and baking cakes and pressing shirts can't be used?"

"I'm not sure," Richie said.

"Are you talking sex, Mrs. Aft?" TH asked.

"Bingo, TH. I am talking sex."

"Wait a minute," Richie said, almost spitting out the words. "You're telling me that our father would get sex out of the officer's wives and that helped them advance their careers?"

"Some of the wives," Marilyn said. "Never me."

"But Logan was one of my father's top deputies," Richie said. "If you didn't participate in his little sex for advancement game then how did Logan rise so far?"

She sipped the whiskey and looked out over the glass. "Logan did a lot of things for Teddy that surpassed me having sex with him."

"Like fixing a murder case?" TH said.

"That's a big one," she said. "I know you don't believe me, Richard, and I doubt if either of the other women will talk, but that is the truth."

Richie shook his head. "How did this little plan transpire?"

"Logan came home one night and said that Teddy would be visiting our house to see me and to be as nice to him as I could be. I told him I was always nice to Teddy. He said he wanted me to be extra nice to him when he came over. He said it would help his career."

TH found his heart beating faster. "What did you say?"

"I told Logan to go fuck himself. If he wanted to advance his career, he could be extra nice to Teddy."

'What did Logan say?"

"He slapped me."

"Do you know if the other women participated in this little game?"

"Based on my conversations with them, I'm going to say yes, but you'd have to talk with them about that, not that they'll talk."

"Why should we believe you, Mrs. Aft?" Richie asked. "You've got to think that your story is just a bit out there."

She placed her drink on the table near her chair and stood up and approached Richie. "Your father came to see me after I told Logan he was crazy. Teddy came and saw me and tried to convince me it was in our best interest if I cooperated in his little game. I politely told him no thanks.

"To that, he grabbed me and forced me to the floor. He ran his hands all over my body and tried to pull my slacks and panties down. I resisted, and eventually, I just spit in his face and called him a vile pig. For some reason this got him to stop, and he got off of me. He left our house without another word after he kicked me hard in the ribs.

"You can believe me if you want; you can also elect to not believe me. I don't care. It was things like this and the way that Skitch Grayson was framed that got me to leave both Logan and Milton. Things are not right in that little town."

•   •   •

Driving back to Milton, TH and Richie didn't speak for the first ten minutes. Richie spent the whole time looking away from TH and out the window. Finally, he turned towards his brother.

"That woman *is* crazy," he said.

TH lit a cigarette and took a drag as he took in Richie's comment. "About which part?"

"I don't fucking know. Maybe the whole thing. The story about dad showing up at their house and ordering Logan to make sure the investigation into Fatty's murder went quickly sounds a little dubious. The part about the evidence planting especially. It's all too far-fetched."

"The sex part wasn't far-fetched?"

"Even more so. Look, I know Marilyn hates Logan Aft. Everybody knows that, but to come up with this sex for advancement story is just not believable."

"We can ask Grace Davis and Ann Smith?"

"I agree with Marilyn. I don't think either one of those women is going to tell us anything about dad that would hurt him. And have you seen Grace Davis? Why would dad want to have sex with her?"

TH laughed. "It had nothing to do with the sex, Richie. It's all about the control for dad. One of those guys could be married to a water buffalo, but dad would have sex with it if it would give him control."

"You're sounding as crazy as Marilyn Aft."

TH threw the cigarette out the window. "There was something that Mary Katz told me about Wilson Garrett. It had to do with the Three Amigos' pension plan. She was sure that dad had something over Garrett in order to get the city council to pass the pensions. She was convinced of it."

"The Fuller murder?"

"No. Why would Wilson Garrett kill Freddie?"

"Makes no sense."

"What about what Marilyn said about the histories of murder in Milton? I don't remember any other murders in Milton besides Freddie's. Think there's something there?"

Richie shrugged. "That we can look into. Maybe your buddy Marks will help us out."

"I can ask him."

"And Marilyn Aft is crazy."

"Maybe, maybe not, but there is one thing we can do."

"What's that?"

"Why don't we ask dad about the Fuller case? Why wouldn't he talk to us?"

"He'll talk to me. He doesn't like you."

Other Sources

Steve Marks sat across from Clarence Johnson and watched him sink his teeth into an enormous jelly roll. The bite that Clarence took was big, demolishing about a fourth of the pastry, but a good portion of cherry jelly squished from the sides and onto his lips. Rather than using a napkin to clean up this mess, Clarence took his right index finger to gather the loose jelly. He then plucked his finger back into his mouth. Marks watched him take another bite, not as aggressive as the first, and then wash it down with a large gulp of coffee loaded with three creams and four sugars.

"You look at Wilson Garrett, and you get the impression that he's just some small town yokel politician. He looks all mild and meek, and with his frumpy little wife and those tub-o-lard kids, you'd think he was this easy going, little man," Clarence said. Clarence was the editor of the County News, Jo Davies County paper, the most reputable news source in the area. Marks wanted to stay away from the Milton Beacon. One, they were more of a local events advertiser. Two, if he talked to anyone at the Beacon, the whole town would know within days.

"I'd never figure him for anything, but that," Marks said, picturing Garrett with his little, colorful bow ties.

"That's his public persona you see," Clarence said. "He wants the people to see that and believe that. He's really a pretty good politician."

Marks shifted uneasily on his chair. He took a sip of his black coffee while Clarence took another shot at the sweet roll. "But that's all I've ever seen," he said. "Wilson has been in office since I was eight. I've never seen him look any different and he always acts like Mr. Small Town."

Clarence was licking his fingers again. "There's your answer. Like all of us, Wilson has gotten older and has sowed his oats and settled down a bit. It was in his younger days that Wilson liked to play a bit."

Marks knew the Trips Aces had been in the water for a long time. "So he was a gambler?"

Clarence smiled, his lips and chin stained by the roll's jelly. "Not that kind of playing, Steve."

Marks was finding all of this hard to believe. "You're talking ladies?"

"Well, I wouldn't call them ladies."

"Wilson liked the hookers?"

"Not liked. He loved them and in the early to mid-eighties, you could go over to Ma Brooks' place on the river and get pretty much whatever you wanted."

"Ma Brooks?"

"Sure, a legal, illegal whorehouse, just on the outskirts of good ole Milton."

"You're pulling my leg."

"Not at all. The house was probably in business for close to fifty years until the public got a little upset and Ma was shut down. Even the damn building was razed."

"I'd never heard about that."

"Like I said, a little before you came along or were old enough to know of such things." Clarence winked at Marks.

"Let's get back to Wilson Garrett. You say he used to frequent this Ma's?"

"I would say he was a God damn regular. If they'd had membership cards back in those days, Wilson's would have been a gold one. If they gave out miles, Wilson could have flown first class anywhere?"

"But he stopped all of that when he got going in Milton politics?"

Clarence leaned forward and spoke softly. "His quitting that scene coincided with politics and with some other stuff."

"You're going to tell me the other stuff, aren't you? You can't keep me hanging like that."

Clarence shrugged. "It's been so long ago, and it probably doesn't matter anymore. Mayor Garrett had a bit of a drinking problem, and occasionally it led to him getting a bit violent with some of the ladies."

"Wilson Garrett?"

"Wilson Garrett and gin were a bad combo. The word was that Wilson would get all drunk on gin and make his way over to Ma's. If the girl he chose was nice to him and treated him properly, there wouldn't be any trouble. If things didn't go the way that Wilson wanted them to, he could get a little nasty with the girls."

"Nasty?"

"Don't act so naïve, Steve. Wilson would slap them around if he thought things weren't going his way."

Marks felt a pinch in his stomach. "Anything ever very serious?"

"Not that I know of. Ma would get upset with him, or the girls would say they didn't want him coming around, but as you know, Wilson came from money. He would come around the next day and give some cash to Ma and some to the poor creature that he assaulted. All would be good until next time."

"That's an amazing story."

"Amazing, yet true. If you look into the history of a lot of people, I'm sure you can find at least one dark secret that they don't want the world to know."

Marks wondered about some of the people from Milton and their dark secrets. "But getting back to my original question about Wilson. Do you think there's anything out there that he could have done that would allow Teddy Brown to hold it over his head?"

"Like I said, this was a long time ago, but Teddy would have been in charge back then. He was in charge forever it seemed. I know that he knew Ma. I'm sure that Ma cut some deals with him, but I don't think from Wilson's drinking to his abusive behavior Teddy would have gotten involved. Wilson always made amends for his sins by making a donation to Ma's favorite charity, her."

Marks smiled. "Ma's not with us, I take it?"

"Dead a long time ago. When they forced her out and razed the place, I heard she went somewhere out west to retire in the sun. She left, her building got knocked down, and Wilson Garrett became the mayor of Milton. I'm not sure you could even find one of the girls that ever worked for Ma. They'd all be in their fifties and sixties by now, but I bet there all gone."

•   •   •

"Marilyn Aft is fucking crazy!" Rachel said.

They were all sitting in her kitchen, smoking, and drinking after Rachel had made dinner. She was standing in the middle of the room staring at her two brothers, a lit cigarette in one hand, and a can of beer in the other. TH and Richie were seated at the table.

"I agree with Richie on that one," she said. "There's nothing more ludicrous than to think that dad controlled those guys so much that he could get sex out of their wives."

"She sounded convincing to me," TH said.

"For a nut," Richie said.

"Anyway, how can you prove something like that?" Rachel said. "You gonna go up to those women and ask them if they had sex with dad? If he told them that would help their husband's careers? They'd laugh right in your face."

TH saw he was losing this battle. "Forget that for now. What about Skitch Grayson and Aft planting evidence on his property?"

"Again she's wrong," Rachel said. "Most of that part of the story came out after both of you guys left home. It was a hot topic for a while. There's a bartender, Gus Morgan, still works out at the Lighthouse Tap. He said that Skitch used to come in there and drink all the time. He's the one that heard Skitch say he had come across some fishing equipment that he was looking to unload cheaply. This happened right after the murder. Aft got a hold of this information, and they went down to Skitch's place and found Fatty's gear. End of the line for Skitch."

"This guy still bartends down there?" TH asked.

"Been there for a million years," she said.

"I guess we can talk to him."

"What about dad? You still want to go up there and ask about the investigation?" Richie said.

"Whoa!" Rachel bellowed. "You two think you're going to go up and see dad and talk to him about the Fatty Fuller case? Are you trying to give him that one little push to the casket?"

"What's the big deal, Rachel?" Richie asked. "Enough people seem to think that Skitch didn't do it. What harm can there be in asking dad his recollections?"

"You'll just get him all worked up over nothing. Skitch Grayson was a bum and a drunk. He saw his opportunity to grab some decent fishing gear and resell it. He conked Fatty on the head and stole the gear. Maybe he wasn't thinking that Fatty would fall into Whisper Creek and die, but he definitely took the tackle. Seems pretty clear cut to me." She pointed her index finger at the two of them, still holding the cigarette. "Also, it didn't take long for the jury to convict him. Don't lose sight of that Starsky and Hutch."

Richie laughed loudly; TH wasn't sure of anything.

•   •   •

TH was tired when he finally crawled under the covers back in his room. His body was struggling to go to sleep while his mind was shuffling all of the thoughts from the Marilyn Aft meeting along with those from the talk with Rachel. Finally, his body won the battle, and he drifted off to sleep.

It wasn't long, but the mind did take over and regain some ground. The first dream showed a boy fishing along a creek. The view was from behind, and you couldn't see the boy's face. You also couldn't see the face of the man who snuck up behind the boy and hit him in the head with a rock. The boy tumbled forward, face first, into the creek. The man could be seen gathering all of the boy's fishing gear and slinking into the nearby woods.

The next few dreams clearly showed the faces of all of the participants. There was one of Skitch Grayson, a younger Skitch, telling a crowded bar that he had some new fishing that he wanted to sell. Then there were multiple shots of Teddy Brown with Grace Davis and Ann Smith. In all of these shots, the couples were talking, laughing, holding hands, sharing a kiss and then disappearing behind a door.

A terrified looking Marilyn Aft was shown on the floor of her living room. Teddy Brown loomed over her. He was snarling and had demon like teeth. There was drool running from the side of his mouth. His eyes were bugging out like a crazed, cartoon character. Teddy was trying to force himself onto Marilyn, but she resisted; she kicked and swung her arms wildly to keep Teddy away. Finally, Teddy gave up and headed for the door, but not without giving Marilyn a hard kick to the ribs.

Finally, a clear image of Logan Aft presented itself. Aft was walking across a moonlit yard and was carrying a number of fishing poles and a tackle box. He stopped by an old wooden shed and was able to easily open the lock on the door. He placed the fishing gear inside of the shed and turned and looked towards the house in the rear of the shot. He smiled widely. His eyes showed an evil gleam.

•   •   •

His phone rang loudly and awoke TH from his sleep. He rubbed his eyes and peered at the clock on the bedside table. It was eleven-fifteen. He grabbed the phone and hit the answer button.

"TH," said a female voice.

TH rubbed his eyes. "It's me," he said.

"It's Cindy, TH."

TH sat up in his bed, still in the dark, images of the dreams still in his head. "Everything okay, Cindy?"

"Everything's fine, TH. I just wanted to call and tell you that I'm sorry for the other night."

"You don't have to be sorry. I understand you're being upset about some of those things."

"No. That's not right. I never should have showed up at your room like that and then attack you for looking into Freddie's murder. I know there's a lot of questions about it, and I just didn't want to hear about it, especially at that moment."

"I hear you," he said. "Maybe we can get together soon and start from the beginning. What do you say?"

There was no immediate response. TH thought he could hear her breathing. "I'm not sure about that, TH. Let me give that one some thought."

"That would be fine," TH said, but then realized that Cindy had hung up.

•　　•　　•

Sleep returned to TH, but it was fitful. The thoughts of the dreams and Cindy's call were making him restless. Twice he sat up in bed to look at the clock on the table. The digital numbers still showed it was the middle of the night. Finally, near six o'clock, he fell into a deep sleep. This didn't last long. This time a pounding on his door awoke him. TH jerked the covers off of him and got out of bed quickly to see who was making all the noise. When he opened the door, he was surprised to see Fred Fuller, Cindy's father standing in the doorway.

"Hope I didn't wake you, TH," Fred said.

TH could see that Fred was dressed for the bank. He wore a slightly rumpled suit, equally crumpled tie, and smelled of a combination of aftershave and alcohol. His eyes were alert, and his face was shaven. What TH had heard sounded accurate. Fred Fuller could drink all night, but still, make it into the bank to perform his duties as its president.

"I was due to get up shortly, Mr. Fuller. Why don't you come in out of the cold?" TH held the door open, and Fred stepped into the room. There were two chairs near a table in the corner. Fred sat in one of them.

Fred waved his arm around the room. "You didn't splurge on the old expense account for this trip, I see."

TH laughed and sat on the edge of the bed. He was wearing his boxer shorts and a tee shirt. "I didn't think I'd be in town this long. I thought I just needed a place to sleep for a couple of nights."

"Doesn't really matter," Fred said, "and I've slept in a lot worse."

TH nodded and then the conversation dropped into an uncomfortable lull. "Was there anything in particular that you wanted to talk to me about, Mr. Fuller?"

"You know, TH, I'm just so damn sorry about what happened with Melissa. She used to come into the bank a lot, and she was such a fine woman. Always said hello. I know the people at the high school loved her, too. It's a great loss for the whole town."

"I've heard that and it's good to hear it from you again."

"And I'm sorry I missed the wake. Cindy told me there was quite the turnout. I'm sure you know I would have been there if I hadn't had some pressing matters to take care of."

Pressing matters like bourbon or scotch, TH thought. "I understand. There's no need to apologize."

"But there is. I should have been there. There's no excuse. The Brown family has come through for us in a lot of ways over the years. I can't think of a better friend that Freddie had other than you. He would always tell us that TH Brown was his best friend. And after Katherine left us, your dad was more than a friend. He knew that I was hurting so he would stop by for stuff for both Cindy and Freddie. He took a very special liking to Freddie. His concern got me through a lot of tough times."

In all of the times that TH spent with Freddie, he couldn't remember them discussing any visits his father had made to the Fuller home. TH thought that was a little odd.

"And what a friend Melissa was to Cindy. She was like the older sister that Cindy never had. It was almost like she shared a bond with your sister.

I think Melissa's passing affected Cindy as much as when Freddie was killed."

This was news to TH. He had no idea that Melissa had any kind of serious relationship with Cindy. "I wasn't aware that the two of them were close."

"Oh, maybe not until later years, but they became closer as they got older."

TH was missing something here and had no idea what it was. "My father have much to do with you before your wife left you?"

Fred Fuller tilted his head and gave TH a curious look. "What do you mean?"

"Did he ever come by your house? You said he came by a lot after your wife left you. How about before that?"

"I'm sure he did," Fred said quickly. "He had some business with the bank, and if he didn't have time to come by during work hours, he would stop by at night, but only occasionally."

"I was just curious. I'm glad he was a big help with you back then."

"It's a shame about his stroke and all. Such a strong figure struck down like that. Such a leader of the community."

"He's not gone yet."

"No, that's right, and he's one tough son of a bitch."

"That he is."

"Well, I really wanted to just stop by and say I was sorry for missing the wake. I need to be going. I've got to open the bank."

"Sure, Mr. Fuller. I appreciate you stopping by."

Fred rose slowly from the chair and extended a hand to TH who shook it firmly. Up close now, Fred's face didn't look all that healthy and alert.

"Stop by and say goodbye before you leave town," Fred said. He started for the door.

"One last thing, Mr. Fuller?"

Fred turned and faced him.

"You ever think back on Freddie's murder? Do you ever wonder if they convicted the right guy?"

Fred stood up a little straighter; his chest came forward in his posture. "I don't think about that time, TH. A lot of me died when Freddie died. A lot of hope went out of Cindy, too. The police, your father's men, found the evidence, arrested Skitch Grayson and brought him to trial. Those twelve jurors heard the case. They found him guilty, and the judge sentenced him. That's what I know and what I remember. There were no other suspects. There was no one with any other motive. It was a just ending to an awful event. It's over, and I really try not to relive it at all."

Fred turned again towards the door and left TH's room. TH stared at the door for a long time. Both Cindy and Fred Fuller were convinced Skitch was the killer. Why were people like Richie, Marks and him thinking otherwise?

•   •   •

TH showered, ran and got coffee and called Richie and Steve Marks. They all agreed to meet at The Dawn of the Day at nine o'clock. Again TH urged Marks not to tell anything to Lou Katz.

"What makes you think that I tell everything to Lou?"

"He is your boss."

"Believe it or not, even in a small town like Milton, he does not follow my every move."

Apparently, Lou didn't have the high regard for control that Teddy Brown seemed to exercise for years.

•   •   •

Marks was sitting in a booth near the back of the café when TH got there. The table was set for three guests, and there was a pot of steaming coffee sitting in the middle of it. Richie had not yet arrived.

"I drove out to see Joseph," Marks said.

"In what capacity?"

"Just a friend, TH."

"How was he?"

"I'd say close to devastated. It's a good thing hunting season is on, or he'd be in trouble. I think being busy helps keep his mind off of what happened."

"Still look bad out there?"

"Not bad. Just empty and quiet in places, like where the animals were. He got a buddy to help him get all of the carcasses out of the barns, and they had a big fire. You could still smell it in the air."

"Did he ask you to look into it?"

Marks shook his head and took a sip of his coffee. "He knows it's out of our jurisdiction. He didn't ask anything like that."

TH nodded as Richie walked up to the booth and sat down. Again, he looked like he'd had a few too many drinks and not enough sleep.

"Doing okay, Richie?" TH asked.

"I'm good," he said. "Coffee would help." Richie took the pot and poured him a cup. He slurped down half of it even though it was piping hot.

"Did you speak with Marilyn Aft?" Marks asked.

"We did. We saw her yesterday. She was very nice to us."

"And is she crazy?"

Richie groaned.

"She might be a little crazy," TH said. "She certainly had some interesting things to say."

Marks sat up straight on the bench. "Interesting things about the Fatty Fuller murder?"

"Definitely that. She said our father came by and ordered Logan to take over the investigation. Told him to speed it up because they couldn't have the people of Milton talking about a murder for a long time."

The waitress came by, but Marks waved her away. "By speed, it up, what do you think he meant?"

TH shrugged. "Coming up with a motive and evidence. What motive did Skitch have to kill Fatty? Fishing tackle that Fatty had? Evidence found in Skitch's shed?"

"But that was where Logan found the gear," Marks said.

"Or that was where Logan planted the gear so he could find it," Richie said from behind his cup. His eyes showed trails of red running through them."

"What I heard was that Logan got a tip from someone that the gear was back there and he went out and found it," Marks said.

"Marilyn knew nothing about this, but our sister Rachel did. She says a guy named Gus Morgan, a bartender at The Lighthouse Tap, heard Skitch telling people that he had some gear that he wanted to unload and for cheap."

Gus Morgan, Marks knew, had been at the Lighthouse forever. He was going to ask him about Ma Brooks whorehouse which had been located about a mile away from the tavern. "I can look into that," Marks said. "What else?"

"She said we should look into the history of murder in the town of Milton. She claimed that Fatty's case wasn't the only one where the investigation might have been handled a bit oddly."

Marks sipped his coffee. "There's not that much in the way of murders in Milton. I'd have to look way back, I guess."

"She just mentioned it."

"So she thought that Logan had planted the evidence to frame Skitch and that there was a history of sketchy murder investigations in the town. Is that about it?"

"Mostly," Richie said, smiling. "Then she broke into the crazy, ludicrous stuff."

Marks poured more coffee for the three of them. "How crazy and how ludicrous?"

"TH, you can do the honors," Richie said.

"She went on to tell us that our father had ultimate control over the officers that worked for him. He controlled every move they made and how they acted. This either helped or hurt them as their careers went along."

"Get to the juicy part," Richie said laughing.

"She told us that Teddy had so much control over those men that he ended up controlling their wives as well. He wanted the wives to treat him as if they were under his command. Do what I say, and things will go okay."

Marks shifted on the bench. "Meaning what exactly?"

"Meaning he wanted sexual favors from the women. In return, the men would be treated quite well by their boss."

Marks cleared his throat. "So the wives of Aft, Davis, and Smith had sex with Teddy to help advance their husband's careers?"

"That was the story except that Marilyn held out after fighting with Teddy. She thinks the other two went through with it, though."

"Well, that is a little crazy. Doesn't mean much, but it sure is an interesting tale."

"I think it means a lot," TH said loudly. "It means that if Teddy had that much control over his men and their wives he could probably get them to do just about anything, like frame Skitch Grayson for a murder."

Marks nodded. As fanciful and ludicrous as it sounded, there might be some credence to what TH said. Did all of this control over men lead to the great pension deals arranged by Wilson Garrett? Did Teddy have some control over Garrett? Suddenly the coffee began to burn in Marks' stomach.

He got a sour taste in the back of his throat. He didn't think it was from the coffee.

•   •   •

The day turned warm and sunny. When TH and Richie got to Marymore, the temperature was pushing near sixty. Sheila Jones once again told them that their father was out on the concrete platform overlooking the bluff. This time she didn't offer to lead them out there to see their father. She said he had been particularly rude this morning and she'd had her fill of him. They both said they understood and started the slow climb up the hill to where Teddy sat.

"This ought to be pleasant," Richie said.

"He's already in a bad mood, and we're going to bring up the Fatty Fuller murder. I'm sure that will cheer him up."

"I'm not sure if anything will cheer him up."

Teddy Brown looked like he had the last time TH saw him. Even with the warm air, he wore the heavy coat, the wool scarf and the cloth hat pulled almost over his eyes. Between the scarf and the hat was about a two-inch slit that Teddy could view the Mississippi and Iowa from. At least today, his nose did not appear to be running.

Richie walked up to Teddy and bent down, so he was eye level with him. "Dad," he said loudly, "it's Richie and TH."

Teddy tilted his head to one side. "Did that black bitch of a nurse tell you I was deaf?"

Richie backed up. "No."

"Then what are you yelling for?"

"I didn't mean to yell."

"What do you boys want?"

TH came around from the side and stood right in front of Teddy. It was clear that their father was in good shape mentally. There was no reason to not be direct. "We wanted to ask you about the murder of Fatty Fuller."

Teddy's head came up a bit. Through the slit, TH could see the one good eye and the one that drooped. "You some sort of cop now, TH?"

"A lot of people in town have been talking lately. There are a number of people who don't believe that Skitch Grayson killed Fatty."

The beady, black eyes shifted to Richie. "Now, you are a cop, Richie. Are you in on this little prank?"

"I don't think it's a prank, dad. I think there might be a good case for Skitch not being the killer."

"A good case, huh? What is this good case?"

Richie cleared his throat. "The two big items are any motive Skitch might have had to kill Fatty and then the act itself. Most people we've talked to don't think that Skitch could have hurt anyone, much less Fatty."

"No God damn motive you say?"

"That's right," Richie said.

"I want you to check something out before you question motives. I want you to go back over the years, maybe twenty or so. You go back into the records, and you'll see old documentation of the number of times that Skitch Grayson was arrested for petty theft. Until he started doing the odd job chores, we're pretty sure he stole stuff and then resold it to make money. My guess is he was arrested three or four times for this. Why'd he do that? Cause he needed money. Go down to the bank and talk to Fred Fuller. Skitch went through bankruptcy and almost lost his place. In the entire time, he'd been here in Milton he has needed money. Is that enough for motive?"

"But dad," TH said, "do you think that Skitch would really come up from behind Fatty and smash him on the head with a rock and then leave him to drown in that creek?"

"So it's one thief defending another?'" Teddy said, laughing. "I once had to go call on the Bush's over on Freemont. Pretty nice couple. Seemed to get along. That is until that night where Alice Bush stuck George in the bicep with a steak knife because she thought he was cheating with another woman from the church. Do you think I expected that, TH? No, I didn't. I didn't expect Skitch to bop Fatty, but that is what happened. The man stole the boy's fishing gear after he hit him on the head. Skitch was bragging about it a day or so later down at the Lighthouse. Aft found the stuff in the shed behind Skitch's house. What's the mystery here?"

TH looked at Richie who shook his head. Both brothers were surprised by the sharpness of their father's memory of the case. His story seemed to jive with the popular one that existed.

"You should know better, Richie," Teddy said. "I can understand TH being confused by all of these rumors, but that is what they are. As police officers, we deal with facts. Those were the facts of the case and the jury believed them. That's why Skitch sat in prison for fifteen years."

Neither boy said anything for a moment. "We're sorry we bothered you with this, dad," Richie said. "We were just following up on some stories."

Teddy laughed again. "Don't come back here with your fucking rumors and your dumb questions."

∙ ∙ ∙

"I don't care how old he gets or what kind of shape he's in, he always manages to make me feel like I'm a five-year-old," Richie said.

TH was already smoking his second cigarette since they'd left Marymore. "He has that talent. You can tell his body took a beating from the stroke, but not his brain. He seemed to remember that case pretty well."

"Let's face it. This had to be the biggest crime committed while dad was the Chief of Police. If his brain is in good shape, which it seems, then I'm sure some of those details are as fresh as yesterday."

"What do you think?"

"About what he said? What's there to think? Skitch hit Fatty over the head with the rock to steal his gear. Then Skitch bragged about it at the Lighthouse where Gus Morgan overheard him. Gus told somebody, and word got to Aft. End of story."

"Really? You think that's all there is to it? Marilyn Aft seemed to think the investigation was rigged. Of course, Skitch said he was innocent. So those two say he didn't do it, while dad and his crew are going to say he did."

"Don't forget the most important people, the twelve jurors, and one judge. The jurors found him guilty, and the judge gave him life. There must have been something there that they heard that convinced them. Remember, the case was taken out of this venue. There's no way dad and his boys were able to cook the case out of Milton."

"So what's next? You're the cop."

"We can ask around a little more, but I don't even know where to begin. Who in this town can tell us something definitive about what happened that night and with the trial?"

TH opened his window and flicked the half-smoked butt out of it. "Marilyn Aft said something about researching the history of murders in Milton."

"And Marks said he'd do a little research."

"Other than that?"

Richie shook his head. "I can't think of anything right now. It may be time to close up shop and head home."

TH knew they had reached desperation time. If they didn't come up with something quick, it looked like there was nothing to find. TH hated to end with that idea. There was no doubt that Marilyn Aft's story of the case was a little out there, but there was something about the way Skitch Grayson told his story. TH believed him.

●　　　●　　　●

The Lighthouse Tap had been a fixture at the northwest corner of Milton for over seventy years. The little tavern was located a little more than a mile from the casino and other hot spots along Brewster Way. When Marks pulled into the tavern's parking lot, he couldn't remember the last time he had been here. The place catered mostly to river people, those that worked the docks, wharves, and barges. Some fishermen, hunters, and snowmobilers would stop during the season, but it wasn't a place for casual, fun-loving drinking. The drinkers that usually came in were hardcore workers who drank to put their tough day behind them. They had little use for recreational drinkers. Marks had never been here for a drink. He had been there because of two fights and once when a longshoremen knifed a ferry operator. He checked his holster to make sure he was armed before he stepped from his car and into the place.

At two o'clock in the afternoon, there were only three tired looking men drinking at the bar. Marks had to wait a minute for his eyes to adjust to the hazy darkness that filled the room. Even though you couldn't smoke in a bar in Illinois the air smelled like cigarettes, cheap cigars, and stale beer. Marks headed across the room to the long bar. He felt his feet sticking to the grimy floor. He found a spot as far from the other three men as he could and waited as the bartender finally turned and worked his way down to him.

"What are you having, bud?" the bartender said. He was a short man, completely bald with a three-inch scar running under the left side of his face. He was maybe only about five-four, but the white apron he wore was stretched out firmly in front of him. The arms that showed reminded Marks of the arms he had seen on gorillas.

Marks placed his badge on the bar. "Gus Morgan?"

The bartender smiled. "I made you for a cop the minute you walked in here."

"That's nice. How are you, Gus?"

"Can't complain. Is Milton sending out detectives now to collect on unpaid parking tickets?"

"I'm not here about that, but I can place a call if you want to clear that up."

"I'm good. What can I do for you, Detective Marks?"

Marks hadn't given his name but saw no reason to be alarmed. Milton was a small town. "You been here a long time, Gus, and I don't mean today?"

"Going on forty-two years. I'll probably die in this bar, but that ain't all bad. I don't want to stay home all day and listen to the old lady. I don't need her to tell me that everything that has gone wrong in our lives is my fault."

Marks laughed. "Maybe that's why I haven't gotten married."

"You don't need anyone pointing out your faults?"

"That and other things."

"So what can I do for you?"

"This may require a little effort. I'm looking for some information going back in time."

"How far back?"

"The Fatty Fuller murder. You remember that?"

"That happened back in oh two, but I remember it very well. It's all anyone talked about for the longest time."

"That's right. Part of the story is that you heard Skitch Grayson talking about selling some fishing tackle that he had recently acquired."

Gus took a couple of beer mugs out of a sink of hot, soapy water, rinsed them and then dried them off with a towel. "What makes you come out here fifteen years later and ask questions about that case, Detective Marks?"

"You know Skitch Grayson is dying?"

"I'd heard that, but if you want my opinion, they should have gave him the chair a long time ago. He was just a worthless drunk. There was no reason for the taxpayers to continue to pay to keep this guy alive for what he did to Fatty Fuller."

"You'd see Skitch a lot?"

"Sure. Whenever he had any money. He used to come in here with Homer Glen, the charter operator, and sit right about where you're standing. Both of them drank nothing but rotgut whiskey. Usually, they'd drink until they couldn't see straight. I don't know how they got home."

"And Skitch was in here right after the murder?"

"Skitch was in here the day of the murder. Homer and he were drinking here that afternoon. Homer left around seven; he had a charter the next day. I would say Skitch left maybe a half an hour later. My guess it was on his way home that he went by Whisper Creek because he knew Fatty liked to fish up there. He caught Fatty alone, bashed him on the head and took his gear. Next day or so he's in here talking about having some new gear to get rid of. Said he could unload it cheap."

"You heard all of this?"

"Yeah. Like I said, Skitch was sitting right here. Skitch wasn't keeping it a secret."

"Then you told the police?"

"Well, I called the Milton PD and asked who was in charge of the case. They gave me to Lieutenant Aft. He came by, and I told him what I'd heard. That was when he went by Skitch's and found Fatty's tackle in the shed back there."

Marks scratched his chin. Here was a witness telling him about Skitch bragging about the fishing gear. Also shooting down Skitch's story about drinking with Homer Glen until late into the night. "Aft and his buddies do any drinking in here?"

"Here? Hell no. If the cops drank in here, I wouldn't have any customers. You know the story, detective. This is a bar for river people."

Marks nodded. "What about Ma Brooks' place?"

"Jesus, you writing a history of Milton or something?"

"Something like that."

"Just so we're clear about Skitch Grayson. I hear these stories once in a while about how he didn't do it and all of that. I think they're horseshit. That man would do anything for a buck, and he was a big liar."

"Forget about Skitch. What about Ma Brooks?"

"What about her? It's no secret that she ran a whorehouse about a mile north of here. She ran that place for years until there was a public outcry to shut the place down. Of course, this outcry came from the wives of most of the men who went into the place. Carol Garrett, the mayor's wife, was one of the ladies who spearheaded the effort to close it. Finally, the cops busted the place and closed it down. The building was levelled not too long after that."

Marks smiled. "So Wilson Garrett was a client?"

Gus laughed. "Back in the day, our fine mayor was quite the character. He liked his booze, and he liked his ladies. Had enough money to pay for whatever he wanted."

"Was he ever any trouble?"

"Out at Ma's?"

"I heard he would get a little rowdy every now and then with one of the girls. So bad, in fact, that he had to pay Ma if he got too out of control."

"I don't like to talk bad about people, but Wilson was not the best drinker. He'd come in here once in a while and leave pretty drunk."

"Wilson drank here. I thought you said you were a bar for river people."

"Wilson's daddy owned a pretty good sized barge and tug company. That makes him river people. Plus he spent a lot of money."

"You ever hear of him getting out of control out there, doing something that might get him into trouble?"

"Nothing like that. Mostly what I heard is what you said. He'd get a little drunk, rowdy and then he'd have to pay off Ma before she would let him back in the place."

"And all of the girls that worked out there, they are probably all gone?"

"They were prostitutes. A couple of them may have become dancers, but most probably went where they could ply their trade. The only one I know that is still kind of around is Valerie Plume. Real sweet girl. She used to stop in here after a long night and have a drink. We got to be pretty good friends. When the house was shut down, she moved to Freeport to start up something new. She'd had enough of that trade."

"Think she's still down in Freeport?"

"Sure is." Gus reached behind him to a counter behind the bar. He grabbed an old card and placed it on the bar in front of Marks. It was a Christmas card. "Like I said, sweet girl. Sends me a Christmas card every year. I guess that's what I get for being nice to her after those long days at Ma Brooks."

•   •   •

TH was already in a bad mood when Marks called him. Talking to Richie hadn't helped. Richie had been swayed by the meeting with Teddy and was considering going back to Kansas City.

"We don't have any real evidence that says that Skitch wasn't the killer.

All we have is his story and some rumors from Marilyn Aft. I don't think we are going to find anything else," Richie said.

"Why don't you give it a few more days? You said Karen wasn't around anyway."

"I don't know, TH. All of this driving around and getting nowhere is giving me a migraine."

"Don't let dad get to you. He's got that way of intimidating people."

"What are you talking about? Yeah, dad gets on my nerves, just like anybody else, but that has nothing to do with my decision here. It's what we know. I just think we are wasting time."

"One or two more days?"

"I'll think about it."

"What about Melissa?"

"Seems like there's less there than the Fatty Fuller murder. Let me think about it a little."

TH was hoping that when Marks checked in that there would be some better news from his meeting with Gus Morgan.

"As far as Skitch goes, I don't think that I picked up anything to help us and probably found two things that hurt us."

"Such as?"

"One, Gus Morgan swears that Skitch was bragging about some new gear that he'd picked up recently that he wanted to unload cheaply. This was right after the murder."

"That's not good. What else?"

"This one kind of ruins the Homer Penn alibi. Gus said that Skitch and Homer were in the Lighthouse the day of the murder, drinking pretty heavily. Homer left earlier than Skitch because he had an early charter the next day. Skitch hung in there for about a half an hour and then left. Gus remembers it was close to seven-thirty. This would have given Skitch plenty of time to get over to Whisper Creek."

"Teddy said that Skitch was always in money trouble and wouldn't pass up any opportunity to make some easily. "

"There you go. If he thought he was just knocking Fatty out and was going to steal his gear that makes sense. I'm pretty sure that Skitch wasn't a cold-hearted killer. His intent was to steal the gear and sell it. When he heard Fatty died, he was in a bigger hurry to unload it."

"You believe that?"

"My mind is telling me that, and it's starting to make sense."

"Are you going to bail out on the investigation?"

"It's not an investigation, TH. We're just asking some questions."

"You know what I mean."

Marks sighed deeply, thinking of the Wilson Garrett/ Valerie Plume angle. "Not just yet, but I need something solid pretty soon to keep me spending time on this."

Marks sounded a lot like Richie, two cops parroting each other. "Okay, Stevie. I'll be in touch."

●　　　　●　　　　●

When Marks hung up with TH, he wasn't sure what he wanted to do. Nothing he had heard seemed to point at anyone, but Skitch Grayson, as Fatty Fuller's murderer. The talk with Gus Morgan seemed to solidify that, but there was something about Wilson Garrett that bothered him. Twice Marks had been told that Garrett had been a bit of a wild man when he was younger. Twice he'd heard stories about Garrett where he'd roughed up women and then had to pay to avoid the consequences. Was there something there that allowed Teddy Brown to hold it over the mayor's head, enough where Garrett arranged lucrative pension deals for the Three Amigos? It couldn't be the Fatty Fuller murder, could it? Why would Wilson Garrett kill Fatty? That thought made no sense at all to Marks. Did Valerie Plume, the retired hooker, know anything more that would tell Marks something about Garrett? He wasn't lying when he told TH he needed something more to get him to continue on the Fuller murder. He doubted talking to Valerie Plume would provide that, but he reasoned it wouldn't hurt to talk with her.

●　　　　●　　　　●

The Triple Diamond slot machine that TH was playing was not cooperating. Not one game at the Trips Aces had cooperated with TH since he had hit town. No doubt that playing video poker and slots was all luck, but even TH felt his bad run was a little unreal.

The game he was playing was located about a hundred feet from where Cindy Fuller was dealing blackjack. Where TH had an excellent view of her, she could not possibly see him. He watched as she expertly dealt the cards out to the players, as she kept the banter going, smiling and laughing at player's comments and jokes. With her good looks and casino personality, TH could see why she was a favorite amongst the male players. Her table was full, the only one of the ten blackjack tables. From where he was she looked happy. TH wondered about this.

TH didn't come to the Aces to stalk Cindy. He had sat down at the game and then noticed how close she was to him. He had come to the casino to play a little, have a drink or two and try to clear his head. What had started out as an inquiry into why his sister had committed suicide had turned into a full-scale reheat of the Fatty Fuller murder case. In truth, they had learned nothing about Melissa, but maybe they really didn't want to. When everyone started mentioning how Skitch Grayson had cancer and how he didn't kill Fatty, things took a turn. Now he wondered if they were really getting anywhere with that.

The only plusses to their cause was Skitch Grayson telling them he hadn't killed Fatty. This was not news, nor was it helpful. Marilyn Aft, a Skitch supporter, provided little for proof other than to say that her husband and Teddy might be behind framing Skitch. This didn't hold much water because TH knew that the two men she hated most were Aft and Teddy Brown. Maybe she was a nut. The sex for promotion stories she told seemed to give some credence to that.

Meeting with Teddy had done nothing, but dissuade Richie. Their father insisted that Skitch was the killer, that the man was a drunk and a thief, always looking for easy ways to make money. This, their father had said, could be proven by reviewing police arrest records. Maybe Skitch had only intended to knock Fatty out to steal his gear. Maybe murder was nowhere in his plans.

With the call from Marks, there was proof from a witness, Gus Morgan that Skitch had bragged of selling some fishing tackle that he had recently acquired. Along with that was the fact that Skitch had been drinking with Homer Glen the night of the murder, but Gus' story didn't mesh with Skitch's. Homer had left the Lighthouse Tap at seven; Skitch followed about a half hour later giving him plenty of time to get to Whisper Creek, conk Fatty on the head and steal his gear. If, like Teddy had stated, Skitch was a serial liar then why should they believe him over Gus Morgan?

TH slammed his hand on the button that said Maximum Bet. The first

Triple Diamond showed, the second came up, and this was followed by a blank. The payout was twenty-five dollars. Anything else would have paid hundreds.

"Fuck," TH said a bit too loud. He looked towards where Cindy was dealing. She seemed to be looking right at him after his vocal reaction, but there really was no way she could see him.

"Tough luck," a guy playing the game next to TH said. "Rarely do you get the two Triple Diamonds. Really tough luck."

"Yep," TH muttered. Was it just tough luck or was it just the continuation of a bad week? It occurred to him that Melissa had just killed herself a few days ago. Maybe he should do a little something about that before he left town. The Fatty Fuller murder seemed a little futile.

More Clues

TH was having breakfast alone, playing more with his eggs than eating them, and sipping the same cup of coffee until it got cold. He wasn't really hungry and wasn't sure why he'd come to breakfast. With both Richie and Steve Marks getting ready to bail out on the Skitch Grayson inquiry there seemed only one thing left to do in Milton. TH wanted to talk with Margaret Hatch, the teacher friend of Melissa's, who had said that all of the blame for Melissa's death fell on the Brown family. What had she meant by that? Did she know something that no one else knew?

He tasted a piece of greasy sausage and quickly washed it down with coffee. He decided he wasn't hungry just as his cell phone rang. It was seven-forty-five. It was Steve Marks.

"Call to put the final nail into the coffin?" TH said.

"TH, you'd better get a hold of Richie and get over to headquarters as soon as you can, and I'm talking about within the half hour."

"What the hell happened?"

"Just get over here."

TH hung up and called Richie. "I'll be there in fifteen minutes. Marks wants to see us."

"He say why?"

"No. Said we needed to get over there as soon as we can."

"This can't be good."

"That was my thought."

•   •   •

When he picked up Richie, TH could see that his older brother had been drinking a lot the night before, maybe the effect of the meeting with Teddy.

"Tough night?" TH asked.

"Let's just get this over with."

They drove in silence to police headquarters which was located across the street from the Milton City Hall. As they pulled into the Police Department parking lot, they could see Mayor Wilson Garrett entering the building.

TH thought how silly he looked in his ill-fitting suit and bow tie.

They walked into the lobby of the building and asked for Marks. They waited a few moments, and a uniformed officer came and got them and led them to a conference room that overlooked the parking lot. All of the blinds on the windows had been drawn. The officer told them to be seated and that Detective Marks would be in shortly.

"This seems kind of formal," TH said.

Richie suddenly was more alert. "This seems like an investigation of some sort. They want to show us something important."

"Related to the Fatty Fuller murder?"

"I doubt that. This has the feel of something current and important right now."

They both sat back in the chairs they were in and waited quietly.

They waited about ten minutes. The only break in the wait came when an assistant brought in a pitcher of water and several glasses. She said nothing but poured each of them a glass of the water.

When Marks finally entered the room, he looked both frazzled and exhausted. He wasn't wearing a suit jacket, and his tie was undone, and his shirt was rumpled. In his hand, he carried a letter sized, manila envelope. Behind him came the tall, lean figure of Lou Katz. Like Marks, he looked stressed, but his shirt looked newly pressed, the tie still perfectly knotted.

"Wow, all the top brass in the place," TH said.

"What's going on here?" Richie snapped. "This is giving me the impression that you think we're involved in something gone wrong."

Marks looked over at Lou. "Show them the pictures," Lou said.

Marks began to undo the clasp on the envelope. TH could see that his hand was shaking. He wouldn't look at TH.

"You okay, Stevie?" TH asked.

Marks didn't answer. Instead, he removed six photos from the envelope and placed them on the table. The shots were all in color and were of a woman. They were all headshots, but weren't very good. The reason for this was the woman's face had been beaten so badly it was hard to recognize who she was.

"Anybody you know?" Marks asked.

Richie, who was used to seeing crime scene photos, shook his head. TH was taken aback by the photos. "Should we know this person?" he asked.

"You should. You saw her the other day. It's Marilyn Aft."

"Marilyn Aft? Who did this to her?"

Now Marks looked directly at TH. "That's what we are trying to figure out."

"You don't think we had anything to do with this, do you, Steve?" Richie asked.

"According to a neighbor, the last car that was seen at Marilyn's house fit the description of the rental that TH is driving. The neighbor saw two men get out of the car; those men fit your description."

"This is bullshit," Richie said. "We told you that we went there and talked to her. Our car was in the drive. We talked to her, and we left. She was one hundred percent alive when we left her."

"Calm down a minute," Lou Katz said. "We don't think that you guys had anything to do with the murder, that is, physically."

"What the hell does that mean?" Richie said.

"It's this Fatty Fuller thing," Marks said. "Suddenly you guys start poking around, and Marilyn Aft ends up dead. This is the same Marilyn Aft that told you guys that Skitch Grayson was innocent and that her husband, and this department, may have helped to frame him."

"You told Lou?" TH asked Marks.

"I had to as soon as we got word of this murder. It's one thing to be asking some questions. It's quite another thing when one of the people who gets asked the questions ends up with their face beaten in."

"No clues?" Richie asked.

"None really. There were no signs of any forced entry, so it looks like Marilyn knew the killer. She was murdered right in her living room. It appears she was hit in the head several times with a very heavy, blunt weapon. A crowbar is the first guess. Other than her body, blood and brain fragments there is no evidence that anything happened at the house."

TH felt the anger rising in him. "Where was Aft when this supposedly happened? He's one of the only ones that she could get in trouble with what she said."

"Logan was in Milton the last two days; he never left the town," Lou said.

"And Jack and Ben Smith?"

"Wait a God damn minute, TH," Lou said. "You're out of line. These men that you mentioned were all police officers under your father. Suggesting that they had something to do with this crime is ridiculous."

"Anything missing at the house?" Richie asked suddenly.

"No evidence of any theft of anything," Marks said.

"Then somebody went to that house with the sole intent of killing Marilyn Aft. Who would have any motive to kill her other than some of the people in this department who she fingered as framing Skitch Grayson?"

"That's crazy," Lou said. "There was no framing of Skitch Grayson. The department got a tip from Gus Morgan that Skitch had some fishing gear he wanted to unload. Aft checked, and it was Fatty's tackle. That tied him directly to the murder. He was arrested, tried and convicted. It's all in the record. Any talk of there being a frame-up is absurd."

"We were just asking around based on some rumors that we heard," TH said.

Richie sighed heavily, his face red from anger. "If there was no frame up then why would somebody visit Marilyn right after we were out there and bash her head in? Don't you think that's quite the coincidence, Lou?"

"That I'll agree with you on," Lou said.

Just then the door to the conference room was opened and Logan Aft, followed by Jack Davis, entered the room. Aft looked wild-eyed and his hair was standing up on end, signs of being just awoken.

"Logan, I told Marshall to keep you in my office until I was done with the Brown boys," Lou said.

"Fuck that," Aft said. "I want to be right here and look at these two scum bags who struck down an innocent woman in her own home."

"You might want to shut him up, Lou," Richie said.

"That's enough Logan," Lou said.

Aft turned towards Lou. "Shut the fuck up yourself, Chief," he blurted. "These two son of a bitches went out there and harassed Marilyn about something, and now she's dead. I know they went out there looking for dirt on me, trying to discredit my record."

"You're crazy," Richie said.

Logan Aft lunged at Richie and threw a big right hand that caught Richie on the left side of his face, sending him sprawling to the floor. Before Aft could do anything further, Steve Marks had him in a headlock, totally binding his movement. This caused Jack Davis to draw his forty-five and point it right at TH's chest.

"Wait a fucking minute," Lou yelled. "Jack, holster your weapon."

"I heard these two might be armed," Jack said.

"They're not armed," Marks said. "Put the gun away."

Richie was slow to get up, rubbing his chin; TH stood still, his heart hammering as he looked at the hole at the end of Jack's gun barrel.

"These two motherfuckers had something to do with my Marilyn getting murdered," Aft yelled as Jack holstered his gun. "I want them arrested."

"We have no reason to believe that TH and Richie had anything to do with Marilyn's death. We have no cause to arrest them. They were seen out at her place and have admitted that they just talked to her. She was alive when they left," Lou said.

"You've got to at least get some DNA, Lou," Aft moaned.

"They are not suspects," Lou said. "Now, I'm going to have Steve let you go Logan. I want you and Jack to go down to my office and wait for me. If you can't do that, I will have to have you escorted from the building. Do you understand?"

Aft got a calm look of understanding on his face. "I do," he said. He looked at TH and Richie. "This ain't over by a long shot."

Marks let him out of the headlock, and he plunged out of the conference room with Jack Davis on his heels.

"Sorry about that, Richie," Lou said.

"I should press charges, but I won't."

Lou nodded. "We're pretty much done here. You guys are good to go, but if you can both stay around town a couple of days until the dust settles on this thing, I would appreciate it."

Back in TH's car, he cracked a window and lit a cigarette. "You need some ice on that."

"That and a whiskey. There's both back at Rachel's."

"Guess you can't leave town for a bit."

"Somebody went out and killed Marilyn Aft right after we talked with her about Fatty Fuller. Why the hell would I leave town now?"

"So who gets your vote?"

"The killer? Aft for sure."

"With help from Jack and Ben?"

"No. This he did solo, but somebody tipped him off that we were out there talking to Marilyn."

"One of the neighbors?"

"Had to be. How would he know that we'd been there without someone telling him?"

"And why would he return to see Marilyn and kill her?"

"That's easy TH. By talking to her we were getting close to striking a nerve. Aft knows a lot about the Fatty Fuller case and whatever he thought Marilyn knew about it has been silenced."

•   •   •

Steve Marks returned to his office and closed the door after the questioning of the Brown brothers and the incident with Logan Aft. He was shaking. He knew that TH and Richie had nothing to do with the murder, but the neighbor had identified their car and described the two of them. They had to be brought in for questioning. What he was more upset about was Logan Aft barging into the conference room and then swinging on Richie Brown. The Three Amigos having anything to do with the justice system of Milton was wrong. He didn't care what deal Teddy Brown had cut with Mayor Wilson Garrett. The Amigos reign needed to be over and soon.

As he was brooding, sitting in his chair with his feet up on the desk, something that Marilyn Aft had said to the Browns was rattling around in his head. She told had told the brothers to look into the history of murder in the town of Milton. Like Lou Katz, Marks had been on the force eleven years, since his college days at Marquette University. Since that time there had been no murders in the town of Milton. Technically, Marilyn Aft had been killed in the nearby town of Cook, so the record was intact. What murder history was Marilyn talking about? The only other murder that Marks was aware of was the Fatty Fuller case, and that had been fifteen years earlier when he was still in high school. He got up from his desk and started downstairs to the records department.

The records department was located in the basement of the building. It was getting close to lunch and Marks was hoping the manager, a bookish, nosey, middle-aged man would not be around. Marks was looking for Tammy Glaser a cute, chubby redhead who flirted with Marks whenever he was down there. As luck would have it, the manager was out, and Tammy was sitting in her cubicle, eating a yogurt and staring at an open program on her computer.

"Don't hurt your eyes looking so hard at that screen," he said.

Tammy Glaser looked up and smiled. "Hello, Detective Marks. Did you just wander down to records to give me tips about my eye care?"

She really was cute, and if Marks wasn't with Tori, he'd have to think about it. "Actually I'm interested in something historical about our fine town."

She scooped the last bit of yogurt out of the container and into her mouth. "Crime history."

"We don't have crime in Milton, but something like that."

She laughed. "What exact historical fact are you looking for?"

"Well, I know there's not much, but I want to know about the history of murders in the town. Of particular interest are those cases within the past forty years so 1977 and on."

"This have anything to do with Marilyn Aft?"

"If I told you, I'd have to kill you, but maybe."

"That's too easy. There have been only two murders in Milton in the last fifty years. I know this because we had to give the town PR department something about crime for their summer flyers, you know, the ones that say great middle-American town with low crime?"

"No crime but a casino, strip clubs, and poker rooms."

"That's the one."

"So two in fifty years?"

"Yep. The Fatty Fuller murder back in 2002 and the Arthur Kimbro case back in 1977."

"What happened with Arthur Kimbro?"

She shrugged. "Just some black guy who decided to go to the casino with his white girlfriend. Some redneck farmer from Iowa, name of Herb Varner. Didn't like what he was seeing and shot poor Arthur dead in the middle of Brewster Lane. A bunch of people saw the shooting, and soon Mr. Varner was trying to head back over the river and into Iowa. Three of our finest, including Chief Brown, gave chase. They did manage to find Varner's car off the road and in a ditch about a half mile from the Route 20 Bridge but never found Varner. Neither did the Illinois or the Iowa State Police. The guy vanished. Technically, even though everybody knows who killed poor Arthur, the case remains open."

Marks ran his hand back through his hair. He felt a bit of a headache coming on. "You said Teddy was out there. Who were the other Milton cops?"

"You're not stumping me, Detective Marks. That would be Jack Davis and Ben Smith. Teddy was in one car; the two of them drove together in another vehicle."

"You're sure about this."

"Like I said, I had to do the research, and their names were there."

"Huh," Marks said. "Thanks for in the info, Tammy."

"Your welcome, Detective Marks, but I wouldn't mind a cocktail if you ever wanted to buy me one."

He smiled. "I'm almost a married man," he said.

"But not yet."

●   ●   ●

Marks went back to his office and reached into his desk for his small bottle of ibuprofen and the pint of Dewars he kept there. He popped two of the pills into his mouth and washed them down with the scotch. This might make his headache a little better, but didn't help him solve anything. The Brown boys had gone to see Marilyn Aft, asking questions about the Fatty Fuller murder case. Within that discussion, she had told them to look at the history of murder in Milton. In fifty years, according to Tammy Glaser, there had been two murders. They had discussed the Fatty Fuller murder, so Marilyn had to be talking about this Arthur Kimbro case. What could be wrong with that? This guy Herb Varner had shot Kimbro and fled, never to be found. What did this have to do with the Fatty Fuller case? How, if anything, was Mayor Wilson Garrett involved? That was well before his time in office.

Marks felt his temples tighten. He took one more gulp of the Dewars and hoped the ibuprofen kicked in. He was more confused than ever. He returned his attention to his notes from the meeting with the Browns and the report he owed the PD from Cook regarding Marilyn Aft.

•   •   •

It was after lunch by the time that TH arrived at Milton High School. He was hoping that he could get a chance to meet with Margaret Hatch, Melissa's friend, to discuss what she meant by her comments at Melissa's wake. Margaret had virtually attacked Richie, Rachel, and TH at the wake insisting that Melissa's suicide was to be blamed on all of them. TH wanted to know what she meant by that.

TH hadn't been in the old building since his graduation fifteen years before. He was told that Margaret had a class and then a free period. He was allowed to wander the halls until her class let out. TH went down near the gym and looked at all of the old trophies on display in the glass case. Prominently shown was the runner-up baseball trophy from the Class A state championship.TH smiled as he looked upon it. He was deep into memories of that season when the bell that sounded the end of classes went off. He quickly made his way to the teacher's lounge where he asked to see Margaret Hatch.

TH took a seat in a small conference room as he waited for Margaret. She had been quite upset with the family at the wake. He hoped she would be a little more subdued today, but a thought crossed his mind that she might not even want to meet with him. This was dispelled when the door opened, and Margaret Hatch entered. Again, as she had looked at the wake, she was a bit frumpy, dressed in a plain black dress with a white necklace. Her hair looked mussed, and she had on a little too much make-up. She didn't smile as she took a seat at the table across from TH.

"Thanks for seeing me, Margaret," TH said.

"I don't have a lot of time since I need to get ready for my next class. I'm only doing this for Melissa. I don't think she'd want me to be rude to you."

"I appreciate that. I hope it doesn't take that long."

"What can I do for you, TH?"

TH cleared his throat. "I don't want to sound accusatory, but at the wake, you said to us that a lot of the blame for Melissa's suicide rested with our family. I was wondering what you meant by that."

She shifted on her seat, clearly nervous. Thru the make-up on her face, TH could see dark circles under her eyes. "In the weeks before Melissa died, she complained to me about the meanness that your father showed to her when she visited him at that nursing home. She said that his attacks had turned particularly vicious during her past few visits. She told me that what your father said to her was making her ill when she thought about it."

Now it was TH who shifted on his chair. "What was he saying to her?"

"That's just it. She would never tell me exactly what was said. She only told me during her most recent visits that your father had attacked her and made her feel pretty useless. I got the feeling that he degraded her pretty badly."

TH knew that his father's words could be vicious, but what would he have said to Melissa who was a regular visitor? Why would he have been so mean to her? "My father can get way out of line with his comments, so I'm sure there were some mean things said. Did this attack happen during one particular visit?"

Margaret shook her head violently. "She told me that she went to see your father on several occasions to get him to take back what he said and maybe get him to apologize, but the last I heard was that these efforts proved to be a waste of time. She even said that he reiterated what he said and got viler with his descriptions."

"But no content was disclosed?"

"None, ever. Whatever your father said was kept a secret, but I could tell it was tearing at her."

"Did you ever think to mention this to Bob Booker?"

"TH, Melissa and I were friends. She told me these things in confidence. I didn't feel right going to her husband about it. I also didn't think that she'd go as far as she did. Maybe had I realized how bad it was I would have gone to someone about it. I felt it would be better to keep the whole thing under wraps."

TH nodded. "Now, to the second part. Why were you so upset with us?"

Margaret crossed her arms over her chest and gave TH a defiant look. "Melissa told me you all knew how your father could get. She said you were all treated in the same fashion. You all got the same treatment. She couldn't believe that your father wasn't talking to Rachel the same way that he talked to her. Rachel had been the one in the most trouble. How had she escaped his wrath? It bothered her that this behavior had gone on so long and no one talked about it. No one was able to get your father to stop."

"Stop what? The nasty comments that he made to people when they came and visited him?"

"That's what I got out of it."

TH knew that Rachel had said their father could be vicious when she went and saw him, especially since the stroke. Richie and TH had seen him so little that his comments hurt, but had no long-lasting effect.

"You know, there was something else, TH," Margaret Hatch said. "Your father and his police force ruled this town with an iron fist for over forty years. You still get the feeling that he is in charge. I think Melissa was very worried that if she made too big a deal about what your father was saying to her something bad would happen to her and her family, maybe to Bob Booker. Maybe she felt like ending her life was just an easier way of dealing with things."

•   •   •

Steve Marks was surprised to see the Booker Real Estate sign on Ben Smith's lawn. More surprising was the smaller *Contract Pending* sign hanging from the first sign. Steve didn't know that Ben and his wife Anne were selling their house; he also didn't know if they were downsizing or planning on leaving Milton. Marks made the assumption that there really was a lot about Milton that he didn't know.

Ben Smith answered the door after one ring of the bell. He had once played linebacker for Iowa and still maintained an athletic build, other than the spare tire he had wrapped around his belly. He was over six feet tall, wide at the shoulders, and had a thick neck. His hair, a chestnut brown, was streaked with gray.

"Didn't expect to see you out here, Steve," Ben said.

"I hadn't planned it. Something came up, and I wanted to ask you about it."

"Well, don't stand out here in the cold. Come on in."

Ben led Marks to an office that was located just off of the kitchen. Ben pointed to an old chair in front of a bookcase and Steve sat down. "Can I offer you a beer or anything else to drink?" Ben asked.

"No. I'm good. I don't want to take up a bunch of your time."

Ben laughed. "Retirement gives you too much time. Sometimes it's hard to fill the day."

"Speaking of retirement, I noticed the sale sign on your lawn."

Ben shrugged. "It was time, you know. I'm too old to be a real cop, and this deputy thing is kind of a farce. We're going to close in mid-November and then off to Arizona. Getting ready to give Lou my papers."

"You don't say. I thought you two were Milton lifers."

"Milton is a nice town, and it's been good to Anne and me, but it's time to move on," he said. "What was it that you wanted to talk to me about?"

"I had the Brown brothers in today to talk to them about somebody seeing them up by Marilyn Aft's house before she was murdered."

Ben waved a hand at Marks. "That's a terrible thing that happened to Marilyn, but the Brown brothers didn't have anything to do with that."

Marks thought Ben answered a little too quickly. "Why would you say that? Do you know something?"

"I don't mean it that way, Steve. I know TH and Richie. These are good guys. They wouldn't have anything to do with something like that."

"But no ideas?"

"Not really. It did cross my mind that Logan Aft has pissed off a number of people over the course of his career. It could be somebody seeking revenge on Logan."

"But not Logan himself?"

Ben's face scrunched up. "No way! Logan may be an insufferable asshole, but he is not a murderer."

"I don't think so, either."

"What were the Browns doing out there anyway?"

"According to them, they were poking around, asking questions about the Fatty Fuller murder case."

Ben laughed. "What the hell would they be asking questions about that for? That case was what, 2002 or so. Skitch Grayson was caught and sent to prison."

"That's just it, Ben. With Skitch Grayson getting cancer and then getting released his name is back in the news. There's a lot of talk about him not being the actual killer."

"That's bullshit, too," Ben raised his voice. "He was the only one with any motive, evidence was found on his property, and he had no alibi. Nothing points to anyone else being the killer."

"That's pretty much what the case file says."

"It wouldn't say anything different because that's what happened," Ben said, his face getting redder. "You didn't come out here to ask me about that, did you?"

"Not the Fuller case, but Marilyn had some interesting comments about that."

"Sure she would. She hated Logan, and she was crazy. I'm sure in her mind she had concocted a number of theories about everything that he ever did."

Marks caught himself looking at two photos of a younger Ben Smith that were side by side on the bookshelf. One showed a much younger Smith in Iowa football uniform; the other was a picture of Anne and Ben on their wedding day. Ben was smiling broadly in both. Now he was not smiling. "We all know Marilyn was a character, but she did say some interesting things. In particular, she told the Browns that they should do some research on the history of murder in our little town."

"Murder in Milton?" Ben laughed again. "What's there been, five?"

"More like two in the last fifty years. In 2002 we had the Fatty Fuller murder. In 1977, there was a murder of a black man, Arthur Kimbro. An Iowa farmer named Herb Varner shot him dead in the middle of Brewster Way and then tried to high tail it out of town."

"That one I do remember," Ben said. "We heard that Kimbro had been shot and that the shooter was seen heading for Route 20 and the bridge over the river. We put out an APB and headed in that direction."

"Who's we?"

Ben scratched his chin. "It was Jack Davis and me in one car and Chief Brown in the other."

"No Aft?"

"I don't know where Logan was. Anyway, we followed the road along the river until just before the bridge turnoff. We saw a car, which later we found out was Varner's. The car must have hit something because it had a flat and had skidded off the road. It was in some high grass about twenty feet from some thick brush. The driver door was wide open, but there was no sign of Varner. He must have taken off on foot through the brush. We tracked him a bit, but there was no sign of him. "

"And Herb Varner was never found?"

"Not a trace. We were looking, the Illinois State Police were looking and so were the Iowa State Police. The guy vanished."

"End of the case?"

"Not really. The case remains unsolved, but that was over forty years ago.

My thoughts are that Herb Varner is dead."

"What kind of guy was Varner?"

"What kind of guy?"

"Yeah. What was he like? You guys must have looked into him."

Ben rubbed his chin. "From what I remember he owned a soybean farm about twenty miles west of Dubuque. Had a wife and three kids, if I recall. Seemed normal to me other than he shot this black kid, Kimbro, because he was with a white girl."

"There's no doubting that Herb Varner shot Kimbro. A couple of people saw it, but the guy just disappears, leaves his wife and kids, his farm and everything else behind? No one ever heard from him? He never needed any money or anything like that?"

"I'm not sure what you're getting after, Steve, but that's the story. The guy killed Kimbro and took off. He might have been looking at a death sentence, or at least life, if caught. Maybe he figured that was the best option."

The way Ben told the story it was hard to not believe his reasoning. "What about Wilson Garrett?"

"Jesus, Steve. You're all over the board. What the hell do you want to know about Wilson Garrett?"

"I was interested in what happened out at Ma Brooks' place."

Ben laughed. "A lot of men got laid out at Ma Brooks' place."

"I understand that. I was curious about what happened with Wilson Garett out at Ma Brooks' place."

The serious look returned to Ben's face. "You're starting to make my tummy hurt a little, Steve. You've asked a lot of questions about a bunch of things, but I really don't know what you are after."

What was he after? "It just kind of started with the Melissa Brown suicide. That caused the first big question. Then the talk of Skitch Grayson and the Fatty Fuller murder, which got Marilyn Aft talking about the history of murder in Milton, which got us talking about Herb Varner murdering Arthur Kimbro and then disappearing. Somewhere in all of that talk came the story of Wilson Garrett once having a wild streak and getting rough with the ladies out at Ma Brook's, so rough that he had to pay Ma to keep everything quiet."

Ben's mouth was hanging open; his eyes were staring at Marks. "You're not thinking that all of that stuff is connected, are you? If you are, you might want to talk with Lou about getting some time off."

Marks ran his hand back through his thick hair. "I don't know that any of them are connected, but they all seem a little confusing, none of them seem to make sense."

Ben threw his hands up in the air. "Jesus H. Christ, Steve. If the old man heard you talk this way he'd have you busted down to a patrol cop. What's all the mystery? Skitch Grayson killed Fatty and was tried and convicted. Herb Varner, no mystery here, gunned down Arthur Kimbro and disappeared. Sure the disappearance might be a bit strange, but the guy hasn't turned up anywhere. Lastly, yes, Wilson Garrett used to become a bigger, meaner man when he drank. He did get a little rough with a couple of the ladies out at Ma Brooks' place, and he paid her for the inconvenience. That was years ago. All of this was years ago. All of it has been settled, so I'm not really sure why you are out here asking me about it or what you are aiming to do with anything you might find, which is going to be not much."

Marks knew he'd reached the saturation point with Ben. He knew no more answers were coming his way. He also knew that Ben hadn't told him that much and was getting upset. Something wasn't adding up. "I didn't mean to get you all riled up, Ben. All of this stuff happened before I got on the force, and with Marilyn Aft, it just got my brain going."

Ben was smiling now. "The biggest cases always produce the biggest questions. That can cause the mind to wander. My recommendation is that you stick to some of the current problems that face the force today. Not anything you can do about all of those old cases, anyway."

Marks nodded. "That's probably the best advice that anyone has given me in a long while."

Ben was nodding his head, and his smile had grown.

Unchained Secrets

The day had been hot and humid. Even when the sun went down and darkness took over the heat and humidity were in the air. The air conditioner in the house wasn't doing the trick. TH's room felt like a sauna. He hadn't had the best of days, and now the hot conditions were making it tough to sleep.

When the day started, TH hadn't minded the heat. He loved to play baseball in the warm weather. He loved the high school doubleheaders. It was the summer before his sophomore year, and school would be starting soon. The baseball season was about to end.

What TH hadn't expected, and it was a first for him, was that he would go hitless in the two games that day and that he would strike out five times. His team lost both games, and he blamed himself for the losses. He was only fourteen at the time and immature. Losses and his bad performance would stick with him for days. This day was no different.

When he got home in the late afternoon, he showered and spent a good part of the evening staring at the TV, but not really seeing what was on. He spoke little to his family. They knew it was best to just leave him alone on a day like this. Nothing would make him feel any better. He went into his room at nine o'clock, turned off the lights, and tried to go to sleep. Maybe sleep would help him forget the awful day.

Because of the warmth in his room, he slept only in a pair of boxer shorts. He never got under the sheets. For a while, he thought he would never get to sleep, but eventually, he drifted off. He slept solidly for a couple of hours until the sound of his bedroom door being opened awakened him. The door had a chronic squeak that acted up as soon as you opened it, regardless of how quiet you were trying to be.

TH heard the squeak and looked toward the door. Someone had entered and closed the door behind them. TH's stomach jumped a bit, but then the figure was sitting on the edge of his bed.

"You doing okay, TH?" he heard his father ask.

TH rubbed his eyes and propped himself up on one elbow. "I'm fine, dad," he said.

"I wanted to check on you and make sure you were doing okay because of how upset you were tonight."

"What time is it?"

"It's a little past two."

Two o'clock in the morning seemed like an odd time for a parent to be checking on you in your room.

"I'm really doing okay, dad. You didn't have to get out of bed and come in here and check on me. Today was just a bad day. I'll get over it soon enough."

There was no response for several moments. He could hear his father's breathing. It was labored. For the first time, TH felt tense. Something wasn't right.

"I want you to know that I am here for you," his father said. "Whatever it is you want, you let me know, and I will take care of it. Do you understand that?"

TH swallowed hard. "Yes, sir."

"We are a family, a team. The most important team. We'll do whatever we need to do to take care of each other."

TH wasn't sure what to say. "I understand."

Again there was the strange silence and the heavier breathing. His father placed his hand on the top of TH's foot, just below the ankle. TH tensed at the touch.

"It's going to be okay," his father said.

"What is, dad?"

His father's hand started to slide up his leg, slowly caressing the lower leg, the knee and then his lower thigh. The hand was warm, almost too warm to believe it was just a hand.

"Try and relax, son."

The hand came up higher on the thigh, massaging the deep muscles. It began to reach for the groin area.

TH quickly swung his left hand from the other side and grabbed his father's hand, pushing it away as his body slid farther from his dad. "What's going on here, dad," TH said sharply, loudly.

His father got up from the edge of the bed. "I just wanted to make sure that you were doing okay. I was worried about you."

TH was breathing fast and was sweating more than he had been. "I'm okay. I just want to get back to sleep. I just want to be left alone."

"That's fine, son. I'll leave you be. I was just concerned." TH heard his father back away from the bed, open the squeaky door, and leave his room.

TH let out a deep breath and got out of bed and locked his door. He crawled back into the bed and was soon shivering. He pulled the sheets and covers over him, but it took the longest time to stop shaking. He didn't think it was from being cold. Finally, he stopped and then he began to cry. He couldn't understand what was happening. The whole sequence didn't make any sense. It probably never would. The only thing he knew was that he would never speak of this night to anyone. That and he would never go to bed at night without locking his bedroom door.

•   •   •

Valerie Plume agreed to meet with Marks at a local Freeport coffee shop. She hadn't been hard to find. She was listed in a Freeport phone book, and the listing showed her home address as well. In her day she might have been a beauty, but age had taken its toll on Valerie. Marks pegged her to be about sixty, but she might have been younger. It was hard to tell through her lined face and nicotine-stained teeth. The hair on her head was a reddish brown, dyed. Her fingernails were chipped and maybe bitten. She looked old and tired.

It took Marks over an hour to get to Freeport. Then he waited in the coffee shop for Valerie to show up. He had no idea who he was looking for. He had no picture or description of her. He'd been there about twenty minutes when Valerie walked up to the booth he was sitting in.

"Detective Marks?" she said.

He smiled. "How'd you know who I was?"

"You're the one person in here who looks like a cop."

She sat down across from Marks and ordered a black coffee. The waitress came and filled her cup and gave Marks a refill. Valerie sipped the hot coffee and then emptied a creamer into it.

"Gus told me that you seemed like an alright guy," she said.

"You called Gus?"

"Right after you and I spoke. It's not like cops from Milton come to visit me every day. A woman in my past profession doesn't have the best of memories of the police."

"Get busted much?"

She laughed. "More like hassled. Especially when I was at Ma's. They'd take you into the station, threaten you with a bunch of bullshit and then let us go. Ma had the whole thing greased. I think they just took us in there to make the public think they were doing something. Eventually, the outcry got too loud, and they had to actually do something. That's when the house closed down."

"How long were you out there?"

"About ten years. Ma was real good to all of us. I liked it. I liked the area. I had some friends, like Gus Morgan."

Marks sensed that maybe there was more to their friendship than her stopping at the Lighthouse for a drink. "It's not a horrible place to live," he said.

"There are a lot worse," she said, taking a sip of the still steaming coffee. "I'm sure you didn't drive all the way here to go over my career at Ma's."

"Not all of it, but maybe just a small piece."

She placed the coffee cup back on the table and raised her right hand to her mouth. She nibbled at her finger, but then stopped. "What piece would that be?"

Marks instinctively looked around the room. There was no one in the place that he knew. "I'm interested in a former client of Ma's. I'd like to know what you know about Wilson Garrett."

Valerie Plume closed her eyes for a moment, and when she opened them, she looked sadder. She took another sip of her coffee and looked towards the door. Marks thought she might be contemplating leaving. "Wilson Garrett, before he got into politics and found himself that plump, little wife, was a pig, an animal."

She was staring hard at Marks; there was an intensity in her eyes. "I've heard that he used to get rough with the girls when he was drunk. I heard that he beat some of them up."

"That's all true," she said. "It would only happen if he drank. If he came in sober, he was an absolute gentlemen. If he was drunk, that was when the trouble began."

"Any specifics?"

She shrugged. "He slapped Jenny Collins a few times. Gave her a nice black eye. He also bit and scratched Linda. Nasty scratches on her back. Some were bleeding."

"But Ma let him back in?"

"It was a business, Detective Marks. He would act up and then come in and pay Ma some money, pay the girl he attacked some money and then be on good behavior for a while. Ma let it go on. She figured if she cut him off he might get his father to voice a complaint and have the whole place shut down. It was easier just to deal with his bullshit once in a while."

"Was he ever a client of yours?"

She smiled. "Client, that's a funny word, but yes he was. I got him on a good night. He was a perfect gentlemen."

"Ma never had to call the cops on him; things never got that bad?"

"Just once, but it wasn't his fault."

"Ma called the cops on Wilson when it wasn't his fault?"

"He was with this girl Corinne one night. She'd only been there about a month. It wasn't until she was hired that Ma found out she had a drug problem. She told Corinne to cut it out, or she was gone. Anyway, Wilson paid to have a girl overnight. Nothing physically bad happened, but when Wilson woke up, Corinne was dead. She OD'd during the night. He got Ma, and they called the cops. A pretty stout group showed up. Chief Brown, Ben Smith, and that asshole Aft were out there. They got the body out of there without anyone really knowing anything about it. It saved Ma and Wilson a lot of problems. It was like she was there one minute and gone the next."

"Nobody went to the wake and funeral?"

She laughed. "Corinne was a drug addict, but she was also a mean spirited bitch. Some of the girls, not all, were happy she died. We heard her body was sent back home to Ohio where her parents were for the burial."

"How was Ma about this?"

"She was upset, but I sensed it was more of a business thing. She didn't want girls dying in the house. She also didn't want any of it leaked outside of the house. If she found out that you were spreading stories about it, you would be gone."

"And things went back to normal for Wilson Garrett?"

"Oh, no. As far as I know, that was the last time that Wilson stepped foot inside of Ma's. I think the whole thing, the OD and the cops scared the hell out of him."

A dead girl and a body shipped out to Ohio, and nobody talked about it, Marks thought. "You know this girl Corrine's last name."

"Riley, Corrine Riley. A lot of girls change their name or maybe use like a stage name, but not Corinne. She used her real name. She liked the Irish sound of it."

Marks nodded and looked out the window where the sun was starting to peak through thick, late October clouds.

•   •

In the later afternoon, Marks found himself back at the cubicle of Tammy Glaser. She was talking on the phone and smiled at him as he stood near her. She brushed her hair away from her eyes with her free hand and then made the "one-second" signal. He nodded and waited patiently. Finally, she hung up the phone.

"Twice in one week, Detective Marks. People might get the wrong idea and start talking."

"Let them talk. We could use a little rumor around this quiet place."

"That's the truth, but I doubt you came down here again to start rumors flying."

"I'm looking for something, anything that you might happen to have, on a woman named Corrine Riley. She was a prostitute that used to work out at Ma Brooks."

Tammy scrunched up her face. "You looking for an arrest record?"

"Maybe, but actually I'm looking for something that she indicates how she died and what happened to the body. This is probably going to be at least twenty-five years or older," he said, referring to the time before Wilson Garrett was in office.

"You do bring a little excitement to the job." Tammy's fingers glided along the keyboard and Marks could see her entering some different programs and prodding through different windows. She finally opened one and made a telling sound.

"You find something?" Marks asked.

"This has got be it."

"What have you got?"

"Corrine Riley, age twenty-four, found dead in a ravine along River Trail Road on the morning of April 19th, 1987. The report says that it was suspected that the girl had been doing drugs and had ended up walking along the trail and stumbled into the ravine which was a good forty feet below the surface of the road. It says she suffered severe head injuries that were likely fatal."

"Toxicology?"

"Cocaine at an obscene level. Alcohol, too."

"Who found her?"

"Random 911 call from a pay phone. Hikers the report says, but nothing to indicate who they were."

"That makes sense."

"This makes sense? What are you looking for, Detective Marks?"

She really was a pretty girl. Maybe a little plump, but cute. If not for Tori? "I'm not sure. Does that report tell you anything else about her?"

"It was discovered that she was from Akron, Ohio. Parents were Patrick and Sharon Riley. The body was shipped there as soon as they were located."

"Nothing more?"

"Notes from calls that Ben Smith made to the parents, nothing crazy there and also notes from a call Ben made to Ma Brooks. Apparently, someone knew that Corrine had been working out there."

"What do those notes say?"

"It says, 'Ma Brooks said Corrine Riley had been in her employ but disappeared the night before the discovery of her body. Corrine had a history of being unreliable and of using drugs. She had been warned by Ma Brooks that her job was in jeopardy if she continued the erratic behavior.'"

"God damn," Marks said. "God damn!"

"You're freaking me out a little," Tammy said, looking around the little area. "What is going on here?"

"Quiet down a little, and I'll buy you that cocktail. I can't explain it down here."

"I have a right to know," she said, her voice cracked a little.

"You do, and I will tell you. One more thing before I go. What do you show for arrest records for Wilson Garrett?"

"Mayor Wilson Garrett? Mr. Goodie Two Shoes?"

"That's the one."

She went into another program and entered the mayor's name on a search line and hit enter. The computer made a light sound as it wound through its memory. Finally, it stopped. "Not one thing."

"Fuck me," Marks said. He turned and started for the stairs.

"Detective Marks," Tammy called out. "You just can't leave."

He turned to face her. "I have to go. We'll have that drink. I promise. Keep all of this to yourself, Tammy."

Marks ran up the stairs, leaving Tammy looking around the deserted Records area. She liked Marks and wanted to go for a drink with him, but his recent requests and behavior were scaring the hell out of her.

•   •   •

Marks had just made it up the stairs and was turning towards his office when he looked out of the window that showed a clear view of the receiving area where new arrestees were processed. An unmarked car was idling there, and he saw Logan Aft get out of the front seat and open the rear doors. The first person to get out of the back was Jack Davis. The second person to follow, hands cuffed behind him, and looking quite drunk, was Joseph Running Bear. Not only was he clearly drunk, but it looked like Joseph had been in a fight with a real bear.

Marks ran out of the side door just as they were about to lead Joseph into the holding area for the jail. "What the hell is going on here, Logan?" Marks yelled.

Logan Aft turned to look at Marks. "What's it look like to you, Steve?"

"Why do you have Joseph in cuffs?"

Aft walked towards Marks, leaving Joseph and Jack Davis by the jail entrance. "We got a call from the bartender down at Lifers. He said that Chief Joseph was in there drinking a lot of whiskey and talking up a storm. Said the Chief was ranting on about somebody killing all of his animals. Said that my name came up. Said the Chief kept saying that I would get mine soon enough."

"So you arrested him for what, drunk and disorderly?"

"That and suspicion."

"Suspicion of what?"

"Murder!"

Marks laughed. "Who do you think Joseph murdered?"

"The way he was talking I have to think he had a hand in murdering Marilyn. If he was thinking that I was behind all of his animals being killed and that he was looking for revenge, then why wouldn't he start with Marilyn?"

"That's crazy, Logan?"

"We'll see."

Marks brushed past Aft to take a look at Joseph. The big Indian's shirt was torn in multiple spots, there was blood on his left elbow, one knee, and his face had a number of new looking bruises. "What the hell happened to him, Jack?"

"He's awful drunk, Steve," Jack Davis said. "He could've fell a couple of times."

Joseph had his head down and looked ready to pass out. Marks bent down to talk to him. "Joseph, it's Steve Marks. What the hell happened to you?"

Joseph raised his head and looked into Marks' eyes. "Somebody needs to take care of Aft," he said.

"See what I'm talking about, Steve. He wants me. Why not start with my family?"

"Marilyn wasn't part of your family anymore, Logan and, anyway, Joseph wouldn't go all the way to Cook and murder her."

"Like I said, Steve, we'll see. Right now, we've got him for the D and D charge. We'll have to wait until he's sober enough to ask him about Marilyn."

With that, Jack Davis yanked open the jail door and led Joseph into it. He was followed closely by Logan Aft who wore a big smile.

•　　•　　•

TH had called his sister Rachel earlier in the day, but she was back working a shift at the Walmart and wouldn't be home until four o'clock. He was waiting for her in his rental when she pulled her own car into the driveway. TH didn't know if her kids were around, but he did know that Richie had gone off to see Billy Tasker again. He was glad. He wanted to ask Rachel a couple of questions on his own.

"You're not looking for Richie, are you?" she said as she got out of the car.

"No. he told me that he was going to see Billy Tasker. I just wanted to talk to you."

She stopped and gave him a look. "What's with the real serious tone?"

"Just some stuff I want to talk with you about."

"About what, TH?"

"Can we head inside?"

"Sure. I don't think the boys are around yet."

They went inside and got settled inside of the kitchen. Rachel opened up two Buds for them and lit her own cigarette. TH noticed that her Walmart blazer looked a little tight on her.

"That must have been a hell of a punch that Aft threw at Richie. He's got a nice shiner to show for it," Rachel said.

"It was a cheap shot, but it was loaded. Knocked Richie off his feet."

"That Aft, he's something else."

"He's just a God damn thug. Always has been."

Rachel took a swig of her beer and then a drag off the cigarette. She flicked a large ash into an overflowing ashtray. "So what's with the surprise visit?"

"No surprise," TH said, sipping his own beer. "I went and saw Margaret Hatch."

Rachel pulled out one of the kitchen chairs and sat down. "Why would you go see her? She's just a frustrated old ninny. I never understood why Melissa was so close to her."

"Maybe Melissa felt that Margaret was somebody that she could confide in."

"Confide in about what?"

"Do you remember when we were at the wake, and Margaret attacked us saying that we were responsible for Melissa's death?"

"How could I forget that? But the woman is nuts."

"You think a lot of people are nuts. Anyway, I went and saw her. I asked her what she meant by those comments."

Rachel cocked her head to one side. "I can't wait to hear what she said."

TH slapped his hand on the table. "I'm not fucking around here, Rachel."

"I don't think you are. I just don't trust much of what Margaret Hatch says."

"Hear me out. She said that dad said some pretty mean things to Melissa during some of the visits that she made to see him."

Rachel blew out a huge puff of smoke. "Dad says mean things to everyone, you included."

"Apparently these were real mean."

Rachel shook her head. "Most of the time we went up there together. If dad was mean to anyone, it was me. I never really heard him say anything terrible to Melissa."

"Didn't you say you hadn't been out there together for over a month?"

"It was something like that, a month, five weeks."

"Maybe it happened then."

"What happened? Dad was an asshole to all of us. He called me fat and stupid. I think, because of my great marriage record, that whore came out of his mouth a few times. I guess he could have called her some bad names. She did marry Bob Booker so stupid wouldn't be too nasty."

Now it was TH shaking his head. "No. Margaret said that Melissa told her that dad had made some awful comments to her, stuff that all of us were aware of. Margaret thought we could have stopped this stuff long ago."

Rachel stared at him for a moment and said nothing. She sipped her beer and then lit up a second smoke. TH noticed her hand shook a bit. "Something we could have all stopped. I don't know what the hell that woman is talking about."

"You don't recall anything that Dad could have said or did to Melissa when she lived here that would cause her to go into a great funk?"

"Nothing at all. You lived under that roof, too. Dad was a tough guy, a tough father, but I don't think I ever saw him do anything or say anything to Melissa that he didn't say or do to the rest of us."

TH thought of that awful Christmas Eve night from long ago and the summer night where his father came into his room. "I know what you're saying, Rach. I wasn't immune to Dad's criticism, but according to Margaret this was something that made Melissa both physically and mentally sick."

Rachel exhaled cigarette smoke. "Melissa never mentioned anything to me, and we were pretty tight. I would think that if Dad really got under her skin, she would have said something. I don't think it was Dad. I think Margaret Hatch is a little nutty. I think whatever got to Melissa was a lot deeper than anything that Dad could have said to her, and I am pretty sure we will never know for sure."

TH nodded slowly and looked into the sad face of his sister. She looked more worn out every time that he saw her. What he didn't see was any recognition that what he was saying about his father's treatment of Melissa was accurate. Rachel didn't seem to know anything.

•   •   •

"What the hell is going on here, Lou?" Steve Marks said. He was sitting across from Lou Katz on the second floor of the building. He hadn't wanted to sound angry but wasn't sure he'd pulled that off.

"Relax a minute, Steve, and tell me what you are talking about. Bursting in here and making such a wide-open question is not like you."

"It's those two thugs, Aft and Davis. They've arrested Joseph and are planning on charging him with a D and D along with suspicion of murder."

Lou Katz laughed.

"What the hell is so fucking funny?"

"Dispatch took a call that there was a large Indian down at Lifers causing some sort of commotion. We knew it was Joseph, so I sent Aft and Jack. They know how to deal with him the best."

"They do? After what was going on at the wake? Joseph's clothes were torn, and his face looked like somebody used it as a punching bag. Aft said the bartender was saying Joseph was making all kinds of threats against him, threatening revenge."

The smile left Lou's face. "You're kidding me."

"I'm not kidding."

Lou closed his eyes and rubbed his brow with two fingers. "I'll take care of this, Steve. I wasn't thinking right. I'll look into the D and D charge, but I'll make sure that this thing with the murder goes away."

"I don't care how upset that Joseph is with Aft, he didn't kill Marilyn."

Lou waved a hand at him. "You don't have to tell me that."

Marks hesitated for a moment. "There is something else."

"This isn't enough for one day?"

"I'm afraid not. I think there might be a pattern of cover-up within the department."

"Within this department?"

"Yes. I think there is a possibility of a cover-up regarding a high ranking town official. Don't get too nervous because most of the stuff I've been tracking happened before you and I stepped foot into this place."

Lou exhaled. "What exactly have you been tracking, Steve? Please don't tell me that you are getting all hung up on the Fatty Fuller thing. That's for people like TH Brown and Richie. That's not for the police department."

"Richie Brown is a cop, a homicide detective in Kansas City, but just so we're clear it may have started with Fatty Fuller. I was listening to some old theories about that case when something jarred my brain."

"Too hard, I think."

"Listen, Lou. It goes back to the pension deals for Aft, Davis and Ben Smith. How'd they get those and that title of Deputy for Life?"

"That was all approved by the city council."

"Yes, and who proposed it?"

"My understanding was that it was Wilson Garrett."

"Correct again."

"So what's your point?"

"My point is Teddy Brown got Wilson Garrett to push for those pension plans and job titles because he had something on Wilson."

"Teddy had something on Wilson? Our Wilson Garrett?"

"Now you're following along, but I am talking about something that happened a long time ago before Wilson was in office."

"Something over twenty-five years old?"

"Maybe more."

"So what did Wilson Garrett do over twenty-five years ago that would allow Teddy to blackmail him into those pension deals?"

Marks took a deep breath. "I think Wilson Garrett may have murdered somebody."

The look on Lou Katz's face showed that this comment dumbfounded him.

"You don't believe me, Lou?"

"It's not that I don't believe you, Steve. I mean I believe that you think that you are onto something, but what I think is that you have come off the rails a bit."

Marks shook his head. "Not at all, Lou. Will you listen to what I have found?"

"I'll listen, but bear in mind that I know Wilson Garrett. I know him pretty well. You are going to have to do an awful lot to convince me of this. You might have to do more than you would to try and convince me that Skitch Grayson didn't kill Fatty Fuller."

"I still have my reservations about that one."

"Whoa. Let's stick to Wilson Garrett. Tell me quietly and succinctly what you think you have found."

"I got word that in his earlier days Wilson Garrett used to be a little wild and used to go out to Ma Brooks' place."

"The old brothel?"

"That's the one. Anyway, I tracked down this Valerie Plume that used to work out there. She lives in Freeport now. She verified that Wilson used to go out there and get drunk. Sometimes he would get a little aggressive with the girls. When he would get too rough, he would have to pay sort of a fine to Ma Brooks, or she wouldn't let him back in."

"This Valerie Plume was a prostitute?'"

"Yes. Now retired."

"Now you're taking the word of a prostitute?"

"I am Lou. The woman has nothing to gain."

Lou checked his watch. "Go on."

"Anyway, this happened more than once. It was getting to be a problem. Well, this one night the girl that was with Wilson supposedly overdosed and died. Ben Smith, Aft, and Teddy were called. All the other girls were told to get back to what they were doing. I'm thinking that Teddy and Ben got the body out of the house."

"Why is that?"

"Because a hiker called it in the next day. The body was found in a ravine along River Trail. Toxicology report found drugs in the girl's system; the injuries to her head were from the fall. She was quickly shipped back to her parents in Akron, Ohio."

"And Wilson was with this girl?"

"Until the cops were called in."

"You think she was dead in the room?"

"Yeah. The other girls at the house were told that this girl, Corrine Riley, had OD'd. She was dead there. Next day she's found in a ravine. I think Wilson, willingly or not, killed her. I think Teddy and Ben got rid of the evidence and I think that's why the Three Amigos have such a great pension deal."

"Because Wilson pushed it through for them?"

"Bingo!"

Lou's skin tone didn't look right to Marks. He suddenly looked a little pale. "This is a long time ago."

"No statute of limitations on murder."

"Might not be murder."

"Man, Lou, it's something. You can read all about Corrine Riley's death in our files. Ben Smith filed the report."

"Son of a bitch. Nothing in the report about going out to Ma's?"

"Nothing. The reports starts with an unnamed hiker calling in to say there was a body in a ravine. This could explain a lot of stuff, Lou."

"Yeah, but we've got to be sure. We can't just go around accusing people of this shit. This has mega-scandal all over it."

"I wonder what else is out there."

"You're not back on Skitch Grayson and Fatty Fuller again."

"Everything points to Skitch except why he would kill Fatty. That doesn't wash for me."

Lou rubbed his face with his hands. "This is what they call a fucking mess."

"What are we going to do?"

"We need more to move on anything. Something concrete."

"Any bright ideas?"

"Right now, I'm going to go downstairs and figure out what to do with Joseph. I don't want Aft filing any murder charges.'

"He's not going to be too happy."

"Fuck him."

•　　　　•　　　　•

It was late in the afternoon when TH pulled his car up in front of Booker Realty on Main Street. The Booker's, based mostly on Bob's father's hard work and had risen to the top realtor in the county. Bob had worked there since college, and it was said that he did the business a major service by staying out of the way. Those who knew him well said he lacked the drive and killer instinct to be in sales, but occasionally he did sell a house. When TH got out of his car, he noticed there were only a couple of lights on in the office. He hoped Bob was in. He'd gone by their house, and no one had been home.

TH had never been in the office, but it was as he imagined. There was a receptionist's desk and a few chairs in the front of the office. Right behind that were a number of cubicles for the realtors. There was no one working at either of these places. In the back were two offices. One had the lights on. TH headed in that direction.

Bob Booker appeared to be hard at work in his office. He had his head down and was reviewing a rather thick file. He didn't notice that TH had walked right up to his door. TH knocked.

Bob's head popped up, clearly startled. "Oh, Jesus, TH! You scared the hell out of me."

"I'm sorry, Bob. You must have been pretty deep into that file."

"Ah, the old McCandle's house on Third street. It's a National Landmark, but it needs a ton of work. Between the asking price and the rehab, it's going to be a tough sell."

TH was a little surprised that Booker was in the office, but he'd heard that people advised him to get out of the house. He looked extremely tired. "You have a few minutes?"

Bob closed the file and sat back in his desk chair. "Sure, TH. What's on your mind? I only came in here to review a couple of open files and get my mind off of other things."

Other things, TH thought, like his sister's suicide. "I went and saw Margaret Hatch, one of Melissa's friends at the school."

"I wouldn't say they were great friends, but I know her. I'd call her more of an acquaintance."

"She gave me the impression that they were pretty close, confidants at least, especially around the school."

"That might be. I heard she's a bit of a loose cannon. She's been known to tell a few tall tales, if you know what I mean." Bob smiled.

"That may be, but she came up to Rachel, Richie and me at the wake and said it was our fault that Melissa had died. Said we should have known what was going on a long time ago with our father and helped her out."

Bob wore a blank face. "I certainly don't know what she meant by that."

"I didn't either, so I asked Rachel. She had no idea what Margaret was talking about."

"Like I said, Margaret is a talker."

"Maybe, but if it's possible I'd like you to go back a few weeks, maybe a month before Melissa died. Do you remember anything that she might have said regarding our father? Did Teddy happen to say anything to her when she went to visit him that might have upset her? Anything?"

Bob looked off to his left as if trying to remember something. "Your father was never nice to anyone, so it was not unusual for him to say nasty things. I went with Melissa once to see him, and he wasn't very nice to me. He told me I was the wrong one for his daughter. I just shook it off. He was never nice to me."

"But she didn't mention anything that might have stood out? Or maybe she came home once after seeing Teddy, and she was really down?"

"I'm sorry, TH. Nothing like that stands out. I don't think it was ever pleasant for Melissa, or Rachel for that matter, to visit Teddy. He just hasn't been nice to anyone since his stroke. I also don't remember anyone day where Melissa was really down after a visit. If we ever talked about it, she would say things like, 'you know how it is' or 'it's always the same'. I think we got used to the way he was and how it effected people who went and saw him."

TH believed Bob, but he also thought that maybe he was smart enough to have picked up on a change in Melissa's behavior. He was about to get up and leave when he noticed the large tears that were rolling out of Booker's eyes. Bob reached up to wipe them away with his hands.

"You okay, Bob?"

Booker grabbed a tissue from the top of his desk and wiped at his eyes. "I'm sorry, TH. I'm sorry I don't have more answers for you. I wish I knew why she did this to herself. I wish I knew what to tell the kids.

"I mean what do you tell your kids when they ask why their mother killed herself? Not only that, but we really miss her. She was a great wife and a great mom. You know she kept our ship afloat, TH. You know that. I wake up every day and I look at her side of the bed, and I expect her to be there. It hurts, TH."

TH felt awful coming into Booker's office and asking about what Margaret Hatch had said. He should have asked how Booker and the two boys were doing. "I know, Bob. I miss her a lot, and I wish I could have been here to maybe help out a little."

"You want to know the craziest thing? This is just a little weird, maybe a bit paranormal. I can smell her. It's mostly at our house, but sometimes here in the office. I smell her, and I feel like she is here. It's a little frightening, but it is real."

TH looked hard a Booker. He didn't see him as being tired. He saw him as someone who was incredibly sad.

•   •   •

It was closer to seven and TH hadn't heard from Richie all day. He knew when his brother got together with Billy Tasker that the nights got very long. He just wished Richie would stay a little more focused. Something was going on with the Fatty Fuller case based on what happened to Marilyn Aft. There was also something with the statements that Margaret Hatch made about Melissa. Maybe Richie knew something.

TH was finishing up a burger and fries at McDonald's when his phone rang. He checked the caller ID. It was Steve Marks.

"You find out anything worthwhile?" TH asked.

"Not with respect to Fatty, but maybe on something else. Can you meet me around nine tonight at the bowling alley?"

"I can do that."

"Great, but first I have a favor to ask."

"Shoot."

"Get a thousand dollars and get over to the town jail and bail Joseph out. Aft picked him up for being drunk at Lifers. They charged him with being drunk and disorderly. Bond is a grand."

"Aft was the one who arrested him?"

"Lou sent Aft and Jack. Don't ask why. Joseph doesn't look too good, but they said he fell a few times. He was pretty drunk. And just so you know, Aft was trying to arrest him for suspicion of murder for killing Marilyn. Said the bartender at Lifers told him Joseph was threatening revenge on Aft for what happened to Joseph's animals."

"Well, maybe when he was drunk."

"I didn't talk with the bartender, but that's the story. If you can dig up the bail, he can go."

"I've got to get to an ATM, but I can get it. I'll be at the jail within a half hour."

"And the bowling alley at nine."

"Yeah. That, too."

• • •

Marks wasn't kidding when he said that Joseph looked a little beat up. When TH picked him up at the jail, he looked like he had been in a pretty good fight. The shirt he wore, a button down work shirt was torn in several spots. One elbow showed through the cloth. One knee of his pants was torn, and blood was evident on the leg. Joseph was also sporting a black eye and some good scratches on his face.

"You don't so look good," TH said when Joseph climbed into his car.

"Don't feel all that good."

"Do you remember much?"

Joseph laughed. "I remember going to Lifers. That much I recall. I remember ordering the first whiskey. Then things get a little fuzzy."

"Word has it that you were pretty drunk and were spouting off about getting revenge on Logan Aft."

Joseph squeezed both eyes together and then opened them. He sighed heavily. "I don't remember that, but it's probably true. Aft is at least one of the ones that killed my animals, and I have been thinking about it."

"Probably not such a good idea to announce it in public."

"Apparently not."

"Do you remember fighting with anyone?"

"Nope. I guess I didn't do very well."

"Do you have a coat?"

"In my truck."

They pulled into Lifers parking lot and found Joseph's truck. TH was surprised that it looked like nothing was wrong with it.

"Thanks for bailing me out, TH. I'll get the thousand to you in the next couple of days."

TH put his hand on his friend's arm. "You gonna be okay?"

Joseph nodded slowly. "Didn't hit me right away, but those animals, those stupid cows, pigs, and chickens were like my family out there. It just got to me today. It just hit me that they were gone, that someone had slaughtered them. I needed a drink to calm my nerves. Guess I went a little too far."

"You need to keep calm, Joseph, especially with Aft. I get the feeling that something is going on, something is up with Skitch and Fatty Fuller. I just need a little more time. When I find it, I'm going to need your help. Can you promise to stay out of trouble until I call?"

Again, Joseph nodded slowly. "I can do that, TH."

•   •   •

Unlike the first time they met in the bowling alley, the place was busy and loud when TH walked into the bar entrance. Steve Marks was sitting at the far end of the bar, nursing a gin and tonic. He waved to TH as he headed over to where Marks was sitting.

"Okay to talk here?" TH asked.

"What are you having?" Marks asked as the bartender came over. TH ordered a beer. "It's as safe here as anywhere. I think the word is starting to get around."

TH sipped his beer. "What word would that be?"

"I think something is up. I think this little poking around on Fatty Fuller is making a few people anxious and I think it also opened some other doors to things that have been going on here for a while."

"What kind of things?"

Marks took his time and explained the history of Wilson Garrett's past and the death of Corinne Riley.

"So you think that my father was able to coax the pension deal for the Amigos out of Wilson when he got to office because of what happened at Ma's one night with this Corrine Riley?"

"Seems logical, doesn't it? Wilson fucked up, and Teddy helped cover it up. Teddy held onto the card for a long time, and when Wilson got to office and got established, he played it."

"So what makes you think that any of this is related to Fatty and Skitch?"

"Two things really. Why would Skitch kill Fatty? To get some fishing tackle to sell? That's ludicrous. Skitch knew Fatty and liked him. There's no way he kills him to make a few bucks selling some poles and lures."

"The second thing?"

"Marilyn Aft. You guys go talk to her, and she spouts her mouth off about the frame up job the cops did with the investigation. Next thing you know someone bashes her head in."

"Any theories there?"

"None really, not counting Joseph Running Bear. There was no forced entry, no sign of burglary and no struggle. I'd say the killer either snuck in quietly or Marilyn knew the killer and let him in."

"So this somebody who Marilyn knew got the idea she was talking too much about the Fatty Fuller case and shut her down?"

"That's it. Let's think for a minute. Think about Wilson Garrett. Skitch Grayson was an old drunk and an easy target to frame. Did Teddy and Aft use Skitch to cover up somebody else killing Fatty? Were there other ways that Teddy flexed his muscle?"

"There were other ways according to Marilyn Aft."

"Is there something that you didn't tell me from your meeting?"

TH took a sip of his beer and made sure no one was able to hear what he told Marks. "We told you everything, including the bizarre stuff about Teddy controlling the Amigos and their wives."

"I really wasn't buying that part of Marilyn's story." Marks was smiling broadly.

"No laughing matter, Steve. She was emphatic about it. I believed her. Told us she completely rejected Teddy and had a physical encounter with him. He knocked her down and kicked her. This was close to the end of her time with Logan."

Marks dropped the smile and sipped his drink. "So if Teddy has the balls to control his officers enough to prey on their wives, what's to stop him from looking at crimes and the perpetrators to see if there's any gain to made from helping them out? It seemed to work out pretty well with Wilson Garrett."

"So who benefited from the murder of Fatty Fuller?"

The bartender came over, and Marks ordered another round. The noise from the bowling alley was rowdy and boisterous. Pins being slammed into were followed by cheers and jeers from the bowlers.

"That's the million dollar question. It was easy to track the thing with Wilson based on what Valerie Plume told me. I can't go back and look at every person who committed a crime and gave Teddy the thought that blackmailing them would be a good idea."

"That could take forever."

"Or longer."

TH scratched his chin. "Where did the big break come from in the Fatty Fuller case?"

Marks thought for a minute. There was no physical evidence at the scene of the crime. The tip the police got came from Gus Morgan, the bartender at The Lighthouse, when he reported that Skitch Grayson was bragging about having some new fishing tackle to sell. This was the same Gus Morgan that told the stories of Wilson Garrett's past and advised Marks where he could find Valerie Plume.

"You still with me?" TH asked.

"Yeah," Marks said. "I just had a thought. I'm not sure. Where are you at with what you are doing?"

That was a good question. Where was he with the poking around he'd been doing, TH thought. Marilyn Aft was dead, and Joseph Running Bear had all of his animals slaughtered on his property and had been arrested.

Both Marilyn and Skitch Grayson said he had nothing to do with the murder. Then there was the matter of his sister, Melissa. What had caused her to hang herself? What thing or things should the Browns have been aware of as Margaret Hatch said?

"Now you're the one that's off in space," Marks said.

"Off in space, because I hear some things that are mildly interesting, but really have no legs. In other words, I don't have much, and I don't know where I'm heading."

"Welcome to the world of criminal investigations."

A Few Stories and More Clues

The story that Steve Marks had told to Lou Katz about Wilson Garrett was an interesting one. So interesting that it had Lou waking several times during the night to think about it. At breakfast that morning he told his wife Mary about it; he also told her that the Brown boys had been talking to Marilyn Aft shortly before she had been brutally murdered. What Marks had told Lou made him wonder what kind of control had been enforced when Teddy Brown had been the Chief. Had there been something there on Wilson Garrett for Teddy to blackmail him into the deputy positions and favorable pensions for the Three Amigos? Also, did any of this type of control play a factor in the Fatty Fuller case? Was there somebody out there that Teddy Brown was protecting and then blackmailing at the time of the murder?

Lou booted up his computer and found the program he wanted. He typed in the name Corrine Riley and watched as the machine searched its memory. Lou hoped that Marks had been wrong, but Marks claimed to have seen the record. In less than a minute, Lou had his answer.

Corrine Riley, age twenty-four, had been spotted down in a ravine off of River Trail Road by an anonymous hiker who called it into the department. The body, according to the coroner, had been in the ravine for over eight hours. What Marks hadn't said was that there were several possible causes of death. Listed were exposure, it had been nineteen degrees the night before she was found, drug OD, and several head injuries. Corrine's body was loaded with cocaine. The case was listed as an accidental death, the body was prepped, her parents notified, and the corpse was shipped to Akron, Ohio.

Lou sipped his coffee which had gone to almost cool. Things missing from the report that bothered him. What was Corrine Riley doing in the Milton area at the time of her death? Where had she been before she supposedly found herself wandering on River Trail? The report made it seem like she was just there, fell into the ravine and died. She had to be somewhere beforehand to ingest the cocaine. Had it been Ma Brooks? According to Marks, Valerie Plume, the retired prostitute, had made that claim.

Lou scrolled down the page and found what he was looking for. The report, other than the coroner's findings, had been compiled by Ben Smith who confirmed that Corrine had worked at Ma Brooks. Lou shook his head.

•   •   •

A bit later and not too far from Lou Katz' office, Steve Marks was looking at a similar file, but this one was the arrest record for Gus Morgan, the bartender from The Lighthouse. Gus had tipped off Marks on the past of Wilson Garrett. He had also been a key figure in the murder of Fatty Fuller. He had been the one to inform the police that Skitch Grayson was boasting of having some new fishing tackle that he wanted to get rid of. The gear ended up in Skitch's shed and turned out to be stolen from Fatty after he had been smashed on the head.

For the past fifteen years, Gus Morgan's record was clean, nothing, not even a traffic violation. Before that, there was an interesting history. Marks counted four instances where Gus had been dragged in for sale of an illegal substance, marijuana. Gus had paid a fine in each case and been released. There were also charges for selling alcohol to minors, all dismissed. Lastly, The Lighthouse, showing Gus Morgan as owner, had three times been busted for solicitation by prostitutes. In these cases, he had been jailed for short terms and then released.

Marks looked to the ceiling, but there were no answers there. Gus Morgan had broken the law in several cases but had only been fined or given short jail terms. Every case involved a deal with the district attorney. Nothing ever went to trial. Marks couldn't figure out how the law could have been so lenient on Gus, but then there was the case of Ma Brooks operating a whorehouse less than a mile from The Lighthouse. There was nothing legal about Ma's, but yet it stayed in business a long time before being shut down. Why were the police so lax in prosecuting both Ma and Gus. One answer that Marks could come up with was money. He assumed somebody was getting paid to let these two places stay open for business. The other reason, particularly with Gus Morgan, was information. Was Gus getting information and then trading it with Teddy Brown's people so that he got handled lightly? Marks needed a few more answers.

•   •   •

Rachel Brown had an early shift and had gone to work; her children were all off to school. TH and Richie had the whole house to themselves. It was kind of good that the kids were gone because Richie looked awful. The bruises from the cheap shot from Logan Aft didn't help, but Richie's eyes were bloodshot red, his hair was an uncombed, gnarly mess and he reeked of alcohol. He sat quietly in a chair at the kitchen table across from TH. He only stared at his morning coffee.

"You and Billy burnt a few brain cells yesterday, I take it?" TH said.

Richie looked up at TH, squinted a bit, but said nothing.

"I was really hoping that you could help me out with some of this stuff. You look awful, Richie."

Richie shifted on the chair, picked up his coffee, but only looked at it. He quickly put it back on the table. "What would you like me to help you with?"

In Richie's fragile state, TH stayed away from the Margaret Hatch comments about Melissa. "You thought that what happened to Marilyn Aft showed we might be onto something regarding Fatty's murder."

Again Richie looked up and said nothing. He got out of the chair slowly and moved to a cabinet behind him. In it, he took out a bottle of Jack Daniels. He poured a shot into his coffee and placed the bottle on the table. Now he sipped his coffee. "Somebody murdered Marilyn for a reason," he said. "What that reason is nobody knows, except the killer. We are not the police. We can't go questioning people about a murder. We also have no access to anything, like evidence. Kind of leaves us well behind the eight ball."

"So you're done?"

Richie added more whiskey and took a gulp. "I think this case is nowhere. Marilyn told us some great stories, but that was it. The Three Amigos aren't going to tell you shit about the Fatty Fuller case. Their wives, excluding Marilyn, aren't going to tell you that dad used them all, and so what? That wasn't what got Fatty killed. Unless you can miraculously find somebody who knows something substantial, you are just wasting your time.”

TH nodded. “You headed home?”

Richie laughed. “Not today. That’s for sure. I’m close.”

“You don’t seem in the biggest hurry.”

“Yeah, well.”

“Everything okay between you and Karen.”

TH noticed there was no coffee left in Richie’s cup. His older brother poured more Jack in the mug and took a healthy swallow. “Karen thinks that I drink a little too much. She says when I drink that I go to a dark place. I draw into myself, whatever the fuck that means. She says I need to get some professional help and would prefer that I not come home until I do. I haven’t lived in the house for three months.”

“I’m sorry, Rich. I didn’t know.”

Richie smiled lightly. “It’s all on me, TH. I’m a fuck up. I work okay, and then I drink. I drink to help me forget, and then I drink some more to help me sleep. It’s a bad cycle to be in.”

“What are you trying to forget?”

“Life, TH,” Richie said. He took another sip of the whiskey.

• • •

Leaving Rachel’s house, TH had a realization, and it unnerved him. He hadn’t realized the level of dysfunction in his family until now. Rachel had three kids from three different men and was living check to check with help from others. Richie, who he thought was happily married, was an alcoholic with his marriage unraveling. Melissa, the one he thought had the most harmonious life, had something happen to her which caused her to hang herself with a belt from a ceiling fan. TH felt himself shake a bit and felt his temples tightening.

He drove along with no apparent destination and thought about his own relationship with Teddy. Their father had always been tough and demanding. TH thought he demanded too much. He wanted perfection in the classroom as well as on the baseball diamond. There was severe criticism when either thing lacked. Teddy had also wanted both boys to be cops. Not just cops, but Milton cops, following his footsteps. Richie had become a cop, but not until after he went to Iraq and then Kansas City; he’d had no desire to come back to Milton. TH had never wanted to be a cop. With his earlier urge to steal things, he was more on the edge of being a criminal, but looking back on it, he had never stolen anything that would have been a felony until he got to California.

Maybe Richie was right. They'd talked to a few people who had stated that Skitch Grayson hadn't killed Fatty Fuller. So what? They would need a lot more than some random comments for anything to be meaningful, and they weren't getting anything like that. It was funny how during all of this digging around some dirt had come out on Wilson Garrett. That might end up being the more promising find out of the whole mess, but TH felt there was still something there with the Fatty Fuller case. Somebody killed Marilyn Aft shortly after TH and Richie spoke with her. That had to mean something. Right?

•　　　•　　　•

Steve Marks walked into The Lighthouse at just past eleven. Even this early in the day and the place appeared to be in the dark. Marks realized that most of the lighting came from the glow of lights behind the bar. These reflected across the room to give the place that hazy look. Even in the dim light, Marks could make out the short, squat figure of Gus Morgan behind the bar. He was standing with his back against the back counter, arms crossed over his chest. There was no one else at the bar.

"Back so soon, Detective Marks?" Gus asked.

"I've missed you, Gus."

Gus Morgan laughed. "My good friend Valerie says that you looked her up."

"I did, and you were right. She tells an interesting story about Corinne Riley and Wilson Garrett."

"You want something to drink. Maybe a bloody or a screwdriver?"

"I'm good, Gus. You know that story she tells is interesting, but there's questions."

"There's always questions, detective, but none of the other girls saw Corinne Riley that night. We can't be sure that her injuries were caused by Wilson Garrett."

"Don't fuck with me, Gus. You told me a story about Wilson's past, and you gave me Valerie Plume's name. I believe what she told me and you believe her, too. The questions I have don't pertain to what happened to

Corinne in that room or how she ended up in that ditch. They pertain to you."

Gus dropped his arms and put his hands on the bar. "Maybe you should leave, Detective Marks."

"Hit a nerve didn't I? You realized that you told me a little too much about Wilson Garrett. You realized that what you told me can get you in trouble."

"You're fucking crazy. In trouble for what?"

"I saw your arrest record, Gus. In some cases, you'd pay a little fine and be right back at work. In other cases, you were doing a few days up at Bridgemore and then getting out."

"They were all kind of minor charges."

"That's debatable. I noticed that the arresting officers were either Logan Aft or Jack Davis or both."

"So?"

"You were working for them. They'd pick you up for something, and probably the first few times it was legit, and they'd plant you in the prison to find stuff out. You were a snitch for them. They used you in exchange for getting yourself out of trouble. If they didn't have use for you, you would pay a fine and be cut loose."

"You are fucking crazy. None of that is true."

"They also used you for Skitch Grayson. They wanted you to tell them that Skitch had shot his mouth off about having that fishing gear, the gear he supposedly took from Fatty Fuller. They used you to set up Skitch and close the case."

Now Gus Morgan smiled. "You are full of shit, Detective Marks. Skitch sat right about where you are standing and was talking loudly about that gear he had. I had heard that all of Fatty's expensive tackle had been stolen. I put two and two together and called Logan Aft."

"That's how it really played out, Gus?"

"Yeah. That's how it really played out."

Marks raised a finger and pointed it at Gus. "I'm working this case now, Gus. It's not Aft or Jack Davis. I'm going to find something, and I'm going to come for you. Your history of being a snitch is going to finally catch up with you."

•   •   •

TH had just pulled into the parking lot of his motel when his phone rang. He was surprised when the register said, Mary Katz. What he didn't want was another lunch where they rehashed old times and missed opportunities.

"Hello, Mary."

"TH, are you alone?"

"I'm in my car."

"We need to talk. It's important."

He could tell from her voice the urgency she felt. "Where would you like to meet?"

"We can't meet. There's too much going on right now."

The only reason she wouldn't meet was for fear of being seen together, TH thought. He looked around the parking lot for any suspicious looking cars. "You sound nervous. Relax and tell me what is going on."

"I don't even know where to start. The last few days have been crazy. Lou is beside himself."

"Lou is upset?"

"Very. I mean, he knew you guys were asking some questions about the Fatty Fuller murder. This didn't sit well with him, but he thought it was harmless."

"Until?"

"Until somebody beat Marilyn Aft to death. The fact that this happened right after you and Richie went to see her sent his head spinning. On top of that, we have Logan Aft punching Richie and then arresting Joseph and wanting to charge him. He thinks Aft in unhinged at this point."

"At this point?"

"More so than normal. Anyway, Lou got to wondering if there could be something up with the murder; Mrs. Aft talks to you guys, and suddenly somebody takes her out."

"All she did was doubt the investigation and the guilt of Skitch Grayson. She told us nothing really important." He left out the part about his father controlling his staff and their wives.

"That may be, but there's still the theory that she may have known something more important and that's why she was killed."

"That was kind of what I thought, but we got nothing like that from her."

"Well, now there's this thing that Steve Marks dug up."

TH thought he should play this one quietly. "I'm a little aware of it, but not much."

"Steve found out that a young woman died out at Ma Brooks' whorehouse many years ago. The young lady had been servicing Wilson Garrett."

"Our Wilson Garrett?"

"That's the story at least. Steve has a witness that says the girl died on site at the house. Says she thought the girl died of an OD while with Wilson. The cops were called in, and the girl was taken from the house. Next day she was found by some anonymous hiker in a gulley along River Trail. Death by exposure and injuries from falling in the ditch. Also large doses of cocaine in her system. The death was ruled accidental. No mention of Wilson Garrett or Ma Brooks."

TH sighed loudly; he felt his heartbeat quicken. "And why do you feel this has caused Lou to get so upset?"

"Wilson Garrett brought forth the motion for the deputy and pension positions for the Three Amigos. I'm sure you're aware that the deputy positons are for lifetime and the pensions are lucrative."

"I've heard that."

"Nobody gets deals like this for no reason. Lou thinks these deals were forged because Wilson owed the Amigos and your father something. He believes what Steve found and thinks Wilson did something to that girl and has been blackmailed. There's no other reason for it."

"How about Fatty Fuller?"

"Same thing, TH, but in that case, no one has any idea of who is being protected or why Skitch Grayson was chosen as the fall guy for the murder."

"Skitch wasn't a model citizen. Serving up the town drunk isn't much of a loss to the town of Milton."

"Exactly."

"But Lou believes this may have happened?"

"He's got the Wilson Garrett case, and there's so much doubt in the Fatty Fuller case that he's thinking there might be something there. He's starting to see a pattern."

Maybe a pattern, but no other proof or witnesses. "That's a lot of good information, Mary," TH said.

"I'm not telling you this for the information quality," she said, raising her voice. "Marilyn Aft is dead, Richie got sucker punched, and I hear Aft, and Jack Davis might have roughed up Joseph. I'm telling you this, so you watch yourself. Lou thinks this a dangerous time. I think it's really dangerous for people like you who are poking around in it."

TH looked around the parking lot again. The pictures of Marilyn Aft's battered face popped into his head. "I hear what you're saying, Mary."

"I hope you do, TH. Lou wasn't himself at all when he was telling me this. He thinks there is a real threat out there. Watch yourself."

"I will," he said, but he realized that Mary Katz was gone.

•   •

TH was just about to step out of his car when his phone rang again. He thought for a moment that Mary had hung up inadvertently. When he pulled the phone back out of his pocket, he didn't recognize the number on the register.

"Hello," he said.

"Is this TH Brown?" asked a woman's voice.

"It is."

"TH, this is Anne Smith, Ben's wife. I got your number from your sister, Rachel. I hope you don't mind me calling you."

"Not at all, Anne. What can I do for you?"

"I'd like to talk with you."

"Now is as good a time as any."

She hesitated for a minute. "I prefer to do it in person. Do you know where the Walmart is in Dubuque?"

This was the same one where Rachel worked. "I do."

"Directly across Twenty, there is a coffee shop called the Morning Bean. Can you meet me there in half an hour?"

TH checked his watch. "If I leave now it shouldn't be a problem."

"I'll be there," she said, and she hung up.

TH got back into the car and started it up. What in God's name did Ben Smith's wife want to talk to him about?

•   •

"I'm pretty sure that Gus Morgan was some sort of informant or prison snitch for Teddy and his boys," Steve Marks said. It wasn't that hot out or in Lou's office, but he was sweating under his suit coat.

"You going to fill me in on how you figured this out?"

"You take a look at his record. There's a number of arrests there. After the first couple, he either settles without a trial, and pays a fine, or he goes into prison for a short period of time. With as many arrests that he had you would think that eventually, they would have put him away for a long time, but that's not the case."

"Because they were using him?"

"Exactly. Something happened along the way where Teddy figured out that Gus had some value by placing him into the system and seeing what he could learn. Obviously, this was after Gus had done something to get himself into some trouble and this ended up being his way out of it."

Lou sat back in his chair and laced his hands together behind his head. "And what exactly does this have to do with anything."

"With Wilson Garrett, we get the picture that Wilson did something bad to that girl. Teddy and friends helped Wilson out of the jam by dumping her body in the ravine along River Trail. Wilson paid them back later with the lifetime deputy and pension deal."

"Where does Gus Morgan figure in the Wilson Garrett case?"

"He doesn't. He has nothing to do with that."

"But?"

"But he does have something to do with Fatty Fuller?"

Lou's eyes narrowed. "Gus Morgan killed Fatty Fuller?"

"No. He killed Skitch Grayson. I don't know who killed Fatty, but I don't think it was Skitch. What I do think happened is that Teddy and Aft needed somebody to cover for the real killer. They settled on Skitch. They knew he would drink down at The Lighthouse. They also knew from their prior histories that they could get Gus to say some things that a drunken Skitch supposedly said. They got Gus to tell them that Skitch had bragged about coming into some good fishing gear and that he was looking to unload it cheaply. This is what tipped the cops off and got them to check Skitch's shed."

Lou closed his eyes and tried to absorb what Marks had told him. Had Teddy and his crew covered for the actual murderer of Fatty Fuller? If so, who was the killer? "You pretty sure about this?"

"I could only piece it together from looking at Gus' record. When I went and talked with him, he denied it, but it made sense to me. You'll also note that there are no more arrests of Gus after the Fatty Fuller murder. It was like he finally got his marker back from Teddy."

Lou massaged the bridge of his nose. "What does this mean, Steve?"

"I think it means we have a couple of murderers out there free and we also have some deputies and a former Chief of Police, who aided these killers by covering up their crimes."

"That's what I thought you were going to say."

"What do we do, Lou? Arrest every last one of them and grill them until they break?"

Lou suddenly felt sick to his stomach. Could you arrest the mayor, former Chief of Police, his top three deputies and Gus Morgan all over suspicion? "Let me think on it overnight and one more thing. Don't tell anyone else about this conversation. I think shit is about to blow apart."

•   •   •

The Morning Bean wasn't hard to find. Directly across from the Walmart was a long strip mall. At the end of the stores, next to a card store, was the coffee shop. TH walked in and looked around. The shop was almost empty. He ordered a coffee and found a spot at a table in the rear of the place.

It was less than ten minutes later when the door opened and an older woman, wearing sunglasses walked in. TH had not seen Anne Smith in years, but she had not changed that much. She was tall and slender and had blonde hair. She looked into the rear of the shop and started towards TH. She didn't remove her glasses until she reached his table. "You look a lot like your father," she said.

"I'm not sure if that's a good thing," TH said. "Do you want something to drink?"

She removed the coat she wore and laid it over the chair next to hers as she sat down. "No thank you. Too much caffeine makes me jittery."

"You wanted to meet in sort on an out of the way place."

She sighed loudly. "Before we start, I want you to know that I think that your father did a lot of good things for the town during his tenure."

TH sipped his coffee but offered no response.

"There was some good, more than bad, but the bad things are the ones I think about late at night. They are probably the reason that I picked to come out here instead of close to town to meet. I'm not sure if it's advisable for us to be together."

"Are you frightened about something?"

She smiled thinly. "You talked with Marilyn Aft. Look what happened to her."

"You really think that Marilyn was murdered because she talked to Richie and me?"

"I do. You know she called me. She called me and told me that she had met with you and that she told you that she thought the investigation into Fatty's Fuller's murder had been fixed."

"I don't know if she used the word fixed, but she had some doubts about how the investigation was conducted. She certainly didn't believe that Skitch Grayson killed Fatty."

"We may never know who killed Fatty Fuller," she said. "I think Marilyn may have mentioned to you that your father tried to control all of us, the men who worked for him and their wives."

"She said something about it."

"And it is true. I know Marilyn fought it and it worked for her. She was looking to get away from Logan for the longest time. That might have sealed it for her. Can't blame her either."

"What about Mrs. Davis and you?"

"I won't say anything about Grace. I have my ideas, but that's all they are. I can talk to you about myself. I was young and stupid. Your father was powerful and influential. Everything he asked for we got paid for in some way. There was always good pay and bonuses. There's the pension deal. It was a sacrifice, but in the end, it worked out. Ben is retiring, and we are moving."

TH swallowed hard. "You don't have to tell me this."

Again she smiled. "I'm an old woman, TH. All of that is in the past, the way past. I really don't think about it, but what I do think about are some of the bad things. I think those are the things that need to be talked about."

"Why are you telling me?"

"To help you understand what you are dealing with. To show you how things worked. And, of course, I can't go to the police with this."

TH finished his coffee and pushed the cup to the side. "Is this about Fatty?"

"It might be, but it started almost forty years ago with the murder of a black man named Arthur Kimbro. A redneck farmer from Iowa shot him dead and tried to run for it. Two patrol cars pursued him towards the

Mississippi. Jack and Ben were in one; your father was in the other. Well, they found the farmer's car, abandoned near the Route 20 Bridge, but no sign of the farmer. He disappeared. Even the Illinois and Iowa State Police never found the guy. There was never a trace of him."

"I'm not sure what this has to do with Fatty Fuller or even Marilyn Aft."

"It's just a pattern of how things worked. I think something happened out there. I think Teddy, Jack, and Ben did see that farmer. I think they helped make his disappear."

"Wait a minute. You think they found this guy and killed him?"

"I don't know for sure, but Ben wasn't himself for weeks. He had trouble sleeping and would mumble in his sleep. A couple of times I could see he had been crying. Of course, when I asked him what was bothering him, he said it was nothing.

"Then there was a case that might have involved Wilson Garrett. Wilson liked to drink and get a little rough at an old brothel called Ma Brooks. Well, this one night Ben got called that he had to get out to Ma's place. He mentioned to me that it looked like Wilson Garrett had gotten out of line and roughed up a girl pretty badly. He didn't think he'd be long."

TH had heard this story from Marks and knew the ending, but played along. "What happened?"

"Ben came home and said it had been a little hassle, but Wilson was fine and nobody at Ma's was hurt. The next day came the story that they found a girl in a ditch near River Trail. She had drugs in her system, and the closest place to where she was found was Ma Brooks. Nobody knew anything, and the girl was shipped home to Ohio to be buried. Again, Ben wasn't himself for a while and his sleep was affected."

"And you think Ben and some of the others helped Wilson out of a jam?"

"That's it exactly. Something happened up at Ma Brooks, and they took care of it. But both of those stories are so old; I'm not sure anything can be done about them."

TH agreed that witnesses who knew anything and that would help were all long gone. "Where does this leave us with Fatty Fuller?"

"I agree with Marilyn that Skitch Grayson didn't kill Fatty. I have no idea who did, but I'd heard ramblings about the investigation. I'd heard from Ben that Teddy Jand Aft were taking care of it. A lot of it didn't sound professional."

"But you have no thoughts on who might have committed the crime?"

"I didn't say that," Anne said. "Your father had a lot to do with the Fuller family after the mother left. He was a bit like a Guardian Angel for them. Everybody knew that Fred Fuller was a weak one and that his drinking was taking over. He needed someone like your dad to step in and help out. Of course, this also led to your father getting a couple of loans at ridiculously low rates. Your father loved to brag about that. He especially liked to brag about the loan he got on the Galena Lake House."

This was the house they would stay at if they went for overnights for hunting or fishing. TH hadn't been there in years. "So my father helped out Fred Fuller, and Fred gave him some loans at low rates?"

"That might be all there is to it, but I'm not sure."

"Anne, I appreciate your frankness today, but I need to know. Do you know something more?"

She shook her head. "I really don't, but I do know one thing that you learn from being around law enforcement all these years. If you can't figure out a motive for a crime, the best thing to do is figure out if somebody benefited from it. This will usually lead you somewhere."

TH looked deep into her eyes. He felt she had told him everything she could. He nodded his head as she got up to leave.

•　　•　　•

"She's right about the Arthur Kimbro shooting," Marks was telling TH. "Teddy, Jack and Ben Smith followed the killer's trail and found his car just before the turnoff for the bridge. It looked like it had spun off the road and had been abandoned. There was no trace of the killer. There never was."

"How'd you know about this murder?"

"When Marilyn Aft told you guys to research the histories of murder in Milton that's what I did. There's been two, Arthur Kimbro and Fatty Fuller."

"What about Corinne Riley?"

"We don't know if that was a murder. I'm pretty sure that girl was dead up at Ma Brooks; pretty sure she died in Wilson Garrett's room. What I'm not sure of is the cause of death. Could have been from a beating which makes it murder. All of those head injuries could have come from falling into that ravine."

"Which makes it what?"

"I don't really know."

"With the Kimbro case, Anne Smith says that Ben was out of sorts for weeks after it happened. She's convinced that something bad happened."

"But we have no idea what."

"Exactly. With Corinne Riley, whatever happened to that poor girl, there was an attempt by Teddy to make sure Wilson Garrett's name was left out of it."

"Agree one hundred percent."

"But what about Fatty Fuller?"

Marks explained about Gus Morgan's history of being a snitch and helping the police.

"You think he lied about Skitch bragging about the fishing gear?"

"That's what I think. They needed to frame somebody and Skitch would be no great loss. They had Gus tell his story about Skitch and the fishing tackle."

"To protect who, though? First of all, who would kill Fatty? Secondly, why would my father and the police protect him?"

"Both good questions. I don't see anyone murdering Fatty to frame Skitch. That's too ridiculous. Maybe somebody was just going to rob Fatty, and when they clunked him on the head, they accidentally killed him. That doesn't make sense because they didn't take the gear and it ended up in Skitch's shed."

"Then why and who are still the questions. Anne Smith said to find out who benefited from the crimes. She also told me my father got some pretty good loans out of Fred Fuller. Said he bragged about it quite a bit."

"So your dad was using Fred to secure favorable loans. Did Fred kill Fatty and your dad helped protect him because of their financial arrangement?"

"It occurred to me, but then I'm not sure Fred could kill anyone, especially his own son."

"That sounds unlikely. What are you going to do?"

"I was going to check with Cindy one more time. She had mentioned that my dad used to come around there a lot. He was always helping them out after Mrs. Fuller took off."

"Can't hurt to ask a few more questions and it has to come from you since we are not really investigating anything to do with that."

"But you kind of are."

"Kind of, but rather than go after it from that angle, I think Lou is considering asking Logan Aft a few questions."

"I'm sure that will go well."

"Logan will say he talked to Gus Morgan and that Gus told him about the gear. He'll say he found the gear in Skitch's shed like he has a hundred times before. That's what Logan will say."

"Somebody must know the fucking truth."

"Oh, somebody does, TH. The hard part is getting someone to tell it to us. That and finding the proof to back it up."

TH found Cindy Fuller working the same blackjack table as the first time he visited her at Trips Aces. He sat down at the table and played a few hands, losing quickly. Cindy was joking and playful with all of the players. She didn't treat TH any differently. As he continued to lose, she smiled at him.

"I've got break in ten minutes," she said.

"I'll be in the bar," he said.

He bought a beer and found a table that looked out over the casino floor. The table game area wasn't as crowded as the slot area. There were loads of people, mostly older people, popping their money into the one-armed bandits. TH wondered if there was more to life than that, hoping to pop a thousand nickels.

Cindy came in a few minutes later and sat across from him. He noticed that she had untied her hair and refreshed her bright lipstick. She looked good. "I didn't know you were coming out to see me."

"I didn't know until just a little while ago."

She tilted her head to one side, giving him a quizzical look. "What made you realize it?"

"There's a good chance that a witness in Freddie's case may have lied when he told the police that Skitch Grayson took the fishing gear."

She stared at him intently. "I know I blew up at you the last time and then I apologized, but I really meant it when I said that my father and I wanted to let sleeping dogs lie."

He nodded and sipped his beer. "Even if it means the wrong man was convicted and spent all of that time in jail?"

"I don't mean that. It's just painful to hear. Ever since Freddie was killed, there's been these rumors about who the killer was. It's exhausting to hear it. I know my father and me would like all of that talk to end."

"There's been a couple of crimes committed in Milton that appear to have been covered up by the police. There's a chance that this may have happened with Freddie."

She laughed. "A cover-up. Come on. That's probably the most absurd thing that I have heard yet. Who are the police covering up for?"

"Don't know. It's just a theory."

"It's a lousy theory. If somebody lied and it led to Skitch getting convicted, that's wrong. Maybe the real killer is out there, but the idea of some cover-up is ridiculous."

A woman about fifty feet away yelped out as her machine hit a winner. She celebrated a short while and then pushed the PLAY button again, sure to give back her winnings.

"I don't want you to get mad at me, but I was kind of wondering when my father started to come by and offer his help at your house? Was it before or after Freddie was killed?"

"What does that have to do with anything?"

"Cindy, look, I'm not trying to upset you. Skitch Grayson is dying. I'm not so sure he was the killer. If I can clear his name before he dies, I think that would be the best I can do for him."

"Why?"

"Because my father is the one that sent him to prison."

She crossed her arms across her chest. "It seems your father was coming to visit for the longest time. I remember him being there when Freddie was really small. He used to bring Freddy and me little gifts. It seemed like it went on forever."

"But more after your mom left?"

"Yeah, of course, but my dad was a complete wreck when Mom left. He was really drinking a lot. Here he was with two little kids, one with Down Syndrome, and no one to help raise them. Your father was a big help. Always has been."

"When you told me before that my father had helped you out did you mean as a family or personally?"

"I meant both. He helped my father a lot, and he helped me a couple of times when I had some trouble with Troy. Minor stuff, but your dad intervened, and everything got settled down."

"I take it your dad would help out my father if he could on a loan or anything else associated with the bank?"

She shrugged. "You'd have to ask my father about that. What he did at the bank was his business. I don't ever recall him discussing any of that with me."

That seemed logical. If there were any favorable loans given to Teddy by Fred Fuller they had been handled discreetly.

"You don't think my father had anything to do with any of this?" Cindy said abruptly.

"With killing Freddie? Absolutely not."

"That would be a stupid thought," she said. "Why aren't the police looking into some of this if you are so sure that people have lied and maybe the right person didn't get caught? You're good friends with Steve Marks. He's the lead detective in Milton now, isn't he?"

"He is the lead detective. That's true."

"What's his position in all of this?"

"He was the one that found out that the witness may have lied. He's the one that told me about it."

She looked surprised. "But the police haven't started any official kind of investigation?"

"Not yet, but I know that Steve plans on meeting with Lou to discuss their next course of action. I think they might bring in Logan Aft and ask him a few questions."

She looked at her watch. "I've got to get back," she said. "I'm not sure what all of this means, TH, and I'm not thrilled to be talking about it, but I hope you find the right killer. I mean, if Skitch wasn't the one. Like you, I'd hate to see him die before somebody clears up his name.

•　　　•　　　•

After hearing from TH, after his talk with Cindy Fuller, Marks called down to Tammy in Records. There was too much flirting going on with her when he went down there in person.

"What can I help you with, Detective Marks?" she asked. Marks could detect the tone, not all businesslike.

"Looking for anything that you may have on Troy Stripling and Cindy Fuller. I guess she was Cindy Stripling back then. Any domestic stuff?"

"Give me one minute," she said, and Marks realized he was on hold.

He didn't think this was much of a lead, but anything might help. Teddy helping out Cindy with her crazy husband, even though unusual, wasn't incriminating.

"It says here," Tammy said, "that there were a number of disturbances called in three, four years ago. Most were called in by neighbors, but one by Cindy. We sent out a car on each one. Each one was settled without arrests."

Nothing there thought Marks. "Anything else?"

"Nope. I knew Cindy a little. Marrying Troy Stripling not the brightest thing that she could have done."

"Not somebody I'd want my daughter marrying?"

"I heard he was trying to get into one of the bridesmaid's pants the night before the wedding?"

Marks laughed. "Sounds like Troy."

"Cindy was no angel herself. A couple of years before she married Troy she had to run off to Milwaukee to get an abortion. Would never tell anyone who the father was."

Marks felt his mouth drop open. "You're sure about this?"

"One hundred percent. She told some friends, and it got out. About the abortion, not the father."

Marks wasn't sure it meant anything. It couldn't mean anything. The alleged abortion had occurred after Fatty had been murdered. Nobody was taking any revenge on Cindy for that. At least he didn't think so.

•   •   •

The day that Fatty Fuller was murdered had been a hot one. It was also the last day of the summer season for the Milton High baseball team. The game, a meaningless affair, had gone on forever. Both teams trudged through the innings at a monotonous pace. TH couldn't wait for the game to end. What had been the most exciting part of the game was that Cindy Fuller showed up. She was there as a chaperone for Fatty. Fatty was the team manager and a favorite of all the players. They would joke with him and kid him as he sat in the dugout. Cindy stayed a safe distance away from the players, but TH could see her clearly. He could see her long, reddish hair fly as the breeze blew. He could also make out her long, athletic legs. She had helped this view by wearing very short, denim shorts.

The game ended a little after four, and after joking a bit with the other players, TH found himself driving home. It was funny. As soon as he was in his car and on the way home he missed baseball. With the end of the summer season that also meant the end of summer break. School would start in a few weeks. His senior year and then off to college. He caught himself looking back at the diamond. One more season, one more year of high school and then he was off in search of his future.

He had gotten home, showered and had dinner with his father and two sisters. His dad asked each of them how their days had been. Nobody had anything particularly interesting to say.

"How was the game today, TH?" his father asked. He was chewing frantically at a piece of pork chop.

TH shrugged. "Not much too it. It was the last game of the summer, and I don't' think either team wanted to be there."

His father swallowed his food and took a sip of his beer. "That's the problem these days," he said.

TH wasn't sure what he meant. "What is the problem?"

"You kids. That's it. You are all too privileged to understand what is important and what isn't."

TH felt himself about to laugh but smiled broadly instead. "Dad, these are exhibition games, nothing more, and it was like ninety-five out there."

His father's face turned bright red. TH looked at his sisters, but they both had their heads down.

"So when you get on the force here and you think a day is slow and your body and your mind go into remission, what the hell are you going to do when something happens right in front of you, and you have to make a snap decision?"

"I think that's a little different than a baseball game."

"You're damn right it is, but my point is the same. Whether it's school, a baseball game or working in the police department, you have to be ready all the time. You have to give one hundred percent every day. There's no taking a day off. That shit doesn't work anywhere, especially in the streets."

Now TH did laugh. "Dad, this is Milton, Illinois, not one of the bureaus of New York."

His dad's hand came down and smashed hard on the top of the table. Memories of the Christmas Eve dinner hit TH hard. Only this time, he was the target. "I don't want to hear that garbage coming out of your God damn mouth. You don't belittle this town or the police force. Our record is one that speaks of safety for the townspeople and the lowest crime rate of many

158

towns this size. Don't disrespect it and don't take days off. You'll end up a loser if you do. Do you get me?"

TH felt himself trembling. "Yes, sir."

"Now you may be excused from the dinner table."

TH looked down at his half eaten dinner. "But I haven't finished eating?"

"Think of that when you're working a double some day and your feet hurt, and you're starving. Give that some thought. Now off to your room."

TH looked to his sisters again, but their heads were pointed down at their plates. He got up and left the table and returned to his room. Closing the door, he realized two things. He was really hungry, and he would never be a Milton cop.

It was after nine when TH heard the doorbell ring. He had been waiting for his father to go up to bed so that he could make a kitchen visit. The doorbell being rung several times brought him out of bed and into the area leading to the front foyer. His sister Melissa answer the door. She turned and looked into the living room.

"Dad, it's Mr. Aft. He says he needs to talk with you right away."

TH stood still and heard his dad's recliner chair coming back to its normal position. His father walked into the foyer and opened the door to speak with Logan Aft. TH couldn't hear anything. Both Aft and his father were talking quietly. Finally, his father closed the door and announced loudly to his family. "I've got to go in for a while. Something bad has happened."

"What is it, dad?" TH said.

His father stared at him for a minute. TH thought he might be about to tell him he was still grounded. "Somebody hit Fatty Fuller over the head with a rock, and he fell into Whisper Creek and drowned. I've got to get down there."

Both Rachel and Melissa screamed out in horror. TH couldn't believe what he had just heard. He just saw Fatty a few hours earlier.

"What have these God damn, stupid people done?" his father said. Then he turned and ran up the stairs to get his uniform on.

Closer

When TH awoke, his first thought was about the late night call where Steve Marks had told him about Cindy Fuller getting an abortion. Cindy had always been a little bit of a wild child, but TH never thought she was reckless. He couldn't imagine her getting pregnant without wanting to. The thought seemed inconceivable to him, but he wasn't sure any of that mattered. What did her pregnancy and abortion have to do with anything?

His second thought and the one that had him wake up several times during the night was the comment his father had made after he got the news the Fatty had been murdered. "What have these God damn, stupid people done?" his father had raged. When TH had first heard the words, he thought his father was talking about some unknown person or persons. What if he had been talking about somebody that he knew? What if he'd been speaking about the actual killer?

He got up and showered as fast as he could and headed directly for Rachel's. He wanted to get to her before she took off for Dubuque.

TH pulled in behind Rachel's car and breathed a sigh of relief that she was still home. He didn't see Richie's car anywhere. He turned off the car and headed up the drive. The doorbell was answered after one ring.

"He's not home," Rachel said. She looked like she was finishing up her makeup. She was wearing the Walmart smock.

"If you're talking about Richie, I didn't come here to speak with him."

"Come on in, but I don't have a lot of time."

"This won't take long."

They went back to the kitchen and TH took a seat at the table. Rachel stood nearby and lit a cigarette; she didn't offer him anything to drink.

"A little feisty this morning," he said.

"I'm just busy, TH. I've got a job that I hate, and my kids drive me crazy. On top of that my two brothers won't leave me alone."

"I shouldn't be around here much longer, and I think Richie is leaving soon."

She exhaled a large plume of smoke. "So he says. What drags you out here this morning?"

"Do you remember the night that Fatty Fuller was murdered?"

"Well, yeah, sure. What about it?"

"Do you remember what dad said?"

She put her arms up into the air. "I think I was too shocked to remember anything. That and it was fifteen years ago."

"I clearly remember him saying, 'What have these God damn, stupid people done?' "

Rachel took a drag off of the cigarette. "I do remember him saying something like that, now that you mention it."

"Who do you think he was talking about?"

"I don't think he was talking about anyone. I just think he was speaking out loud, talking in general."

"You don't think he was talking about a particular person?"

"Not at all. Who did you have in mind?"

TH shook his head. "No one, really. I was just wondering."

"I really think you and Richie should head home. All of this trying to figure out why Melissa killed herself and who killed Fatty Fuller is just agitating people. On top of that, you guys talked with Marilyn Aft, and right after that she gets her brains bashed in."

"Did you know that Cindy Fuller had an abortion?"

She stopped smoking and looked at TH. "I had heard that some time ago, but I don't think that has anything to do with what you're looking at."

"I don't either. Some stuff comes up, and it bothers me. I'd like a few more answers."

"Like what Margaret Hatch told you about us being to blame for Melissa's death?"

"That does bug me."

"That woman is a crackpot, TH. I wouldn't take anything that woman says for fact. I have no idea what she was talking about."

TH thought about the strange visit his father had made to his room on that late summer night. He wondered.

"I've got to get going," Rachel said. "The problems at the Walmart are never-ending."

TH laughed. "I can imagine."

"What are you laughing at? Do you know how many kids come in there and can't find the condoms? I am providing a public service."

"Well, I'd hate to keep you from your appointed duty."

•   •   •

TH found Fred Fuller behind his desk at the bank. Fred greeted him warmly and invited him into his office. Once he got inside and could really look at Fred did he see what kind of shape he was in. Fred's brown hair was matted a bit from the line of sweat that ran along his forehead. His eyes looked slightly bloodshot; his nose was traced with thin, little red lines. The suit he wore was rumpled, the tie hadn't been tied correctly, and his shirt was frayed at the collar. Fred was drinking a cup of black coffee. TH wondered if anything had been added to it.

"Getting about ready to head home, TH?" Fred asked.

TH thought that was an odd question to open with. "Probably in a couple of days."

"Been up to see your old man?"

Another strange question. "I've seen him twice. I don't know that I'll see him again before I go back to California."

Fred's eyebrows raised at that. "Not even to say goodbye?"

"I'm not sure, Mr. Fuller. You know my father, and I weren't that close."

"He's a tough one to get close to."

"That he is, but I hear he was pretty close to you guys."

Fred took a sip of the coffee and winced a bit. The coffee wasn't alone in the cup. "He used to help us out a bit."

"After Mrs. Fuller left?"

"I don't remember exactly. It might have been after she left."

"But Freddie was definitely around?"

Fred rubbed his forehead with the palm of his hand. "Oh, sure. Teddy used to bring him toys."

"And did he continue to help you out right up until the time that Freddie was murdered?"

Fred Fuller stared straight ahead. He took another sip of the coffee. The sweat beads on his forehead intensified. "What's with all the questions, TH? Your father was a good man. He was good to us. He helped us out a bit after

Katherine left. What's the big deal?"

"There seems to be some new evidence that indicates that one of the key witnesses in Freddie's case may have lied to help set up Skitch Grayson."

Again, the dumbfounded look. "Well, that seems a little improbable. They did find a good portion of Freddie's fishing tackle inside of Skitch's shed."

"On the night that Freddie was killed my father said very loudly, 'What have those God damn, stupid people, done?'. Do you have any idea who he was talking about?"

Fred laughed. "I have no idea what Teddy meant by a comment like that. Maybe you should ask him."

"I don't think he'd be much help to me or anyone else."

"Why would you say that? He was the Chief of Police. I would think that if they convicted the wrong man, he would be the first one to want to make sure that things were straightened out."

"Unless he had something to do with it."

Fred grabbed the coffee cup with both hands and raised it to his lips, but never sipped it. He put it back on his desk. "You're not making a lot of sense. You're trying to tell me that Teddy was responsible for setting up Skitch Grayson for the murder of my son?"

TH noticed a large scar that ran along the back of Fred's hand. "Maybe. There has been an uncovering of crimes that have an element to a cover-up in them tracing back a while in Milton's history. So I'm going to ask you again. Do you have any idea what "people" my father might have been talking about?"

"Are the police involved in this? Aft and Jack Davis are still down there. I think Ben Smith is on his way out."

TH nodded. "I think Chief Lou Katz and Detective Marks are involved now. I think they are starting to piece some things together."

Fred turned his swivel chair a bit so he could look out his window. The lone tree in his view had lost most of its leaves. He turned back to TH. "Those were very tough times for us," he said slowly. "Trying to raise Freddie was a lot of work. Katherine did as good of a job as she could, but it got to be too much. The stress was too much. That was why she left. After she was gone, Teddy tried to help, but it wasn't the same. I had to work. A lot of the stress fell to Cindy when she was home. She became a bit of a surrogate mom for Freddie. Other than school, he became her life. Once the day help would leave it was up to Cindy to take care of her brother. It started to wear her down. I could see what it was doing to her."

TH felt his stomach tighten. "Did you do something, Mr. Fuller? Something to help Cindy?"

He shook his head from side to side. "Not at all. I could never do anything to hurt Freddie."

"Then what are you talking about?"

"I just want you to understand what it was like back then. My wife had left me with a young boy with Down Syndrome and a young girl. I had no idea what to do. I started to drink. I started to drink a lot. It was an awful existence. When Freddie was killed, as bad as it was, it was like a weight being lifted from us. We were relieved when they found the killer and then when they sent him away. It was just best that the whole episode was over. Do you understand, TH?"

"I'm trying to."

"I don't know what this supposed witness lied about and I don't know what people your father was referring to when he made that comment. I only know what I know. They caught Skitch Grayson, and they convicted him. As far as I am concerned he is the one that killed Freddie. I know Cindy believes that, too. These rumors that get kicked around from time to time are just nonsense. That's really all I know."

·   ·   ·

For anyone who went past TH's car, they were probably sure that he was having a breakdown. He swore out loud many times and pounded his fists on the steering wheel column. Only a sore finger made him stop this behavior. He ran his hands through his hair and started the car.

"We're finished," he said. There was something there. He was sure of it, but unless somebody cracked there was no need to go on. These little hints that kept coming in, the ones that said there had been improprieties in the investigation, were vague. They were like little teasers. There was nothing meaty enough in any of them to prove anything. This little game they were all playing was becoming a bit of an up and down rollercoaster ride. It was becoming a waste of time.

He was about to pull out of the bank parking lot and head for no place in particular when his cell rang. He didn't want to talk with many people, but when he saw it was Marks, he answered.

"Where are you?" Marks asked.

"I'm just leaving the bank. I had a rather unrevealing talk with Fred Fuller."

"Well, we must have revealed something."

TH sat up straight in the car seat. "Why do you say that?"

"Gus Morgan was found about an hour ago. Somebody took him out in back of The Lighthouse and put two bullets in the back of his head."

"Jesus."

"Who did you tell what I found out about Gus?"

"Only Cindy and Fred Fuller. I just left Fred's office so unless Cindy told him, he's only had the news for about twenty minutes."

"I only told Lou. My guess is that Cindy told somebody and somehow it got to Aft and his crew."

"Where are they?"

"They are all at home, but Lou told them all to come in to talk. We think their alibis will be airtight."

"Sure they will, but you know they did this. You know they probably killed Marilyn Aft, too."

"Let's not get ahead of ourselves. We are going to question them and see what we can find. Lou is about as tight as I have ever seen him."

"I can't imagine why. This is getting completely out of control."

"Which is why I am calling you. You need to stay low, real low. My thoughts are they are going to come for you. At this point, I will put nothing past them."

TH thought about the warning Mary Katz had given him. "Can't you just arrest them?"

"For what. In Marilyn's case we have no evidence, nada. In Gus' case, same thing. Somebody got him to take one last look at the river and then shot him in the head. Must have been after hours. Nobody heard or saw a fucking thing."

"You really think they'll come after me?"

"You are the one asking most of the questions. We should have told you to stop it. It was police business."

"But until we started asking around, the police weren't doing a whole bunch, and Skitch was rotting away a day at a time."

"Okay. Forget what I said. Just keep an eye out. Do you have a gun?"

"Yeah. I have one."

"Don't be afraid to use it if these guys come calling. I don't think they are going to ask you a bunch of questions."

•   •   •

It was less than a ten-minute drive to the house that Anne Smith shared with her husband, Ben. The little ranch looked quiet on this morning. A for sale sign stood in the front yard. There was only one car sitting in the garage that was open. It was a van. TH figured that this was the vehicle that Anne drove. He also knew the Amigos had been issued department Fords. Ben had been called into headquarters about the Gus Morgan shooting. Anne Smith was home alone.

The look that Anne gave TH when she answered the door was one of fright like she had seen a demon. She took a step backward after she opened the door.

"I'm sorry, Anne," TH said. "I need to ask you a couple of more questions."

She looked up, and down the little street, she lived on. "Come in. We only have a short time."

"Ben was called into headquarters, I hear. A man named Gus Morgan was executed behind The Lighthouse last night."

She tilted her head to the side. "Ben said he was a questionable character."

Anne was dressed more casually than she had been the first time they met. She looked like she was in the throes of packing. "He has a checkered past from what I've heard. He also may have lied to the police during the Fatty Fuller murder case to lead them towards Skitch Grayson."

"I don't know anything about that."

"But I think you may know some things that may help us get to the bottom of some of this. I understand that you might not have wanted to tell me about them, but I really need some help. We're kind of spinning in mud."

Her look relaxed a bit. "I don't know what you think I know or what of value that I can tell you."

TH realized for the first time how tired all of this was making him. How could he get Anne Smith to tell him anything of value? "We've discovered a pattern in a number of cases that my father oversaw where his department may have covered for some of the actual perpetrators of the crimes. You know about Arthur Kimbro who was gunned down in town by a white farmer. Nobody ever caught the farmer; no one has ever seen him again. There was also the case of Corrine Riley found in a ravine along River Trail. Records show she had cocaine in her system and fell into the ravine. Others say she may have met foul play out at Ma Brooks while servicing Wilson Garrett."

"I've told you what I know about those two cases. I've pretty much told you that both of those cases were a little mysterious, that the truth hadn't come out."

TH put up his hands. "I know. I know you told me that. I don't care so much about those. I care about Fatty Fuller. You told me a little, but I think there is a lot more that you could have told me."

She continued to look right at TH, but she started wringing her hands together. "I'm not sure what you want me to say."

"Anne, it may not matter to you, but it does to me. I don't think Skitch Grayson killed Fatty. I think my father and his men, including Ben, may have helped him cover for somebody who did. Skitch is dying. I want to find the real killer before it is too late."

"First of all," she said angrily, "Ben was not involved at all in the Fatty Fuller investigation. That was your father and Logan Aft with help from Jack Davis."

"You've got to tell me, Anne. This nonsense of these cover-ups and my father's control of things has got to stop. The truth needs to come out."

She nodded and sat down on a sofa in the room. She looked outside as the wind blew dried, dead leaves across her lawn. "For the longest time, I knew that something would come along and one of these cases would blow open. I knew the truth, as you call it, would be out in the open. I knew it, and I feared it because life would never be the same for any of us."

"I'm really trying not to ruin anyone's life."

She laughed. "It will be hard for you not to. With those cases you mentioned, there are probably good reasons for arrests and charges for Aft, Jack Davis, and Ben."

"And my father?"

She laughed again. "I didn't mention him, TH, because I figured that you knew that he would be right there at the top."

"I'm sorry. It was a stupid question."

"This whole lie is stupid and for what? So that a couple of people could go unpunished?"

"That's what it looks like."

"Shameful," she said. "I want you to know that I don't know what happened to Arthur Kimbro's killer. I don't know what happened between Corinne Riley and Wilson Garrett. Lastly, I don't know who killed Fatty Fuller."

"But you know something?"

"Yes, I know something. A long time ago, before Fatty Fuller was even born, there was a terrible accident out on Route 20. A sedan with a dad and mom and two kids was going east. Another sedan, one male driver, was going west. The single male driver was drunk, over two point zero. He swerved and clipped the families' car, not much I heard, but enough to send then careening down into the woods along the road. They might have been okay if the car hadn't hit an oak and burst into flames. All four members were DOA."

"And the single male driver?"

"Drunk, but not drunk enough to be able to think. Knew he had caused the accident. Pulled over, got out and ran to where the other car left the road. By that time the car was in flames, and there was nothing he could do. Going back to his own car he stopped long enough to throw a punch at the roof of his car. It opened up a gash on the top of his right hand. It required something like twenty stitches to close. It was a nasty gash, and the scar is still there.

"The man did the right thing. He got ahold of Chief Brown and reported what had happened. The Chief told him to go to the hospital and get his hand treated. Teddy told him he would take care of everything else and he did. He called Ben and told him to get right out to the site. Ben got the fire department and a rescue squad out there. By that time everyone was dead. The case was opened as a hit and run. I suppose it may still be open."

"And you think this has a lot to do with the Fatty Fuller case?"

"There's no doubt about it. After the crash, the man who injured his hand was never arrested or charged even though the police knew who he was. He never spent one day in prison, but he got a sentence that was a lot worse than going to any prison."

"I'm not sure I follow."

"Teddy owned that man and his family after that. He got what he needed from the man, and I am pretty sure he got what he needed from the man's wife. It was a total control issue. Like I said, the man never went to prison, but his family was ruined by your father."

"But you are not going to tell me who this man is?"

She smiled. "I won't explicitly tell you anyone's name in any of these cases, and it's really because I don't know for sure, but I know about the man who hit the family and bashed his own hand. That one I'm sure of and I'm not going to tell you. I'm not going to tell you because you can probably figure it out."

TH thought for a short moment and thought he knew who she meant, but it still didn't make a lot of sense how it tied into the Fatty Fuller murder.

"You really need to be going. I don't suspect that Ben will be down there that long. If he catches you here, I'm not sure what will happen."

"I understand," TH said.

"I'm sorry to have to be vague, TH," she said. "It would be easy to blurt out names of people that I suspect, but that wouldn't be right, because I am really not sure."

•   •   •

TH called Marks as soon as he got away from the Smith home. Marks had just gotten out of the meeting with Lou Katz and the Three Amigos.

"How did that go?"

"About as well as expected. All three knew nothing, and all three had good alibis. Coroner thinks Gus Morgan was shot about three in the morning. Everybody we talked with said they were home sleeping."

"Guess the wives could confirm that except that Aft has no wife."

"Says he was home. Might be hard to disprove."

"Like everything else."

"I'm in a bit of a rush here, TH. Anything else I can do for you?"

"One thing. It appears there was a hit-and-run a long time ago on Route 20. A family of four got killed. Case has never been solved from what I was told. I was wondering if you could verify that this accident even occurred. It may lead to someone else who was being protected by Teddy."

"Do you want to give me your source?"

"I will, but not right now."

"Okay, TH. I will see what I can find, but I am warning you. You are getting in a little deep on this stuff. Watch your back."

TH hung up the phone and headed back towards the motel. He wanted to get his gun out of his bag and make sure it was loaded.

●   ●   ●

He believed Marks when he said that they would be coming for him. He wasn't afraid but knew it was a reality. He also knew it was true when Tiffany Gold stepped out of her Lexus as TH pulled into the motel parking lot. TH cut the engine and saw Tiffany wave at him. He got out of his car and walked towards her. It was getting late into the morning, and Tiffany wore an open coat, showing a short black, tight skirt.

"Surprise, surprise," TH said.

"I didn't think you'd expect to see me out here," Tiffany said.

She stepped forward and gave TH a hug. He was very conscious that this was an extraordinary event.

"When I saw you at my sister's wake, I wasn't sure that I'd see you again," TH said.

She opened the coat a bit for a better view. "Disappointed?"

"Not at all. You look great."

"Thanks, but I'm actually here on a business matter."

"Should we go inside?"

She briefly looked around the lot. The whole area was quiet. "I don't think we need to. I'm just hoping that you can help me."

"Why don't you tell me what it is you want?"

"For about six months I lived with a guy named Taylor Ashford. His family owns the largest John Deere dealership in Iowa. To make a long story short, the live-in deal didn't go all that well. I don't think his family cared for the fact that I was an exotic dancer."

Among other things, TH thought.

"Anyway, we broke up, and I left his house. When I did, I forgot to bring with me one of the only things I have from my mother. It's a set of silverware, sterling silver."

"Why don't you ask Ashford to give it back to you?"

"I have, TH. He won't. I don't think he was happy with my attitude and with me moving out. After all, he did get me this." She pointed at the Lexus.

"I don't suppose you'd give back the car for the silver?"

She smiled. "I still have a key, and I know the silver is on a serving piece in the dining room. It's in a cherry case."

"Sounds easy enough. What about Ashford?"

"Away on a hunting trip up in Ontario. The house will be completely empty. All you have to do is go in and grab the silver and leave."

He'd heard that same line a hundred times in his racket. Most times it was accurate. A few times he had been shot at. "You can't just go grab it?"

She made a silly face. "I could never handle doing that."

"I can make a run up there and grab the silver."

"What is your fee?"

"A hundred an hour. Starts when I leave here and ends when I get back."

She handed him an envelope. "Here's three hundred, the key and the address. It shows up on Google. A little hard to find. The house is set back in the woods, away from the road. Very quiet."

Too quiet, thought TH. If there was ever a description of a set-up, this was it. "I can go tonight," he said. "You're sure no one else is going to be near this house?"

She raised her eyes and looked squarely at him. "The house is deserted. Taylor lives alone. There will be no one else anywhere near that property."

Her face, beginning with the eyes, looked so sincere. He almost believed her for a minute.

•　　　•　　　•

Back in his room he found the gun, a light Walther, and loaded it. He knew he had some calls to make, but he suddenly felt very tense. He took several deep breaths and lied down on the bed. After a few minutes, he felt better. He sat up. As he did, his phone rang. It startled him.

"Your hit and run," Marks said, "was over thirty years ago. A nice little family returning from a trip was run off the road and into a ditch. The car hit a tree and exploded. Everybody died."

"Thirty years ago?"

"Close to it. Unsolved."

"That's the one."

"Want to tell me who your source is yet?"

"Steve, trust me on this. I don't want to get anybody in trouble over this. I want to make sure of a few things."

"If this fucks up any kind of investigation, this could cause a lot of problems for you. You know that."

"I know. I hope that very shortly I can give you a lot more information than I can right now."

"If you are still alive."

"Yeah," TH said. "If I am still alive."

When Marks hung up, TH made the calls he needed to make. He suddenly was very tired. As tense as he'd been, he seemed to find a resolve and relaxed. He lay back down on the bed and closed his eyes. It wasn't long before he was asleep.

The Murder of Fatty Fuller

The house that Taylor Ashford lived in was easy to find. It was on Google as Tiffany had said. Located a little south and west of Dubuque, it was located in a development of large homes, on big lots and divided by thick expanses of trees. Even this late in October it was difficult to see one property from another. As TH pulled down the long drive to Ashford's place, he realized how secluded he was.

The house was a two-story, Georgian style and looked too big for a bachelor to live in. The entire front of the house was fronted by a large porch. On the beams that lined the top of the porch were lights that shined across the drive that TH parked in. The first thirty feet or so of the lot in front of the house was lit up.

TH walked nervously up the stairs and inserted the key in the front door. For a moment, the key stuck and TH wondered if Tiffany had given him the right one. He jiggled it a bit, and the lock snapped open. He reached into his pocket for the small flashlight he brought along and turned it on. It wasn't hard to find the dining area that Tiffany described and the cherry box holding the silverware was right where she said it would be. He grabbed the box under one arm, after examining the inside, and retreated his steps to the front porch. Closing the door behind him, he went down the steps.

Too easy, TH thought to himself. He reached for his keys.

"Well, what do we have here?" The voice was loud and scratchy and came from TH's right. When he looked that way, he saw Logan Aft coming out from behind a huge oak. He was holding a shotgun in front of him.

"Mr. Aft," TH said calmly. "I was just retrieving an article of importance for Tiffany Gold. You know her, I think."

"Looks like a burglary," Aft said. From behind him, Ben Smith appeared; his gun was down at his side. From TH's left, in front of his car, was Jack Davis. He also had a shotgun, but it was pointed right at TH.

"Don't think so," said TH. "Tiffany hired me to come out here and get the family silver from this nice house. Why don't you call and ask her?"

Aft smiled. "You're right, TH. There's no reason to bullshit each other. Your days of playing junior detective are over."

"Why all of this, Mr. Aft?" TH asked. "Why did it have to be this way?"

Aft lowered the shotgun. "That's a fair question, and it deserves a fair answer. Your daddy is a good man, took care of his men and took care of Milton. There were a few things that he asked us to do. Things that protected a few people that made mistakes. That's all it was. Just mistakes people made that needed to be fixed. Nobody got hurt."

"Not Skitch Grayson?"

Aft turned his head to the left and spit into the grass. "Skitch Grayson was a drunken bum. Sure he went to jail, but he didn't have to worry about bills or health care or meals any longer. The State of Illinois took care of Skitch."

"And Corrine Riley, Ben?" TH asked. "Do you remember her?"

Aft looked back at Ben. "Tell him, Ben. Doesn't matter now, anyway."

In the light, TH saw Ben lower his eyes. "That girl was dead when we got there. The coroner was sure it had been the drugs that killed her."

"Not the punishment that Wilson Garrett gave her?"

"I don't know," Ben said. "We'll never know."

"What about the farmer who disappeared after shooting Arthur Kimbro in the middle of town? Who were you protecting on that one?"

"That's enough," Aft said loudly. "You know a lot, TH. As a matter of fact, you would have been a good cop if you'd listened to your father. I can't tell you anything more."

"Like who killed Marilyn or Gus Morgan?"

Aft smiled. "Like those two," he said. "Like I said, you should have listened to your father and become a Milton cop. You would have made a good one. Instead, you became an asshole."

Aft's gun moved upward only a couple of inches. The first shot hit him in the jaw right under his nose. His jaw exploded, and Aft was knocked backward onto his butt. The second shot hit Jack Davis in the center of his forehead. He staggered about six inches and fell into a heap. TH dropped the silverware box and dove behind a pillar on the porch. When Ben Smith realized what was going on, he stepped forward and raised his gun. The next shot came from behind him and hit him between the shoulder blades. It missed his heart, but the hollow point bullet ripped a gaping hole in his stomach and exited through his sternum. Ben dropped his gun, reached for his belly and dropped to his knees.

Logan Aft knew he was dead. He knew this was his final moment. Missing most of his jaw, he scrambled to his knees and found the shotgun. The pain he felt was excruciating, but he had one more thing to do. He turned back towards the porch and saw TH crouched behind the pillar. He began to raise the shotgun. The final shot of the night hit him in the heart. His eyes popped wide open for a moment, and then he fell backward.

As TH saw Richie appear from the woods behind where Ben Smith was kneeling, he got up from the porch. The gun he had was still in his pocket. From his left, he saw the large figure of Joseph Running Bear emerge from the trees. The rifle he had used to kill Aft and Jack Davis was still trained on Ben Smith.

"I missed Aft on the first try," Joseph said.

TH stepped down from the porch and vomited onto the drive. "He looks pretty dead to me dead to me," he said, wiping his mouth.

"I was trying for his mouth to shut him up for once."

All three now had Ben Smith surrounded. He was still on his knees, and blood was trickling from his mouth. He looked up at TH. "Didn't mean for it all to go this way."

"Why don't you lie down, Ben. We can get an ambulance for you," TH said.

"I'm dead, TH. Tell Anne, I'm sorry."

TH knelt down and looked Ben in the eyes. The old cop's eyes were still clear. "What happened to the Iowa farmer that shot Arthur Kimbro?"

Ben grimaced, but held TH's gaze. "The turnoff for the 20 bridge, about fifty yards from the road, near a utility box. He's buried there. Teddy shot him twice in the back of the head." Blood started trickling from Ben's mouth.

"And Fatty Fuller. Who killed him?"

"The murder of Fatty Fuller." Ben coughed hard, and the pain was evident on his face.

"Come on, Ben."

Ben smiled through blood soaked lips. "Aft was right. You would have made a damn good cop." He took one more big gasp and then pitched forward onto his face. Richie stepped forward and grabbed his wrist for a pulse.

"He's dead," Richie said.

"What do we do here?" Joseph asked.

"Richie and I will call Steve Marks," TH said. "They came here to kill me. It just didn't work out that way."

Joseph looked over the three bodies. "Good assessment. You might have made a good cop."

• • •

TH knew the apartment complex that Tiffany Gold lived in. He had found a directory that told him that she was in Building C, Unit 210. He followed the signs to Building C and trudged up the stairs to the second floor. The cherry box, now chipped in several spots, under his arm. When he got to 210, he hit the doorbell.

Tiffany Gold looked more than surprised when she opened the door and TH was standing there. She looked terrified.

"TH," she said. "I didn't expect you this late."

"There was a bit of a distraction, but I've got your silverware." He stepped into her unit and put the box on a table.

"I guess I should say thanks," she said.

"That is what you paid me to get for you," he said. "But now just a bit of advice. I think now would be as good a time to get your shit together and leave town. Those other three assholes came out there to kill me; you only set me up. There was good cause to kill those three. With you, it would just be murder. Tonight would be a good time to go."

"TH, they had me. They had me on a couple of charges. I had to do it."

"I don't care, Tiff. I don't care. Just don't be here tomorrow."

TH left the apartment and got back to his car. He had never thought of the little motel room as comfortable, but now he couldn't wait to get there.

• • •

Steve Marks was leaning against his car in the parking lot of the police department. It was a cold, cloudy start to the day, the last day of October. It was Halloween. He waved as he saw TH's car pull into the lot. TH pulled over close to him and got out.

"So what do you think?" TH asked.

"Well, we finished talking to Joseph and Richie earlier. Their stories matched yours. Those three guys went up there to kill you. There's no doubt about it. It's also known that Richie was using a throwaway, a gun with no record. Bullets untouched. Joseph's a little trickier, but he too was certain he didn't touch the bullets used. No prints on the bullets and no weapons found."

TH lit a cigarette and sat on his hood. "So?"

"So, as I advised the Dubuque detective, we had heard rumblings of the three of these guys may be involved in some narcotics deals. What this looks like to us is a drug deal gone bad. We sent our coroner's vans up there to retrieve the bodies. Dubuque was pretty happy to be done with it. The bad thing is the press might not leave Lou alone for a while."

"How did Anne Smith and Jack's wife take it?"

"Surprisingly in stride. It was almost like they expected a call like this one day. They were kind of living in the shadows for a while, with all of the secret stuff. Now that is over."

"You check on Tiffany?"

"The apartment door was open, and she and most of her clothes were gone."

"You think all of this is going to fly?"

Marks shrugged. "You guys aren't going to tell anyone what happened. Lou and I aren't going to say that three of our deputies went up there to murder you. Tiffany Gold is long gone. The two wives don't even know what was going on. I think it's pretty solid."

"Still kind of hard to believe. It's like something out of the Wild West."

"Is it really, TH? With all the bullshit that's gone on here for years? I think this ending fits right in."

"Not quite the end."

"Aren't you leaving yet?"

"One more call to Fred Fuller."

"Then you promise that you will leave."

"I promise."

"Oh, by the way, we're sending a crew out to the turnoff for the Route 20 Bridge. I don't know if we'll find anything and if we do if we can identify who it is."

"I can only tell you what Ben said."

Marks nodded. "We'll see."

"And my father?"

"Need the body first."

⁕   ⁕   ⁕

"How did you get that scar on the back of your hand?"

Fred Fuller looked down at his hand. It was noticeably shaking. Fred didn't look so good this morning. The last twenty-four hours must have been tough on him.

"Had to be a nasty cut," TH said.

"What do you want, TH?" Fred asked. There were thin lines of blood running through the whites of his eyes?"

TH took a deep breath. "I know about the hit and run. I know that a family was killed. I know the drunken driver smashed his hand on top of his own car, causing a nasty cut. I know that the driver was you."

Fred looked down at his hand examining the old scar. With the finger of his other hand, he traced along the lines of it. The hand shook. "It was one of the worst nights of my life."

"Just one?"

Fred chuckled. "There have been many. So many that I have lost count."

"Let's stick with the night of the crash."

"Crash. It really wasn't much of a crash. I barely clipped them. I think maybe when I veered into their lane, the driver of the other car lost control and that made them go into the ravine. You could see from the damage to my car, that I barely brushed them. That was what made it so easy for Teddy to make it go away."

"He just made it go away?"

"They sent Ben Smith out there to investigate. He found the driver had lost control and left the road, causing the accident. That was pretty much it."

"Until when?"

Fred smiled. "You know the answer to that, TH. You know all of this led to your father controlling my life. From the day of that crash until probably the day that your father had his stroke, he has controlled my life and that of my family."

TH thought of the control factor that Teddy had employed over the Three Amigos' wives. "How did he control your family?"

"It started off by being so innocent. First, it was preferential loans for your home and that lake house. That was easy to take care of, but then he turned up the pressure. He would bring up his knowledge of the crash. He would make me remember what had happened and that I owed him for my freedom."

"How much did you owe?"

Again a slight smile. "The cost, it seemed, was priceless. Teddy wanted to own everything that was mine. It started with Katherine."

TH winced. He shifted on his chair.

"I think, a long time ago, that Teddy would have preferred Katherine over your own mother. I beat him to her and won out. I don't think he ever forgave me."

"I'm sorry."

"You don't need to be sorry, TH. You are not your father." Fred sipped his coffee. "Well, one thing led to another, as you can imagine. We would have to leave when your father came by. The house then belonged to him and Katherine."

TH was having a hard time listening to this story. The implications were so clear. "And all of the help that Teddy gave to you for Freddy after Katherine left."

"You're a smart young man, TH, but I won't drag this out. Teddy was Freddie's father. When Katherine left us, Teddy felt some moral obligation to help us, to raise him."

TH swallowed hard. The news stunned him. "But it was still tough on you?"

"Freddie was always just a little kid. He always needed monitoring. He always needed someone to look after him. As he got older, a lot of this fell onto Cindy. It was very tough on her. She blamed Freddie for messing up her life; she also blamed him for driving her mother away. She had the most resentment of anyone. It was just a sad time."

"Did she know about my father and Katherine?"

"I don't know the extent of that. I don't know if she knew who Freddie's father was. I don't know about that."

"What about the night Freddie died?"

"I don't know why you keep coming back to that."

"I keep coming back to that because a key witness that tipped off the police about Skitch Grayson probably lied. The day after we learned this he was shot in the back of the head by someone."

"Jesus," Fred said. "All of these damn theories about that night. Skitch Grayson was the killer. That's all there is to it. I don't know anything else about that?"

"What about Cindy?"

"What about her?"

"Did you know that she's had an abortion?"

TH saw the Adam's apple in Fred's throat bob convulsively. "I didn't know that. What does that have to do with anything?"

"Probably nothing," TH conceded. "I just keep wondering about those words my father said when he found out that Freddie had been killed. He asked aloud, 'What did those God damn, stupid people do?' "

"Maybe the person to ask about that is your father. I have no idea what he was talking about."

"The night that Freddie was killed, where were you?"

"Pretty well documented. Work until six, the lounge in the Holiday Inn until Cindy called and told me Freddie was missing."

"Did you know that Freddie was going fishing that evening?"

"I didn't. It was a spur of the moment thing."

"So who knew he'd be down at Whisper Creek by himself?"

TH saw the look of horror on Fred Fuller's face. The thoughts of his father's total control of the Fuller family, Katherine Fuller leaving, Cindy's frustration with being Freddie's guardian and then her abortion exploded in his brain. He thought he might actually be sick. He got up from his seat, a bit wobbly.

"Where are you going?" Fred asked. "You can't possibly believe that she had anything to do with this. That was her brother."

"There's too much there, Fred. I have to know the truth in this?"

"You're all crazy," Fred shouted as TH left his office. "You all should have just left this alone."

• • •

Cindy Fuller told TH that she would meet with him before her shift at the Trips Aces. He was waiting for her in the lounge that had been completely decorated for Halloween. Everything was orange and black. There were ghosts and goblins everywhere. He didn't order a drink, and he wasn't playing video poker. He was almost too nervous to deal with this. His hands shook. It seemed surreal.

Cindy arrived about twenty minutes before one. Dressed in her white shirt with the bow tie, hair glistening and eyes alert, she looked fresher than TH remembered seeing her. Seeing her now made him realize where the lifelong crush came from. Why hadn't things gone a different way so long ago? How had things become some messed up and confused along the way?

"My father called me right after you did," she said. She took a seat across from him in the booth. "We talked for quite a bit."

"I'm sure that was an interesting call."

She brushed some of the red hair off of her forehead and tugged at the bow tie. It looked a little tight. "All my life, at least as long as I can remember, Freddie was there. It didn't seem like I could do anything without him being there. It worked on me, and it dragged me down. I resented him for it. I resented that he was my brother, or half- brother, if that's the right call. What is it when your mother has a child by someone else?"

TH wished he had ordered a drink. He looked at Cindy. She looked calm. It looked like maybe she was unloading a burden.

"I didn't know about the hit and run for a long time. It was well after my mom left us with Freddie when my father sat me down and told me the truth. I love dad, drunk that he is, but for all of us it would have been better had he gone to prison for what he did."

"I'm not sure that would have been better," TH said.

She smiled and placed her hand on top of TH's. "We'll never know that will we? Anyway, what we do know, is that the accident opened the doors for your father to get into our lives. He got to my father and got some great financing on some loans. Not so bad for just that. Then he got to my mother, someone who he longed for forever. I wonder if his come on line had anything to do with fuck me or your husband goes to jail for killing a whole family."

She was looking straight into his eyes, hauntingly. Her tone of voice wasn't normal. He slid his hand from under hers. She smiled.

"Anyway, Freddie came along, and life went on for a while. Your dad still came around and acted like we were all his private property. Looking back I can see how much strain this had on my mother. The problems with Freddie, my dad's drinking and Teddy Brown controlling you, it all had to wear her down. After a while, she just split.

"Picture this. Freddie is about four, I'm about eight, and my mom leaves.

My father goes deeper into the tank, but Teddy Brown was there for us. In a way, he actually held us together for a while. He did help us get by."

"You don't have to tell me all of this if you don't want to."

Her hand covered TH's again. "I have to," she said. "It would have been okay if Teddy just gave us gifts and money. That would have been fine if he just came and went, but that wasn't Teddy. He was giving a lot to us, but he wasn't getting anything in return. He had a drunken banker in his pocket and a son with Down Syndrome. What the fuck was he supposed to do with all of that?"

TH shook his head. He felt nauseous.

"Do you remember the night that Freddie's zoo burned down?"

TH lifted his eyes to hers. "How could I forget?"

"Your father's men did it. I heard them talking. It was Aft and Jack Davis. Your father heard that Lenny Granier was harassing me. He had them torch the zoo and frame Lenny. It was just something else your father did to try and get what he wanted."

"What more could he want?" TH asked. His heartbeat wasn't resting, and he felt perspiration running down his sides.

"He wanted me, TH. He waited and waited. He was very patient, but I would cry to him. I couldn't cry to my own father. There was no use. I would cry to him, and he would soothe me. Eventually, he took advantage of me. It went on for a long time, longer than I care to remember. It's the biggest single reason that I never gave you a second look or chance. How could I date you while I was sleeping with your father?"

TH's stomach tightened, acid hit the bottom of his throat. "I really don't need to hear all of this. I'm sorry."

"So am I, TH, but you need to hear it. It will clear things up." She paused and took a deep breath. "When I got pregnant, I was so down, so lost. I had no idea what to do. That was when your father sent your sister Melissa over to counsel me and be my friend. You know what, it worked. She was a great friend and confidant. She held my hand for a long time until Teddy arranged an abortion up in Milwaukee. Once that was all over, Teddy stopped coming by. I'd see him, and he was cordial and all that, but he never stepped into our house again."

"But what about Freddie?"

"What about Freddie, he asks? Freddie was still my problem. Other than work, dad was useless. No help at all. Freddie was my responsibility."

"And it got to be too much?"

"Not at all. I was so used to it. It became part of my day. That was all. After the abortion and Teddy leaving us alone, I wanted to get along with my life. I was going into my junior year; you were going to be a senior. I wanted to start living my life. I had to do that without Freddie being there all the time."

TH felt his palms getting sweaty. He felt sick. "How could you do it?"

"I knew where he fished along Whisper Creek. I knew it was a secluded spot. I went out there about a half hour after he did. I snuck up on him and found the biggest rock I could handle. I swung it as hard as I could, and he went out cold. He fell face first into about two feet of water. I knew he would drown."

"And you felt nothing?"

"At first I was startled when I saw his blood flow into the creek, but then I felt relief. I felt free for the first time in my life, but I also knew that telling your father might mean he'd enslave me again, but he didn't. I told him what I did, and he took over. He didn't want anyone hearing anything about his control of us. Your father had Logan Aft get out to the site and find the body and gather the fishing gear. Somewhere along the way, the plot was hatched to pin it on Skitch Grayson. I just sat back and watched."

"With no remorse, Cindy?"

"I don't think I felt any. Why would I? I knew what I had done."

TH swallowed hard. "I wish I knew what was going on back then. I wish I knew how my father acted. I would have done something to help."

She squeezed his hand. "Nice of you to say that. Maybe it would have helped me. Maybe it would have helped Melissa and Rachel."

"What are you talking about?"

"Don't be naïve. Your father was a fucking predator. Do you think your own sisters avoided him?"

There was a stabbing pain at his temples. At the same time, he felt heat around his ears. Visions from the night that his father entered his room came back to him. "Melissa's suicide?"

"I don't know for sure," she said, "but all of that haunted her. We talked a lot. More than most knew. Her past started to bother her and Teddy made some awful remarks to her when she went to visit him. I think maybe she wanted to quiet the demons."

At a loss for words, TH felt himself sliding out of the booth and standing.

He was shaking.

"What do I need to do, TH? Do I need to talk with Lou Katz and Steve Marks? Do I need to turn myself in?"

TH focused for a minute on Cindy. She didn't look very pretty any longer. She looked like a murderer. "You're so fucking late with all of this. Skitch Grayson, an innocent man, has sat in prison for fifteen years. Now he is dying of cancer. I know that your life was horrible in many ways, but you had no right to deprive him of his."

Cindy nodded slowly and for the first time showed any emotion. A large, single tear rolled down her cheek. "I'm sorry, TH," she said.

•   •   •

The wait was driving TH nuts. He had called Rachel and found that she wouldn't be back home until three o'clock. She had to be there for the Halloween trick or treaters. She also told him that Richie was stopping by to say goodbye as he was about to head back to Kansas City. TH stopped at Lifers and had a couple of beers. He needed to settle down a bit. The last words from Cindy had fueled his temper. The beers weren't doing that much to calm him.

It was funny how he had missed all of the Halloween decorations on Rachel's street. Maybe they hadn't been there and had just been put up on the last day. Now they were prominent as the children were beginning to go out to load their bags with candy. Rachel's house, as gloomy as it normally looked, spotted two glowing Jack-O-Lanterns. TH felt anything but the spirit.

Rachel and Richie were out in the back of the house; TH was glad that her children were not around. His older brother and sister were having a beer in the last few hours of sunshine. It was still crisp outside, but nice. Rachel also cradled a cigarette.

"You made it sound like it was a little urgent that we talked," she said.

"Cindy Fuller admitted to me that she killed Fatty. She is going to tell Steve Marks."

Rachel's mouth hung open for a minute. "Why would she do that?"

"Taking care of Fatty was getting in the way of the rest of her life. In a way, she snapped."

"That's crazy," Richie said.

TH felt a surge of temper. "You know what else I learned?"

Rachel and Richie could both sense that something was up. "What's wrong, TH?" Rachel said.

"I found out that dad was Fatty's father. He'd had a long time forced relationship with Katherine Fuller and Fatty was the result."

"Jesus," Rachel said.

"Yeah, and later he preyed on Cindy. He got her pregnant, too, but she got an abortion up in Milwaukee."

Rachel flicked her cigarette away and kept her eyes to the ground; Richie bolted back a good amount of beer.

"The more I hear about dad, the more I realize what a fucking animal he was, the more I realize what a good decision I made by leaving. We should have all left."

"What's your point in all of this, Theodore?" Richie said. The beer bottle was resting on the table. His hands were balled into fists which hung at his sides.

"Cindy also told me that during her pregnancy and long afterward she had a good friend and confidant. That *someone* was Melissa. You see they became special friends because they shared a bond. They had both been abused by our great father."

Richie stepped around from his side of the table, closer to TH. "That's enough, TH."

"There's a few other tidbits that she enlightened me about. She told me that dad had abused Rachel as well. Melissa told her this. Then she went on to tell me that dad was making crude and disgusting comments to Melissa when she went to see him. Cindy was pretty sure this was eating at Melissa when she hanged herself."

Rachel's head was hanging down, and she began to sob. Richie got up very close to TH. "You need to shut up right now. You don't know a fucking thing," Richie said.

"I think I'm entitled to a few answers. Primarily, what was going on here? How did this get so out of control?"

"Your little girl friend doesn't know everything. She had her little turn with dad, but she didn't go through what we went through."

"What the fuck are you talking about, Rich? What do you mean what we went through?"

With that, Richie drove his right fist hard into the spot just below TH's sternum. Whatever breath was in TH was knocked completely out. He gasped heavily and fell to his knees. He thought he might pass out.

"Richie, don't," Rachel said.

Richie knelt down next to TH who was searching for air. "What I'm talking about, TH, is something you might not be able to grasp. You can't grasp it because you were the lucky one. You were the one that got away. You see the rest of us, all three of us, were dad's victims. Every fucking flaw that we have can probably be traced back to how dad treated us. For the most part, we coped. Melissa, for whatever reason, stopped coping."

TH tried to say something, but no words were coming. He was trying to regain the proper feeling in his lungs.

"You don't need to say anything, TH. We know you didn't know. You don't even have to say that you're sorry. We get it. Just don't criticize us for the way that we handled it, because you don't know what you are talking about."

•   •   •

Ten minutes later they were all sitting at the table. Each had a fresh beer and Rachel, and TH smoked cigarettes. Calm had returned to the little yard.

"So is this the end of our family?" Rachel said. "Do I have to die, too, before you come back to Milton?"

"You'll outlive me," Richie said.

"I'm serious," Rachel said.

TH flicked the smoked butt into a stand of bushes. He didn't know. He didn't know when or if he would come back.

"I guess I'll come back if Marks needs us for the shooting, but right now I need to go home and fix my family," Richie said. "Just because the one I had here got a little fucked up doesn't mean the one in KC has to be that bad."

"TH?" Rachel persisted.

"We'll see," he said. "This trip has kind of taken it out of me. Right now, I need a little break from Milton."

They all laughed. They all needed a little break from each other. Nothing more was said for a few minutes. Then the front doorbell rang with the first horde of kids seeking treats. Rachel handled the children while both Richie and TH went to their cars. There were no hugs or goodbyes. There were no promises. They all figured they might see each other again. *When* was a big question. Right now it was best to be alone.

There was ten PM flight to Los Angeles. TH had plenty of time. He checked with Steve Marks for any updates. Cindy Fuller had turned herself in and was waiting to be indicted; her daughter was staying with a friend. A complete set of human bones had been unearthed by the turnoff for the Route 20 Bridge. It would be a while before they could be positively identified, but Marks was certain they were the bones of Herb Varner, the man who had murdered Arthur Kimbro. The skull sported two large bullet holes. With the only two witnesses to the crime dead, Lou Katz was reviewing his options with the Legal Department before he made any move on Teddy Brown. TH wasn't surprised by any of the developments. He told Marks to let him know if he was needed back in Milton for the shooting deaths of Aft, Davis and Ben Smith. Marks didn't think so. A drug deal gone badly had produced no witnesses or evidence. Right now, the Dubuque police weren't sure who they were looking for.

There was maybe a half hour of sunlight left when TH parked the rental at the foot of the hill that led up to Marymore. It was getting cold, so he pulled his hood over his head and put on gloves. As quickly as he could, he made his way through the woods leading to the peak that held the concrete viewing area. He was certain he had been unseen.

When he got to the viewing area, he was a bit winded. He took a minute to catch his breath and sighted his target. His father was sitting in the wheelchair and facing west as the sun descended quickly behind the bluffs on the opposite side of the Mississippi. TH walked on the viewing platform and circled its perimeter. The spot that his father was looking over was the steepest. There was a significant drop off to the rocks and woods below. He approached his father and removed his hood. His father didn't raise his eyes, continuing to look ahead.

"Your three fucking morons tried to kill me near a house out near Dubuque," TH said.

"That may be the smartest thing you've ever said," Teddy responded.

"But they are all dead now."

Teddy didn't blink. He didn't make any kind of movement.

"I learned a lot the past couple of days. For a while there, it was nothing and then, all of a sudden, the faucets opened. I learned that you shot Arthur Kimbro's killer, that Fred Fuller killed a family while driving drunk and that you were blackmailing Fred. I learned that you were Fatty's father, that you got Cindy Fuller pregnant, sent Melissa to her as a counselor, and paid for an abortion up in Milwaukee."

Teddy raised his head to look at TH. The skin of his face looked grayer. The eyes more rheumy. "You are boring me, TH," he said. "Those things, nasty as they were, were necessary. It's all about control."

The urge to slap Teddy crossed TH's mind. He took a deep breath. "Like you controlled the men that worked for you and their wives as well."

Teddy shrugged or shivered. TH wasn't sure. "You must have control and obedience if you are to succeed. You must have complete loyalty. There is no other way."

"Same as Wilson Garrett after what happened at Ma Brooks?"

"Wilson Garrett killed that prostitute. That she was a whore was the only reason I let him go."

"That and what he could do for you in the future?"

"You're not as dumb as I thought, TH."

"And our family?"

"What about our family?"

"You had to have that control and obedience there, too?"

"It was the only way."

TH got down close to his father's face. He could smell something medicinal. "Control had to include abusing and raping them?"

Teddy smiled. "When gaining control, you must use every available tactic. It's the only way that you will be successful."

TH looked at the gully in front of him. Ending this all would be too easy. "That was all a long time ago, but you must have said something to Melissa recently that made her kill herself."

A bit of spit ran down Teddy's chin. He smiled. "I don't understand that," he said. "When she came I always told her that she was my favorite."

TH felt the burning feeling at his ears and at the bottom of his throat. He could see the drop off to the gully, not that many steps away. He stepped behind the wheelchair and kicked off the break. Grabbing the handles firmly, he stooped to say something into his father's ears. "Regardless of what condition you are in, you don't deserve one more day on this fucking planet."

"You going to kill your old man, TH?" Teddy asked. "Guess you'd be a killer just like me. Surprising, considering you couldn't kill that deer."

TH let go of the handles and took a deep breath. He reached into his pocket and took out the small recorder that had been running the whole time. "You think all of those people in that town still love you?"

Teddy issued a small laugh. "They always will."

TH shoved the small recorder in Teddy's face. "Even after I play this recording for them?"

Teddy tried to make a quick grab for the recorder, but he was much too slow. "You little motherfucker. You give me that, TH?"

"No, dad, not this time. This time I am in control. The people of Milton will hear this tape, and it will bring clarity and resolution. This tape is for them, for Melissa, Richie, and Rachel. It's also for me. This is the last thing I'll ever want from you."

TH turned and started back to his car. He could hear the rant that began from his father the moment he left him. His vocabulary, especially the foul words, hadn't failed him at all.

•   •   •

He was maybe halfway back to his car when he started to cry. There were intervals of sobbing and just whimpering. He couldn't totally get himself under control until he got to the Interstate 39 turnoff at Rockford. Finally, he settled down. He thought of his father, tormented out on that ridge, watching his image flow down Whisper Creek as Fatty Fuller's blood had. TH knew there was a good chance that Lou and Marks would come after his father for killing Herb Varner. That was probably enough. He picked up the recorder from the seat next to him and ejected the tape. He opened his window. He thought for a moment, but he was right. That was enough. He tossed the tape onto the freeway pavement.

The End

NOTE FROM THE AUTHOR

Word-of-mouth is crucial for any author to succeed. If you enjoyed the book, please leave a review online—anywhere you are able. Even if it's just a sentence or two. It would make all the difference and would be very much appreciated.

Thanks!
John

About the Author

John Sturgeon is a retired insurance agent and the author of the *Levee District Series*, published by Black Rose Writing. *The Murder of Fatty Fuller* is his first stand- alone novel. John lives in Wheaton, Illinois with his wife, Mary.

Thank you so much for reading one of our **Crime Fiction** novels.
If you enjoyed the experience, please check out our recommended
title for your next great read!

Caught in a Web by Joseph Lewis

"This important, nail-biting crime thriller about MS-13 sets the
bar very high. One of the year's best thrillers."
–*BEST THRILLERS*

View other Black Rose Writing titles at
www.blackrosewriting.com/books and use promo code
PRINT to receive a **20% discount** when purchasing.